RIPPLE

An Agent Victoria Heslin Thriller – Book 4

JENIFER RUFF

COPYRIGHT

BOOKS BY JENIFER RUFF

Chapter 1

Move. Move. Move!

The young woman staggered from one tall tree to the next, pressing through the dark woods. Spindly branches caught on her sleeves and snapped as she pushed them aside. Her head throbbed and tears streamed from her eyes. She forced herself to keep going, stumbling toward the road, shaking her head to clear it. Her limbs were too heavy. Her legs wouldn't respond. Bile rose into her throat.

He must have drugged me!

Through the forest, white Christmas tree lights sparkled from one of the enormous houses. Someone might be home there. With fear choking her voice, all she could manage was a single, high-pitched shriek. She needed help, but didn't want to draw him straight to her.

Leaves crunched nearby.

Her heart leapt as she wheeled around.

"I will find you," he hissed through the darkness.

The thump of heavy footsteps grew closer. Clawing the thick bark of a tree, she tried to stay on her feet, but her body gave out. She fell to her knees, collapsing onto her side. A patch of snow and pine needles pressed against her bare skin, stinging her cheek.

He's almost here.

Trying to be invisible, she held her breath, even as it begged to escape her chest. Could he hear her heart slamming against her ribcage like a cornered rabbit with no defenses?

The footsteps stopped.

Is he gone? Please make him go away.

Thick fingers squeezed her forearm and yanked her from the forest floor.

I didn't tell. I promise. I told nothing. I've never told anyone.

She willed him to hear the truth in her unspoken words and believe her.

He lugged her through the woods in his arms.

Toward the lake? Or back toward the houses? She wasn't sure.

Her mind clouded like the dense fog that hung over the lake in the early mornings. Through her confusion came the sound of water slapping ominously against the shore.

He stopped. A gate clicked open and then shut next to her head as he walked through. His boots thumped across hollow wood. With one sudden jarring motion, he heaved her away. She landed hard, her head slamming against a solid surface.

The floor rocked.

It's the drugs.

No, I'm in a boat.

Reeling from the sudden pain, she struggled to sit up, straining to lift her head off the floor.

The boat's motor started with a deep and efficient purr. Her head fell back. She drifted off again, pulled into oblivion by a force more powerful than her own frantic will to survive.

2

She woke in a daze as he pulled her up by the shoulder and lifted her into his arms again. With one sideways swing, he threw her into the air.

She fell for less than a second before slicing through the dark water. The icy-coldness raced up her nose and shocked her body.

Kick! Tread! Pull!

Her arms wouldn't move, and her feet couldn't kick. Heavy winter clothes and shoes clung to her body and pulled her into the depths.

There was no one to save her now. She was alone with the man who was finally done with her and needed her to die.

She held her breath and struggled but only sank deeper.

The silver moon rippling on the surface of the water looked farther and farther away. Her lungs burned. The pressure in her head felt close to bursting. Colored splotches appeared in front of her eyes.

I never told our secret...

With a gasp, her mouth opened. The murky water rushed in, filling her lungs.

Her body spasmed and her eyes closed.

Chapter 2

One day earlier

The mountains of West Virginia loomed in the distance under thick clouds as FBI Agent Victoria Heslin drove to the house that would trigger a slew of emotions. More than ten years had passed since her last visit to Lake Lucinda. Hard to believe it had been that long, considering she used to love the place. Lake Lucinda meant adventurous hikes with her family and swimming and boating on the lake. She hadn't intentionally stayed away, but when she wasn't traveling for work, she relished spending time alone in her own home. Although, that might have been an excuse. Visiting the lake house hadn't felt the same since her mother died.

Her father tapped the passenger side window as they passed a sign for the upcoming exit. "The last Starbucks for over fifty miles is down the next road. Do you want to stop?"

Gripping the steering wheel with bandaged hands, Victoria glanced in the rearview mirror of her Suburban, first catching a glimpse of her own reflection—unusually pale skin and hollowed cheeks. Her gaze moved to her greyhounds sleeping in the back, curled up on their soft beds, long snouts snuggled into blankets. Although it was December 26th, they still wore their Christmas collars. Big Ed, her largest dog, was lying with his colt-like front legs sticking straight up into the air.

Behind the SUV, a trailer carried three miniature donkeys.

"A gingerbread latte would be a small slice of heaven." She touched the white pearls that surrounded her neck. They'd belonged to a friend who survived the recent plane crash but not its aftermath. "But all the dogs are settled. And the donkeys stopped kicking the sides of the trailer. I want to keep it that way. I'd rather not stop, unless you need to."

"I'm not the one with the latte addiction." Her father chuckled. "I'm fine with driving straight through. We don't have more than an hour."

When they finally exited the four-lane highway, the scenery summoned memories from her youth. Emerald trees with thick needles covered the hills on either side of the road. Crumbling stone walls stretched across fields. Every few miles, a modest church with a spire and a sign with removable letters appeared like clockwork.

"I had the house cleaned and the boat tuned up." Mr. Heslin rolled his window partway down. Chilly air whistled into the vehicle. The dogs jumped up and pushed into each other, lifting their noses as they clamored for space near the window crack. "The lake is extra quiet and peaceful in the winter. That's what your mother loved most about the place."

"I'm just going to relax there," Victoria said. "I didn't even bring my laptop." She had a feeling her father's request to visit their lake house might have something to do with keeping her distracted until her official recovery period ended and she returned to work.

"I've got some news for you." Her father drew the statement out in a way that told her something interesting was sure to follow.

Her mind raced through possibilities but came up blank.

5

"Your brother and Minka are at the lake house."

"Really? He didn't tell me he was going to be there. I can't wait to meet Minka." Victoria grinned, picturing the tall attorney with striking cheekbones and shiny, long, brown hair. She'd only seen one picture of Alex's current girlfriend, so her mind was filling in the blanks. "Do you think there are wedding bells in their future?" As soon as she asked the question, she wished she could take it back because of what might come next—her Dad wondering aloud if she ever intended to get married.

From inside the center console, Victoria's phone vibrated, rattling the hard plastic cupholder. The car's navigation screen lit up, telling her it was Ned calling. She pressed the green button. "Hey. You're on speaker. My dad's here."

"Hi, Mr. Heslin."

"Hello." Victoria's father leaned toward the navigation screen. "How are you feeling?"

"Better. I went for a run today—"

"Should you be doing that?" Victoria asked. "Is running okay?"

"It was more of a jog. My first one since we've been back. Doctor approved. Anyway, a reporter followed me and by the time I was done there were four of them asking me questions and filming me. Is that unreal or what?" Ned's tone was upbeat, absent any self-pity. How many people could maintain that attitude after what he'd been through, not to mention corrective surgery to repair the damage frostbite had done to his face? Ned was resilient. One of many traits she admired about him.

"That's a big part of why I wanted to get away from the city," she said. "The media didn't seem to be losing interest."

"Are you still on the road, or have you reached your lake house yet?" Ned asked. "Lake Louise, right?"

"We're still on the road and reception is a little spotty through the mountains, so I might lose you. And it's not Lake Louise." Victoria laughed. "It's Lake Lucinda. There's a sad and mysterious story behind the name."

"You can't introduce it like that and then not tell me."

"Okay. This is way before our time, but everyone around the lake knows the story. Here's the gist of it. Lucinda Lee was born here, in the mountains, then moved to Hollywood and became a movie star. She got pretty lucky with some good parts, then leading roles. During the height of her success, decades ago, she returned to this area and built a vacation home on the peninsula. It wasn't a traditional lake cabin. It was a full-blown estate with a main house and a guest house. And at the time, it was a big deal. Locals drove by to gawk. There was nothing else like it around here."

"Her name sounds familiar now," Ned said. "Maybe I've seen her in an old movie."

"That's not all there is to the story. Lucinda isn't most famous around here for her career or her lavish home. She's famous for her death."

"She was murdered?"

"That's the thing...no one really knows. She was out on a sailboat with her current costar—a man who was not her husband. He claimed to have gone below deck for a nap."

"That sounds suspicious already."

"When he woke...she was gone. Her body was later discovered floating face down in a cove very close to where my parents' house—I mean close to where my father's house is now." Victoria pressed down on the brakes, slowing the car for an approaching hairpin curve. "Lucinda's death remains a mystery.

There wasn't enough evidence to prove anything besides her drowning."

"The book convinced me it was the jealous husband," Mr. Heslin said.

"The book?" Ned asked. "That's why your story sounded familiar. There's a mystery novel about her drowning, isn't there?"

"Yes, a fictional account inspired by the true story. It's called *Lucinda's Secrets*. The author, Judith McPharland, owns a house near my father's. She's written lots of mysteries but that book is her top seller, or it used to be. It's the one that made her famous."

Around the next steep curve, the cell signal disappeared and the call abruptly ended.

"That Ned seems like a nice guy," Mr. Heslin said. "He loves animals as much as you. You've been through a lot together. What's the story there?"

A sharp bark came from the back of the car. Victoria glanced in the mirror again, grateful for the distraction from her alpha female. "Myrtle, be nice. You've got plenty of space. We're almost there."

The roads narrowed further and began to rise and twist. The trees thickened and snow dotted the ground in the shaded areas. Her ears clogged from the altitude change. They'd reached Red Spruce Knob, the steep and winding road that led from the nearest town to Lake Lucinda and the peninsula where her father's house was located. At this juncture, when she was younger, she'd have to set down whatever mystery novel she'd been reading or risk a bout of car-sickness. This is where she would finally look out the window and be surprised by how far they'd come and glad they didn't have much farther to go.

The road dipped back down for the last stretch of the trip. Next came a few miles of modest farm houses and doublewides on mostly weed-infested fields.

We're almost there.

Victoria hit her turn signal and took a right at the top of Peninsula Drive. The scenery changed to professional landscapes. The impoverished homes were nowhere to be seen, replaced by mansions on sprawling lots. In the spaces between the houses and through the trees, flashes of the large lake glimmered in the background.

Victoria peered out her window. "Wow. Things have really changed. The new houses keep getting bigger, don't they?"

"Yes. The property values shot up."

"Are any of the original homes left?"

"Very few. One of the new homes up here belongs to a NASCAR driver. Someone famous. I forgot the name. And two players from the Steelers recently moved here. Drew Bingham remodeled the home next to Lucinda Lee's former estate. Gutted it and had it all redone. Jacob Maxwell-Jones bought one of the last vacant lots."

"Am I supposed to recognize those names?"

"Bingham threw for almost five thousand yards last—oh never mind." He folded his arms and huffed. "And Maxwell-Jones is a linebacker."

"Got it." She shifted her hands on the wheel, flexing her fingers a few times. "Are more of the homes used year-round these days?"

"Almost all of them are vacation homes now. The last time I was here, it was like the whole peninsula was deserted. It's a great place for a getaway, although, there still isn't much in the way of shopping or entertainment. Not enough to keep most people satisfied." He tapped on the side window. "Don't miss the turn."

She steered left onto Peninsula Point Drive. The Heslins' lakefront property came into view—a beautiful stone and stucco home with gabled roofs and two turrets. Woods bordered two acres of fenced land. Behind the house, nestled in the secluded valley between majestic mountains and surrounded by estates, Lake Lucinda sparkled.

"Wow. It's absolutely gorgeous." Victoria stared as if seeing all of it for the first time. The pent-up tension in her neck and shoulders released. Right then, a few days at the lake house seemed like exactly what she needed.

▼▲▼

The inside of the lake house looked just as she remembered. And it smelled the same. Like pine and linen. Welcoming and clean.

Empty beer bottles lined the quartz counter, a sure sign of Alex's presence. The green pottery bowl Victoria made ages ago in art class sat at the end of the counter in the same location it had occupied since her youth. She had never been gifted at creating art in any form, yet her mother had displayed the porcelain dish as if it was a treasure. The "key bowl," as they called it, was the receptacle for any and all keys brought into the house.

The center of the house had an open floorplan, and huge windows dominated the back wall, framing stunning views of the lake. Outside, Victoria's dogs crisscrossed the yard, exploring the fenced perimeter and marking the new territory. The donkeys had found the hay and made themselves right at home, munching away in a covered shelter.

Victoria looked forward to seeing Alex and meeting Minka, but the first order of business was a quick trip to the powder room. When she came out, Alex was descending the center stairway, running a hand through his tousled, blond hair. He had the same blue eyes as the rest of the family. His job as ski and avalanche patrol on the Colorado slopes had given him a glowing tan.

He went straight to Victoria and wrapped her in a big hug. She grunted and laughed as he squeezed her hard. Under his plaid flannel shirt, he was solid muscle and smelled of mint toothpaste or mouthwash.

He stepped back, leaning against the kitchen island, and ran his eyes over her. "My now-famous sister."

"I don't want to be famous. And I've definitely had it with people following me around asking for interviews."

"Let me see your hands. I've seen my share of frostbite, you know." He took them in his own and peered down. "Not so perfect anymore, are you?" He grinned and shook her shoulder playfully.

Leave it to Alex not to feel sorry for her. "I'm fine. Adjusting to my new normal. The stitches are almost healed. I'm lucky."

"Because you'll save thirty percent on manicures—that's not such a bad deal. Can you still fire a gun?"

Victoria laughed. "I'll test my shooting skills on you if you're not careful. Even without part of my trigger finger, I'm still an excellent shot."

That's what I've been telling myself and anyone else who asks. I can still shoot. But how accurate will I be?

Alex looked her up and down. "You're way too thin."

"Yeah, well, you should have seen me a week ago."

11

"It's unreal what happened. I was worried about you. Seriously worried. For a whole week, I thought you were a goner. And the only bright side of the thing was that I was gonna get *all* of Dad's money when he died." Alex's eyes sparkled as he laughed.

Victoria couldn't help smiling. She would have been alarmed if anyone else mentioned a bright side to her death. Only Alex had the personality to get away with saying things no one else dared to say.

"Here I am. Sorry to disappoint you." She gave him a playful, light punch in the arm. It felt good to goof around with him in person. "And no need to apologize again about not being with us for Christmas. Dad and I spent a nice, quiet holiday together. We ate Christmas Eve dinner at the club. Everyone there did a terrible job of trying not to stare at me. At least they didn't surround us and ask questions. Anyway, I finally get to meet Minka. So..." Victoria glanced toward the top of the polished wood staircase with iron railings. "Is she upstairs?"

Alex rubbed his neck and looked past her. "Minka left."

"Left? Like to the store?"

"She's on her way to the airport. Back to Colorado."

"Oh." Victoria didn't know what to think or say. "I hope it wasn't because of us. I hope we didn't crash your getaway."

"No. She wanted to meet you. You would have liked each other."

"Would have? What happened?"

"We had an argument." Alex sighed. "About money of all things. Really it was a simple misunderstanding and I was going to clear it up. She got really upset and before I knew what was happening, she'd left."

"You just spent Christmas with her family. You seemed so serious. I thought she might be *the one.*"

"Yeah." Alex dropped his head and looked away.

"You're letting her go all the way back to Colorado alone?"

"That's what she wanted." Alex crossed to the fridge and opened it. "Look, I'd rather not talk about it right now." He grabbed a soda. "I guess it's a good thing you came, because she took the rental and I don't have a car here."

"I'm sorry she left. I hope you can work it out." Victoria walked back to the mudroom. Alex didn't seem crushed or devastated, so maybe he was the one who had broken things off. It was hard to tell because her brother tended to put up a cheerful front. He hid his emotions well.

Inside the mudroom cabinets, stacks of folded white sheets proved there were still some things Victoria could count on. Each sheet had DOGS written on it in large letters with a permanent marker. She removed a pile and walked from room to room, draping the sheets over couches and chairs to protect them from dog hair and muddy prints, as her mother used to do when they arrived at the lake house. The dogs could sleep wherever they pleased. No worries about damaged furniture.

Victoria finished covering the last chair in the family room as her father entered carrying their suitcases. He stopped to wipe his shoes on the floor mat. "Tori, I detached the trailer and pulled your SUV into the garage." After setting the two suitcases down, he embraced his son in the kitchen. "Great to see you, Alex." He looked around. "So, where's Minka?"

Victoria sighed, hoping there would be no other unfortunate surprises.

13

Chapter 3

The sun had dropped to the height of the mountains. In the fading light, the tallest peak cast a shadow over the valley, blanketing the streets as the Heslins walked the dogs.

Victoria surveyed the home across from theirs. Owned by old George Wilson, it was one of few original structures left on Lake Lucinda and one of the largest parcels of property. George's mobile home looked out of place amidst the multi-million-dollar estates and extra small shielded by overgrown shrubs and trees. Woods bordered each side of every home on the peninsula, but the woods alongside George's house were the most dense and untamed.

After being away for so many years, Victoria was seeing George's place through a fresh lens. Not much had changed. Ragged bushes pushed through the rusting shell of a truck that had been in his yard since Victoria's family bought their home. In the shadows, an old upturned wheelbarrow and a shovel rested against the side of the trailer near an ancient sink.

A seven-foot chain-link fence topped by barbed wire surrounded much of his property. Behind the gate, long spindly cracks and deep ruptures crept across the driveway.

"Why doesn't George sell this place?" Alex asked. "It's a dump, but he'd get a small fortune for the property. He must get offers all the time."

"I'm not sure how he affords the rising property taxes on the land, but I'm glad he's sticking it out," Mr. Heslin said. "He keeps an eye on our home and several others and does minor repairs while we're gone. Last year he found and fixed a water leak in our garage. Imagine if the leak had continued unchecked for months. His fence doesn't bother me. The Roberts—they own the Nantucket House now—offered to pay for a replacement, but George refused."

Victoria let her dogs mill around George's mailbox, sniffing hard. "Remember when George called the police on Alex and his high school friends?"

"He scared the crap out of us with a shotgun," Alex said. "Not the kind of thing you easily forget."

Mr. Heslin shook his head. "George thought kids had broken into our house. I always tell George when I'm coming. Since you and your friends snuck up here, he didn't know it was you. Your friends were a little out of control and George probably saved someone's life on your trip. He's always looked out for you."

"Which means he was always watching me, Dad," Alex said as a gust of wind rushed past, scraping bare branches together. "Don't you think he's a little creepy?"

"I never thought George was creepy." Victoria gave the leashes a soft tug to get the dogs moving again. "He probably wants a simple life away from everyone else. I can relate to that."

"Do you also take your donkeys on walks?" Alex teased as Myrtle surged ahead, pulling hard on the leash in his hand.

15

Victoria grinned. "Not yet. They have names. The big gray one is Oscar. The two browns are females. Arya and Sansa. I should have introduced you."

"I introduced myself. It's funny that you brought them."

"Ned is recovering. And the woman who watched them while I was in Greenland wasn't available. I couldn't leave them with a complete stranger."

Alex's smile grew. "I hate to shock you with this news, Tori, but they're donkeys. They live without babysitters in farm pastures all over the world."

"I know, but mine don't. After what they've been through, they deserve a life of luxury-and ease. Oh, I meant to ask, have you seen any sign of the foxes since you got here?"

"Ah, the foxes. No." Alex laughed. "They're interesting, but I don't miss the way they used to wake us up in the middle of the night, wailing like little demons. They hung around because you used to put food out for them."

That's exactly what she was planning to do before she went to bed. Her dog food contained wholesome nutrients. A little left here and there would be a special treat for the animals.

"I think Judith is here," Mr. Heslin said as they approached the author's home.

Wearing a bright orange parka and a yellow scarf around her neck, Judith stood by the wintery remains of a flower bed, hands on her hips. Her hair consistently looked remarkable because she wore wigs. This one was blonde with loose waves. Victoria had no idea what Judith's real hair looked like. Or if she had any hair at all.

The Heslins stopped at the stone path leading to the front of Judith's house. Victoria waved.

Judith's eyes lit up. "Oh, look who it is!" Waving her arms, she strolled down the front path. "I knew exactly who you all were when I saw the greyhounds in their fabulous coats. Victoria, you look so much like your mother. You really do. Your blonde hair. Same slim, athletic frame." Judith's hands flew to her face and her mouth opened. "Oh...of course...what was I thinking...you've been through so much, haven't you? I was following the story and praying for you." She turned to Mr. Heslin and Alex as if she'd just remembered they were also there. "How wonderful to see all of you!"

Judith appeared not to have aged since Victoria had seen her last, and yet she looked different. Her skin stretched tight over her temples and remained smooth and crease free when she spoke and laughed, displaying no emotion. But her hazel eyes beamed with delight as she focused on Victoria. "Phoebe is here, too. Not right now, she's gone out but she'll be back tonight. The two of you haven't seen each other in ages. Phoebe comes here every so often, and I see Alex and your father occasionally, but you...it's been so long, hasn't it?"

"It has," Victoria said.

"Oh, this is fabulous." Judith clapped her hands. "A wonderful surprise. Phoebe will get such a kick out of catching up with you."

Victoria forced a smile as Alex nudged her shoe and grinned.

When Victoria was younger, the author encouraged Victoria's love of reading by gifting signed copies of every new release. And Victoria had read all of them, staying up long into the night to find out which character was the guilty one. But Judith's daughter, Phoebe, an only child, was a whole other something. She had been quite the bully when they were girls. Disturbing

17

memories crawled into Victoria's mind of the time Phoebe threw rocks at the geese because she didn't want them on her yard. Her aim was mostly terrible, until one of her throws hit a goose head on. Victoria had been horrified and even now, she shuddered thinking about it. Phoebe only laughed, appearing to enjoy Victoria's obvious distress.

"Geese don't have souls," Phoebe had said. As if her opinion on the topic made it okay to harm them.

Victoria wouldn't be entirely shocked if Phoebe had grown up to be a sociopath.

Judith clapped her hands. "You must come for dinner tomorrow. All of you! Oh, it will be so much fun. We have so much catching up to do. And you'll get to meet John."

"We'd love to come." Mr. Heslin said. "We don't have any definite dinner plans while we're here. And if my children don't mind me saying so, none of us are excellent cooks like you."

Judith laughed. "Wonderful. I'm going in now to figure out a plan for our meal."

Great. Can't wait to see Phoebe.

They said their goodbyes, and the Heslins continued their walk.

"Who is John?" Victoria asked.

"I have no idea." Alex turned to his sister. "Judith was awfully excited to see you. She probably wants to pick your brain about Flight 745 for her next book."

"Now that you mention it," Mr. Heslin said, "I don't think she's published anything new in years. Perhaps she *is* looking for some new and exciting insight to get her creative wheels turning."

"Yeah, so she can write another inspired-by-true-events book." Alex pulled back on Myrtle's leash as she tried to explore shrubs lining the road. "Thankfully she didn't turn mom's kidnapping and death into one of her blockbuster novels." He reached into the bushes and pulled the leash free. "Or did she? I've never read her books."

"She did not." Mr. Heslin shook his head. "Doing so would have been in extremely poor taste."

"I like Judith a lot, but money and fame doesn't buy taste," Alex said. "Phoebe's a prime example. Wait 'til you see her, Tori."

Victoria wasn't looking forward to the dinner. Unless their plans changed, she would have to "play nice" with Phoebe.

▼▲▼

"What should we eat tonight?" Mr. Heslin opened the refrigerator door. Most of the shelves were empty. "You didn't do much shopping, Alex." He pushed aside a bag of spinach and picked up a carton of something brown and unrecognizable. "What's this?"

Alex peered around the door. "Got me. One of Minka's vegan things. We need to go shopping. I'll make us a nice dinner."

Victoria hitched up her pants as they slipped down her hips. "I hope you and Minka didn't break up because you couldn't go a day without meat."

For a second, Alex seemed to stare right through her, and she worried that she shouldn't have made a joke about their situation. Then he snapped back.

"You sound pretty concerned about my breakup. Which gets me thinking about how you've never introduced me to any of your significant others. Why not, Tori?"

Victoria shrugged. Her brother was teasing her back, unaware the answer to his question related to layers of protective barriers she'd unknowingly constructed.

19

Alex scooped up his wireless headphones from the counter. "My friends think you're gorgeous. A few of them won't shut up about it. Guess you're too strange."

Victoria landed a punch on Alex's shoulder, this one with more oomph than before. She and Alex had always given each other a hard time, sort of their way of being close.

"No, I get it." Alex plopped down onto the sectional. "You've preferred animals to people since you were a kid. Remember when Phoebe used to knock on the door to see if you could play? You told me to say you weren't here and then you would tiptoe upstairs and hide somewhere with a dog and a book. You always had your nose in a book."

"First off, I hid because it was Phoebe. And anyway, all that reading was the perfect preparation for what I do. It helped me understand people. It helps me figure out motives. And it made me more empathetic. You should try it someday. Reading a book, that is." She laughed. "Now I have an iron gate to keep people from knocking on my door."

"Hmm...who does that sound like?" Alex's smile grew huge as he wagged his finger toward the front of the house. "You and George could be soul mates. Throw a few rescue dogs into his yard and—boom, there you go—he'd be the perfect boyfriend for you. Too bad he's like eighty."

Victoria recoiled. *Could I end up like George?* She checked her phone to see if Ned had tried to call her back since their call dropped.

Mr. Heslin grabbed a glass from the cabinet. "For the record, Alex, George is not eighty. He's only about ten years older than I am."

Alex threw his arm over the back of the couch and smirked. "Okay, then. My bad. Almost eighty."

20

"I turned sixty-two last month," Mr. Heslin said. "And I'm proud of your sister and the career she's chosen."

"Thank you, Dad." Victoria gave her father a quick hug, glad he'd focused on what she had going for her and not what she didn't have. "It means a lot to me that you're proud." She went to the couch and tapped Alex's arm. "Come on, let's see about getting the fridge and cabinets filled."

A few minutes later, she was sitting next to Alex and driving to the nearest shopping center. They were quiet all the way out of the peninsula.

At a stop sign, Victoria studied her brother. "Are you sad about Minka?"

Alex stared straight ahead. "Are you still a vegetarian?"

She laughed. "Yes. Mostly. Listen, if you change your mind and want to talk, I'm here for you. I know I'm no relationship expert, but I am a good listener."

As she drove, Victoria admired the white lights strung around the trees and the bells hanging from the streetlamps. She steered left into the shopping center and parked in front of Prince's Grocery Store, which had been there as far back as she could remember, although the store's facade had been upgraded.

"I'm going to make those oatmeal butterscotch cookies mom used to make." She shut off the car and pulled her grocery list from her pocket. "I have the recipe."

As she opened her door, a silver Range Rover with West Virginia plates pulled into the adjacent parking space. A Christmas wreath with a bow hung from the front of the vehicle. The driver caught up to them in the store's entryway. He was a handsome man with broad shoulders wearing a North Face jacket, a red scarf, and jeans.

21

"Hey. How's it going?" He spoke to Alex and acknowledged Victoria with a nice solid smile, straight white teeth, and a husky voice.

"Hey. It's going well." Alex gestured toward Victoria. "This is my sister, Victoria." He moved his hand toward the man. "This is Harrison Daughton."

Harrison looked to be in his late thirties. Prominent, raised scars lined his face, disappearing under a firm jaw. The scars looked old, from a serious injury, and added an element of interest to his rugged but polished features. The largest of the scars stretched as he smiled. "Nice to meet you, Victoria."

"Likewise," she said.

Alex grabbed a grocery cart. "Harrison lives in Lucinda Lee's former estate."

"Oh. I was wondering who lived there now." Victoria grabbed the handle of her own cart. The front stuck, attached to the others. She pulled and shook it.

Harrison laughed. "Let me help." He placed his hand near hers on the cart's handle.

"I got it," she said, a beat too late to stop him from yanking with her. The cart jerked loose.

"You here for a few weeks?" Harrison looked from Victoria to Alex.

"No. Only a few days." Harrison acted so friendly that she worried they might get another dinner invitation. One was more than enough for her, no matter who was inviting.

"Have a nice visit then," Harrison said. "Happy holidays."

"Same to you." Alex wheeled his cart away. "I'll meet you at the checkout," he told his sister.

Victoria scanned the overhead signs. She and Harrison moved in the same direction at the same time.

Harrison held back and signaled for her to go first. Walking ahead of him, she had a sudden awareness of the view he would have—the view anyone behind her would have *if* they were looking. She usually had a nice feminine shape. Now, her jeans hung from her hips as if she had no rear end.

She swiped flour and sugar off the shelf and into her cart, found the butterscotch chips, and went in search of eggs.

When she'd finished selecting the food she needed, she found Alex and they combined their groceries. Harrison was unloading his cart at the checkout counter. Victoria couldn't help notice his items; a collection of purchases told a lot about a person. Fresh berries, popcorn, apples, milk, cereal, pasta, peanut butter, whole-grain bread, and a box of regular-sized Tampons.

Healthy but simple tastes. And he's not single. Unless the tampons are part of a survival kit. She laughed at herself for over analyzing.

Harrison packed his groceries into a bag as the cashier scanned them. After paying, he waved goodbye to Victoria and Alex.

Outside, a grayness tinged the night sky. Specks of snow swirled to the ground under a bright streetlamp, melting when they landed.

The silver Range Rover drove off as Victoria unlocked her own vehicle. "That man—Harrison—do you know what he does for a living?"

Alex plopped his groceries on the backseat and pulled a bag of chips out before getting into the front passenger side. "I'm not sure if he does anything. Family money, I think. Why? You interested in him? Is he your type? Old money. Fancy car."

23

Victoria chuckled. "No." Not what she had been thinking at all. And the tampons suggested he was already taken. "No," she said again for good measure, so there wasn't any confusion. Although Harrison *was* handsome. "I was merely curious about the other people who own houses around Lake Lucinda now. Besides Judith and George, I don't know the first thing about any of them."

"And that's probably how they want it. People come to Lake Lucinda to get away from everything and everyone else."

Chapter 4

Upstairs, Victoria started the hot water to fill the tub, then returned to her bedroom. From the bottom of her suitcase, she scooped out the small exercise ball provided by her occupational therapist. She sat on the edge of her bed and closed her hand around it, silently counting repetitions, flexing and releasing, channeling strength into what remained of her trigger finger.

On one wall, a collection of her old mystery novels filled a built-in bookshelf. Several of the books had familiar titles and Judith's name printed on their black spines. Skimming through a few of them while she was at the lake might prove interesting, now that Victoria solved crimes for a living.

When the tub was full, Victoria lit the display of candles around the ledge and sprinkled eucalyptus salts into the water. She soaked in the tranquil bath with her feet up on the edge, relaxing and thinking about absolutely nothing until the water grew tepid. Afterward, feeling pampered and serene, she climbed under the soft bedding, moving her feet around to warm up the cool sheets. The thick mattress topper cradled her body and provided an instant reminder of how her mother had made each bed deliciously comfortable. Getting out of bed early to go sailing would be a challenge. But she and Alex had promised their father.

The dogs settled around her; two sprawled at her side, taking up most of the space, and four lounging in dog beds on the floor. Izzy slept in the hallway outside Victoria's room, like she did at home, keeping an eye out for all of them.

Feeling grateful she was at the lake with her family, Victoria fell into a peaceful sleep.

A noise startled her awake.

One of the dogs dreaming? Or was it laughter?

She looked at the clock. A few minutes after midnight. Tossing the comforter aside, she rose and walked to the back window. Moonlight lit a silvery path across the dark water all the way to the end of the yard. Her brother reclined in a patio chair with his feet up and a beer in his hand. Across from him sat a pretty young woman with long brown hair and a serious expression. Flames flickered on top of the gas firepit, casting an eerie glow over both of their faces.

I guess Minka didn't board the plane to Colorado after all. Good. I'm glad she's back and things worked out between them.

Minka looked younger than Victoria expected.

Alex tipped his head back and laughed—the same boisterous sound she'd woken to. The type of laughter that told her Alex had been drinking.

Minka didn't even crack a smile.

They still had some things to iron out. Perhaps Victoria should have insisted Alex take her SUV to the airport and go after his girlfriend.

Across the large yard, the donkeys huddled under the new shelter. They kept their distance and watched Alex and Minka with wary eyes. A passing car briefly cast a streak of light along the side of the house. Minka jumped up from her seat and followed the light with her head. Victoria caught a good view of Minka's beautiful face and a dark beauty mark above her lip.

After turning away from the window, Victoria slid back under the still warm sheets. In minutes, she was dreaming.

A bloodcurdling scream woke her.

She shot up, reaching under her pillow for the gun she kept nearby in her own home. A gun she hadn't brought with her.

Wait—that's not a person screaming. It must be a fox.

Alex was right. The foxes' cries were unsettling, sounding eerily like a woman's terrified wail.

The numbers on the digital clock read 1:30 am. Victoria didn't like being awakened during the night, especially not for the second time. But as she settled back into the pillows, it comforted her to learn foxes were still around and nearby. They were possibly the great, great grandchildren of the ones she used to feed. She was glad they had discovered the food she set out for them.

Chapter 5

Holding a cup of hot tea in the family room, Victoria gazed outside. In the cold morning air, mist rose from the rippling surface of the lake like smoke. It wasn't raining yet, but clouds thickening around the mountain peaks signaled a storm brewing. The higher elevation of mountains could get snow. The valley might only see torrents of sleet and pelting rain.

Inside, looking out, it was deliciously warm and peaceful. Victoria lowered herself onto a large chair and put her feet on the ottoman.

A phone rang from somewhere in the house and then footsteps tapped across the wood floor. Her father entered the open area of the main floor dressed in a thick fisherman's sweater and jeans. He carried the old Tupperware container with the red top, which held the boat keys and the owner's manual and always accompanied him on the boat.

"Morning, Dad." Victoria adjusted a pillow behind her back. "Whose phone is ringing? Does this house have a landline?"

He set the container down on the kitchen island. "Yes. Just ignore it. The only calls are from marketers. But it's come in handy a few times while I was here alone. I used it to call my cell phone when I misplaced it." He opened the Tupperware container and tossed his phone and wallet inside. "Ready for our sail?"

"Oh. I'm so comfortable right now." She wanted to go with him, yet she had no desire to move. Time had slowed down, in a good way, and she was enjoying every second.

Her father gestured toward the windows. "We don't have the best lake weather coming our way. We need to get out on the water while we can."

Victoria had another sip of her tea and propelled herself up. "I'll wake Alex." Carrying her mug, she shuffled back upstairs, sliding one hand over the polished railing, and knocked on her brother's door. "Alex?"

From inside his room, Alex grunted. "What is it?"

"We're going for a sail. Remember? Get up."

Silence.

She drank the last of her tea and was raising her hand to knock again when Alex groaned and said, "It's too early."

"Come on. It's going to rain in a few hours. We have to go now. We promised Dad." She lowered her voice. "I can tell he's into it."

"I'm tired." He sounded grouchy.

"What are you, sixteen? Come on. Get up." Then she remembered Minka. *Oops.* Minka might be in one of the guest rooms, but more likely, she was in Alex's bed right now.

"Go away." Alex grumbled. "I need sleep more than I need a boat ride."

"Okay. Sorry. Go back to sleep." Victoria backed away, slightly embarrassed. Giving her brother a hard time was fun, but not if his girlfriend was there.

"Stay here," Alex called. "Don't go on the boat. I don't want to have to save the two of you."

"You better be joking, Alex. I taught *you* how to sail." She walked away, toward the stairs. While she wouldn't embarrass him, she wouldn't let him get away with making her look less than competent either.

"Is he coming?" her father asked when she got back to the kitchen.

Victoria lowered her voice. "He might have had a late night. I think Minka came back."

A frown flashed across his face. "I didn't see another car."

"Hmm. Strange." Victoria put her empty mug in the dishwasher. "I figured she was staying. There's only one motel in the town. I doubt Minka or anyone else would choose it over your house. She might have gone out for coffee."

"We'll find out when we get back." Her father picked up the container and secured it under his arm. "Let's go. Before it rains."

"Aye, aye, captain." Victoria slid her boots on, grabbed her coat, and followed him out the door.

A great blue heron perched alone on the dock's railing, looking both strange and magnificent with its stick legs and patrician nose. Its presence meant the lake remained free of ice. As they got closer, the large bird flew off.

Victoria reached the weathered boards of the boathouse and inhaled deeply. She flicked a switch on a vertical beam and creaking pulleys slowly lowered the boat into the water. To her surprise, she didn't have to think about what to do to help get the boat ready. Going through the motions was second nature, like riding a bike.

When the boat was in the water, she unbuttoned the cover and peeled the thick canvas back on one side while her father worked the other side. Onboard, she prepared the sails as her father

30

started the motor. He let it run for a few minutes, checked the engine and gauges, then backed out. In spite of repeatedly adjusting her grip to accommodate for her missing fingertips, the entire process had gone smoothly without a word exchanged between them. It was as if no time had passed since they'd last performed the steps together.

They glided silently away from their dock. Victoria's dogs raced back and forth in the yard behind the tall fence, a few of them barking, not wanting to be left behind.

They had the lake to themselves, the only boat in sight. The air was chilly but not too cold. Her father tightened the jib halyard and the forward sail filled with wind. He then hoisted the mainsail and wrapped the main sheet onto the port winch. In a moment they were cruising along at a good clip.

Victoria lifted her chin to the cloudy sky. "This is nice. I'm glad you got me out here."

"Wish Alex had come with us." With the hint of a smile, her father pulled the rim of his hat down.

She recognized the look. Something had him amused. "What are you thinking about?"

"The many times when Alex didn't put the boat on the lift or tie it up. It took me a long while to laugh about it. Especially after the first time."

"Hmm. As far back as I can remember, you've forgiven Alex pretty quickly, no matter what he did or failed to do." Victoria rubbed her gloved hands together. Three half-empty finger sleeves crumpled between the others. "I'm glad Minka is back. I hope things are okay."

Her father brought the boat about, switching both sails' sheets to the starboard winches as he tacked across the lake. "Alex shouldn't have let Minka go off by herself. I can't imagine either

31

Ned or Rivera letting you drive all the way back to the airport alone late at night. I hope they wouldn't."

"I didn't think he should have let her go either. But we don't know the whole story. She might have been screaming at him not to come after her." Victoria brushed strands of hair away from her eyes. "Can we go back to something you said a minute ago? It sounds like you think Ned and Rivera are my boyfriends. That's not the case. Ned works for me—at least I hope he still will, and Rivera is my colleague."

"If you say so." Mr. Heslin leaned back. "And I suppose it will stay that way until you figure out what it is you want."

"What I want?"

A gust of wind surged against the sail. The boat raced forward.

"What you want or who you want. Or if you want anyone at all. Make sure you decide. If you wait too long, you might not get to. One or both of them will eventually move on—not because he wants to, because he sees no future with you—because you don't show him there is one." Holding tight to the sail, he shifted his weight and faced her. "I've lived alone since your mother died, because I was too busy to meet someone else. That was a mistake. Don't make the same one. I want you to have what your mother and I had. Dogs are wonderful, but not the same as having a soul mate. If I get a vote, I like that Rivera fella. He would have moved mountains to find your plane and bring you home. Heck, he pretty much did. However, and I get why you're confused, Ned seems like a good man, too."

Victoria wasn't sure how to respond. He was right. Why was she still afraid of a commitment with Ned? Should they keep moving forward, or should she back off now before they crossed a line that might...what? What did she think would happen? Why did

32

she keep thinking a serious relationship would only lead to heartache or loss somewhere down the line? Ned worked for her, but after everything they had been through together, wasn't it worth risking the relationship to give a stronger, more meaningful one a real chance?

Her father had also mentioned Rivera a few times since they left Virginia, as if he and Ned were interchangeable. No doubt Rivera had impressed her father while she was missing in Greenland. Yet she and Rivera had never exchanged so much as a kiss. Their relationship had been entirely professional. However, she would be lying if she said there wasn't something more brewing below the surface over their last few cases together. The truth was that she had chemistry with both men.

Why couldn't I have met someone on a hike or at the grocery store, where if things didn't work out, neither of us would have so much to lose?

The man from the grocery store popped into her head.

Harrison. He was handsome.

She pushed his image from her mind. She wasn't looking for another guy. And Harrison seemed to be spoken for anyway.

Massaging her fingers and avoiding the tender tips, she took in the opulent mansions along the shore while the breeze blew her ponytail straight out behind her. The newest homes were the largest. They towered on the lots—three, four, even five stories with floor to ceiling windows across the backs. Lake Lucinda offered great opportunities for a peeping Tom with a boat and a good set of binoculars. The exception was Lucinda Lee's former estate. Harrison's home now. Only the rooflines of the house and guest house were visible. Trees and bushes had been allowed to grow tall and full. Apparently, Harrison valued his privacy more than an unobstructed view. She couldn't blame him. When

33

Victoria was a girl, all because of Judith's novel, people visited the neighborhood to see where Lucinda Lee once lived. They'd drive slowly by the mansion and take pictures or park along the street, get out of their cars, and peer in through the ornate front gate. *Lucinda's Secrets* had created such a stir that a few homeowners had moved rather than deal with the intrusion into their privacy. Over the years, as Judith's book aged, the interest waned and the curious visitors disappeared.

As they sailed past a shoal marker mounted on a tall wooden post, her father gestured toward the shore and Enticement Cove. "The cove used to be your favorite spot for swimming."

"Used to be." Shallow water between the shore and the island prevented motor boats from speeding through, making the cove the perfect place to anchor and swim. It also happened to be the location where Lucinda Lee's body was discovered.

Victoria let go of the stanchion and headed toward the stairs in the center of the boat. "I'm going below to check out the cabin. See if it's what I remember."

At the bottom of the steps, a blue banquette bench surrounded a table made of warm teak. Small cabinets and appliances constituted the galley. Light entered through spotless portholes.

With no warning, Victoria's chest tightened. Her lungs constricted.

Has the overhead always been so low down here?

She didn't remember the boat being so cramped. It was closing in on her.

A flashback of Flight 745's first-class wreckage came fast and hit her hard.

Twisted metal. Torn wires. The smell of burnt flesh.

34

A rush of light-headedness made her close her eyes. Clammy sweat beaded her forehead. She grasped for inner strength, not wanting to end up on the deck of the boat's cabin and scare her poor father to death. She'd already put him through more than enough worry for one lifetime.

I have to get out of here!

Gripping the stair railing, she forced one trembling leg in front of the other, pushing through mounting panic, until she made it topside.

She closed her eyes and gulped in the fresh air.

"You okay?" Her father's brow furrowed. "You look a little green around the gills."

"I'm fine." With her gloves wrapped tight around the cold metal railing, she focused on slow, rhythmic breaths.

"You sure?"

She nodded and pressed her lips together. All she could manage in the moment.

"Didn't realize the water would be so choppy already. Feels like we're on the ocean, doesn't it?"

"Yeah, it does."

After a few minutes, she was still a little shaky, but her panic had subsided. Dr. Monroe, the FBI psychiatrist assigned to Victoria, warned her about PTSD and flashbacks. Victoria was supposed to report the incident. And she would—*if* it happened again. For now, it was an isolated occurrence. She had quickly recovered. No sense in worrying anyone. In the future, the next time she had to enter a dark and confined space, she'd be mentally prepared for what might happen and it wouldn't catch her by surprise.

"The clouds thickened since we left the house." Her father loosened the ropes tethering the sail. "Looks like the rain might start earlier than expected. I'm going to turn around and get back before it storms."

They sailed by Enticement Cove again.

A long object floating close below the water's surface caught Victoria's eye. "Hold up, Dad. There's something in the water. Toward the shore."

He pulled the tiller left and loosened the mainsail until they were barely moving.

"That way." She pointed. "See it?"

"No." He squinted at the dark water. "What is it?"

"I'm not sure."

"It's probably a log. These rains loosen the soil and push them into the water. Got to keep a sharp eye out or you'll tear up the keel."

"I don't think it's a log, Dad. Look on the starboard side."

"I see it now." He guided the boat to the right.

She strained to make out the object. "It looks like floating seaweed attached to something." Her bad feeling grew worse. "But there's no seaweed in this lake."

She turned away from the unknown object and grabbed the pike pole from the side storage bin.

The boat drifted within reaching distance. The gnarled branches of a downed tree reached up from under the dark water.

It is just a tree. But the seaweed—what's that about?

Victoria leaned over the side and gently prodded the object, pulling it toward the surface. Dark clothing, narrow shoulders, and a back emerged, floating up from under the water like the head of a crocodile emerging for a breath. What had looked like seaweed was long brown hair on a woman's corpse.

Chapter 6

The corpse's thin arms floated on the gently rolling waves as the Heslins' boat glided past.

"We have to go back." Victoria hung her head and let out a soft moan. "Who could she be?"

"She doesn't look familiar. I'd have to see her face." Her father guided the boat around and pulled in the sail, slowing their approach.

Victoria gripped a stanchion with one hand and leaned out, stretching the pike pole across the water. The hook plopped in several feet shy of the corpse and sliced heavily through the water, back toward the boat.

Trying again, she widened her stance and rose to her tiptoes, holding onto the vessel with one hand and the pole with the other. She let go to use both hands and gain another inch.

The boat moved to the right, jerking her off balance. She grabbed the railing before she sprawled onto the floor.

One more time.

She pulled the pole back, hand over hand, and reached again. The hook fell short and disappeared below the dark water. The pole almost fell from her hand. "This isn't working. Can you drop anchor so I can attach this onto her?"

Her father stared at the body for another second, then returned to the controls and pressed the anchor release button. "Doing it now."

Victoria sent the pole out again, dropping it on the center of the woman's back. Her father held the back of her jacket so she wouldn't fall. Inch by inch, Victoria trailed the hook gently over the dead body and secured the back of the jeans.

She pulled.

The body didn't budge. One leg was caught between the tree branches.

A gust of wind sent stray hairs whipping across Victoria's eyes as she changed her angle and tugged to the side.

The corpse floated free.

"Got her." Victoria kept her eyes trained on the dead body.

Her father's breathing became shallow. "Should we try CPR? Is there any chance we can revive her?"

"No. Rigor mortis has set in. That's a telltale-sign she's been dead at least a few hours. She hasn't been in the water too much longer than that. A day at most."

"How can you tell it hasn't been more than a day?"

"The skin. Her hands are bleached and wrinkled from water absorption, but her skin is still intact. She's not swollen like she would be if it had been a few days. I don't think we would have seen her at all if she wasn't stuck on a branch. She'd still be at the bottom until she bloated and gases sent her up."

He winced. "Should we leave her until the police arrive?"

"No." Victoria's response was sharp and instant. She couldn't bear to leave the woman submerged a moment longer. After seeing the victims of Flight 745 frozen and untouched in the snow day after day for almost a week, she wanted this woman out of the water fast. Leaving her there a minute longer felt wrong. Unbearably wrong. "She could have entered the lake from anywhere and ended up here. Before we move her, we'll take pictures of this location. I can't let go of the pole or I might lose her. Can you get my phone? I think it's in my left pocket."

Mr. Heslin found her phone and took a few pictures. "Oh, God," he said, placing one hand over his mouth and lowering his head. "This poor person."

Victoria looked to the large dock on the other side of the cove. The Heslins' house was close by, but the Nantucket House—a massive, cedar-shingled, gray and white structure with a widow's walk on top—was closer.

Her father slid her phone back into her pocket and returned to the steering wheel.

"You can take us to the Nantucket House dock," she said. "Slowly."

He got the anchor up and they puttered toward the Nantucket House. They didn't have far to go. A wall of large stones sloped down along a wide strip of yard and into the lake. Near the dock, atop a tall pole, an American flag whipped in the wind.

The corpse skimmed through the water face down, hair trailing, creating a gentle, miniature wake of its own. The body was that of a slim woman. Without seeing her face, Victoria wasn't certain about age. Anywhere from twenty to an exceptionally fit sixty-something years old.

Was her death a tragic accident? Perhaps, but fully clothed and in the winter? Unlikely.

Mr. Heslin steered the sailboat alongside the newly renovated dock and shut off the motor. He got out and tied the boat to mooring cleats.

"Do you still have a tarp on board?" Victoria asked, her outstretched arms growing tired from gripping the pole and keeping the body from sinking. The wind swept her hair across her eyes.

"I have a new headsail stowed below. It's never been used."

"Good. Shake it anyway, make sure it's clean. Then can you roll it out flat on the dock?"

Her father climbed off the boat, carrying the sail. Before rolling the material out, he shook it, letting the sheet snap in the wind. "It's ready for her." His eyes dropped to the body, still face down in the water. "How are we going to do this?"

Under the steel-gray sky, the cold water was almost black. There appeared to be no bottom. Victoria dreaded going in, but would if necessary. "I'm going to move her around to the dockside." She scrambled to the front of the boat, guiding the body to where she could reach it from the dock. "Here, hold the hook, please."

Mr. Heslin held the body in place. Victoria leapt off the boat and onto the dock. She pulled off her coat and pushed up her sweater sleeves. Dropping to her knees, she leaned forward until she could grab the woman's shoulders. Cold water traveled up her sleeves, soaking her arms and sending pain through her finger nubs.

"Wait for me." Her father got off the boat again. "Let me—" He gasped as his legs flew out from underneath him. His arms flailed and he fell, smacking the hard surface of the dock hip first.

"Oh, no." Clinging to the corpse so it wouldn't sink to the bottom, Victoria couldn't get up to help her father. "Dad, are you okay?"

He stood slowly, pressing his hand against his side. "I'm fine."

"Are you sure?"

"The dock is wet and I slipped." Grimacing, he took a knee next to Victoria and leaned down.

Victoria's shoulder muscles were tight and cramped. Her back ached, begging her to straighten. She moved a little to the right and bumped heads hard with her father. A sharp jolt of pain shot through her skull. "Ow. I'm so sorry," she said. She stayed focused, wanting to get the corpse out of the water.

Grunting, they lifted the body upward. They scooted back and hauled the corpse with its soaked sweater and jeans onto the dock. Water ran off the dead woman and drenched their own clothes.

"I'll get her feet." Her father moved around to the opposite side of the body.

"You're handling this situation well, Dad."

"I don't know about that, but I'm glad it looks that way to you."

With Victoria gripping the corpse's shoulders and her father cradling the feet, they carried the dead woman to the sail sheet. The body weighed little more than a hundred pounds and was easy to move, once it was out of the water. Strands of wet, tangled hair covered most of the corpse's face and delicate neck. Its skin, where visible, had taken on a ghostly, waxy tinge.

They set the body gently down. Its wet hair slid off to the side.

Victoria caught her first glimpse of the dead woman's face.

Eyes closed. Pale lips parted, revealing the bottom teeth. A dark beauty mark to the side of the nose.

She raised her hand to her heart. "Oh, no."

Mr. Heslin placed a wet arm around his daughter's shoulder. "What is it? You've seen dead bodies before. I thought—"

"Yes, it's not that," she whispered, surprised he'd misunderstood her reaction. She placed her hand on her father's arm and met his eyes. "But it's—," she could barely say the words aloud, "—it's Minka."

Her father cringed as if someone had slapped him. His eyes narrowed, shifting from his daughter to the corpse dripping on the tarp. "No. No."

Victoria held her breath, unsure of what he meant. "No what, Dad?"

"That's not Minka. This girl is much younger."

At first, his words relieved her. The relief was short-lived. Her father hadn't sounded certain. "Have you met her in person? Have you ever seen Minka up close?"

He shook his head. "I've only seen pictures. You haven't met her either. Why do you think this is Minka?"

"Because this is the woman Alex was with last night. Outside. On our patio." She pressed her teeth against her bottom lip, questioning her memory.

What is it about the woman I recognize? It was late at night when I saw her. I was half asleep.

"I didn't get a great look at her. Maybe I'm wrong." She wanted to believe she was mistaken, but she didn't think so. Strong first impressions, the kind that hit swift and sudden like an unexpected kick, were not ones to question. Victoria rarely doubted herself. So why was she doing so now? The answer was obvious. She didn't want to believe Alex's girlfriend, the woman he was with last night, was now dead under suspicious circumstances.

"This can't be Minka." Mr. Heslin's voice was firm. "And I know nothing about Alex hanging out with anyone on our back patio yesterday, other than what you told me this morning." Her father couldn't seem to pull his gaze away from the corpse. His face clouded with emotion. "She's so young. She could be a teenager." After a few seconds, he squared his shoulders and headed back toward the boat. "I'm calling the police now."

Victoria stayed, studying the body.

A touch of frothy foam clung to the corner of the corpse's nostrils, a sure sign the woman had drowned. There were no definitive, visible indications of significant injuries or foul play. Small abrasions marred the hands and face. The scratches might represent defensive wounds or could have come from debris in the water. The fingernails were unpolished. No blood or skin scrapings were visible under the nails, although a microscope might say otherwise. Or the water had washed the evidence away.

The victim wore designer jeans with a double-stitched seam down the side, a sweater that looked to be cashmere, and running shoes. Everything about her seemed familiar to Victoria, like a déjà vu. There was no coat and no purse. Those might be somewhere in the lake. Victoria resisted the urge to check inside the woman's back pockets for identification. The police would arrive soon. As an FBI agent, she could pull rank, but it might cause bad blood going forward. Waiting was the right thing to do.

She scanned the woods bordering each side of the Nantucket House. Had Minka, or her lookalike, walked through them last night or early this morning, scratching her hands on the branches? Or had she come from somewhere else entirely? A boat, perhaps. Or from one of the nearby occupied houses. With the strong wind fueling the current, she could have entered the lake from almost anywhere in the vicinity and been pulled into Enticement Cove. There were many possibilities. Every single one of them seemed a better alternative than the victim ending up in the lake by way of the Heslins' backyard.

A glint of movement flickered in the woods. A flash of red. Victoria leaned to the side, squinting through the trees, but didn't see it again. Had it been her imagination? Or was someone watching them?

Her father's anxious voice broke through her thoughts. "Yes, it's an emergency." He held his phone against his ear. "This is Thomas Heslin. My daughter and I came across a body floating in Enticement Cove. It's a young woman. She's dead."

Please don't let this be Minka.

Whoever she is, she's much too young to die.

Victoria's heart ached for the woman's family. They didn't yet know their loved one was gone. A deep, mind-numbing, incomprehensible pain would follow the news of their loss, a pain Victoria wished no one ever had to experience.

She'd seen so much death recently. And now, death had followed her here, to Lake Lucinda. With that thought came an unsettling measure of guilt, an irrational feeling that her mere presence at the lake had somehow brought about this young woman's tragic demise. Beyond that, an uneasy vibe persisted because Victoria could not dismiss her initial reaction—that the drowned woman was the same woman on the patio with Alex.

Victoria slid out her phone and called her brother.

Oh, God. If it is Minka, how is he going to take the bad news his girlfriend is dead?

And how did she end up in the lake?

45

The phone rang four times and connected to voicemail. Victoria's anxiety grew.

"We were in a boat. Yes." Mr. Heslin was still talking to the police, his tone conveying the serious and shocking nature of the conversation. "We're on a dock near Enticement Cove now. Behind the white and gray house." He gazed up at the Nantucket House, his expression somber. "It has four stone chimneys. You can't miss it."

Victoria tried calling Alex again.

"Hello." Her brother's voice was as groggy as it had been earlier. He must have gone back to sleep, and she had just awoken him again.

"Alex! Thank God you answered. Dad and I are at the dock behind the Nantucket House. I need you to come here right away."

"You crashed the boat?" He sounded more alert.

"No. We found a dead body. And you might know the victim." *I have to tell him in person.*

"What? Who?"

"Just come."

"Okay. I need your car keys," Alex said, all traces of sleep gone.

"They're in the mudroom." She suddenly couldn't recall exactly what she had done with them. "Or in the key bowl. It's not far. You can walk."

From behind her, her father said, "The police are on their way."

"Hurry, Alex." Victoria gazed toward the street, trying to see around the giant house, expecting the police to arrive any minute.

Alex hung up.

Victoria turned to her father. "I'm going to wait by the road." She hoped her brother arrived before the police so she could talk to him first. She picked her coat off the dock and put it on while heading to the natural, wooded area bordering the side of the house. Walking through the trees toward the road, she scanned the area for anything out of the ordinary. Unnaturally broken branches, torn clothing, a purse—anything to help explain what transpired before the young woman ended up in the lake. She emerged from the woods and onto a flagstone path that meandered across the yard between rows of arborvitae and boxwoods. She'd found nothing on her way there.

Shivering in her wet pants and sweater, she pulled a tissue from her coat pocket and dabbed at her nose. Compared to Greenland, this was an annoying cold, uncomfortable, not unbearable. Not the kind of cold that could steal one's fingertips. But being wet had deepened the effect of the chilly air. For a second, Victoria experienced that same tightening in her chest, the quickening of her heart, the tremble inside her bones—then those sensations disappeared.

She shoved her hands inside her pockets. The chill inside her wasn't coming only from the temperature, it was an emotional one. And only Alex had the power to stop it. She needed to hear him say that she had it all wrong. That she'd made a mistake. The corpse wasn't Minka, and it wasn't the woman who was on the patio last night.

And what if it was Minka? She dreaded that Alex would have to see his girlfriend looking pale and lifeless. How would he process this new, terrible reality? He'd also have to call her parents and deliver the worst news of their lives.

Hurrying, she took out her phone, opened Facebook, and typed in Alex's name. He rarely posted, but there was one recent

47

picture. Alex had his arm around a woman with long brown hair. The woman was looking to the side, smiling, her face mostly hidden. A silver necklace with a teardrop-shaped piece of jade rested in the groove of her neck. That was the necklace Alex gave Minka a few months ago. He'd sent Victoria a picture from the store and asked her opinion before purchasing it. Minka was definitely the glowing woman in the photo. It was unclear if she was also the pale, drowned woman they had pulled from the lake.

A flashing blue light appeared at the end of the street. No sirens. Victoria approved of their decision. The young woman was dead. That would not change. Victoria's father had made that clear when he called the police. Sirens would only draw unwanted attention and complicate the investigation by drawing people from their homes.

Where is Alex? He should have been here by now, if he left our house right away.

A sheriff's vehicle with a large side dent drove down the street. As the car got closer, the front door of the Nantucket House opened. An older man with a thick mop of silver hair stepped onto the front porch. The wind billowed his robe around his legs. He watched the sheriff's car pull up in front of the home.

What if the young woman wasn't Minka? What if it was that man's granddaughter? Victoria's heart went out to the old man as he came off the porch and shuffled across the expansive front lawn toward the street.

An officer with a Stetson hat and a badge on his beige uniform exited the driver's side. He was tall and muscular and sported a trimmed beard and moustache. There was something familiar about his walk, the hitch in his bow-legged gait. She might have met him in past summers at the ice-cream store where they all used to go for treats. Or the movie theater that only had

48

two films at a time. Or the boat parties in Enticement Cove where they tied their boats together and listened to music. She didn't socialize as much as her brother had, but had been out enough times to meet most of the people her age. He looked to be in his late twenties or early thirties. Young to be the sheriff. Around the same age as Alex. Maybe he was one of her brother's friends.

A man in his early twenties, wearing an identical hat and uniform, exited the passenger side. He was short by any male standards, but near the sheriff he seemed extra small. He held a black folded bundle in his arms. A body bag.

They strode toward Victoria.

The older and taller of the two spoke first. "I'm sheriff Sean Hayes," he said, with a distinctly southern twang.

The younger man introduced himself as the assistant deputy.

Victoria rubbed her hands together. "I found the body. And my father called it in. He's behind the house at the dock now."

The man from the Nantucket House approached, clutching his robe across his chest. "What's all this about?" He looked between the law enforcement officers and Victoria. "I'm Penn Roberts. This is my house. What's going on?"

"Please return to your house, sir." The sheriff's gaze was steady through red and irritated eyes. "I'll be over to talk to you shortly."

Mr. Roberts wrapped his hands around his shoulders. "Is everything all right?"

"I'll come over once I get an understandin' of what we're dealin' with here." The sheriff was firm but not unkind. After turning away to sneeze against the back of his arm, he waited in silence until Penn Roberts finally raised his hands into the air, said, "all right," and walked back toward his house.

49

The sheriff focused on Victoria as they headed around the side of the house to the backyard. "Your name?"

"Victoria Heslin. I'm an FBI agent. We were—"

"FBI agent?" He stopped and looked at her, his eyes traveling from her face down to her hands. His expression didn't change, but something flashed in his eyes. Recognition.

From the news covering the plane crash, or something else?

"You have a house on the peninsula?" He was still studying her.

"Yes. My father does." She crossed her arms. "Have we met?"

The sheriff responded with, "Hmm. I know who your brother is." He touched the brim of his hat and resumed his long-strided march to the water.

"I'm happy to help," Victoria said to the sheriff's back, now several lengths ahead of her.

The hum of a car engine made Victoria turn. Her SUV pulled to the side of the road and parked behind the sheriff's car.

Alex. Finally.

"My father is at the dock," she told the assistant deputy. "He'll show you where we found her. I'll be right back." Victoria hurried to meet Alex. She was at the driver's side before the door opened. Apparently, Alex was taking his time. When he finally got out, he glanced at the sheriff's car first. "Where's Dad? Is he okay?"

"Yes. Dad is fine. I told you. We found a body floating in the cove. A young woman."

"And you called me because—?"

She placed a hand on his shoulder, worried about how he would take the news. "I'm pretty sure it's the same person I saw you with last night."

"Huh?"

"Last night, I woke up and looked out my window. I saw you sitting around the firepit with someone. I assumed it was Minka. Was it Minka?"

Alex swept his hand over his stubble-covered chin. A fresh cut on his temple, about a half an inch long, had a reddish-black scab over it. "What?"

"Were you with Minka? Did Minka come back?"

Alex didn't answer. So far, he had done nothing to alleviate Victoria's concern. She tapped her foot against the ground, waiting for him to focus.

"No," he finally said. "Minka is back in Colorado."

"You're sure?"

"No, I'm not sure." He pressed his palm against his forehead. "She never answered my texts. She's angry with me."

"Okay. You aren't positive Minka made it back to Colorado, but you weren't with her last night either. So, who were you with on the patio?"

"I don't know."

He doesn't know? What does that mean? Victoria glanced toward the dock. "I only saw her from my bedroom window. It's probably someone else with long brown hair who looks a little like whoever you were with."

"Yeah." Alex trudged down the path leading along the side of the house to the backyard. "If you didn't get a good look at her, it's probably not her. Why would it be? Is she—?"

51

"Is she what?" Victoria asked, passing a bed of dying hydrangea and a striped hammock rocking in the wind.

"Never mind." Alex fell into step beside her.

"What happened to your head?"

He raised his hand toward his head, touching the cut on his temple, but didn't answer.

"The cut you're touching. It wasn't there last night. How did it get there?"

"I bumped into something," Alex answered, placing his hands on top of his head. "I can't believe someone drowned. This is really turning out to be quite a weekend."

"What did you bump into?" Victoria studied her brother's profile as they walked between the woods and a curving patio with an elaborate design of stonework. Alex looked tired and years older than he had yesterday.

How does someone get a cut like that and not remember how?

On the dock ahead of them, the young deputy hovered around, watching like it was his first week on the job while the sheriff pointed here and there, nodding and explaining something. Alex seemed distracted watching them.

"I think I hit the edge of the firepit when I was standing up from shutting it off," Alex said.

"Isn't there a remote to turn it on and off?"

The sheriff looked over at them. "Stop right there." He held up his hand. "Wait with your father for now." He motioned toward Victoria's father, who waited between the dock and the woods in a landscaped sitting area with a scrolled-iron garden bench and two matching chairs. Victoria and Alex joined him.

52

Yellow tape surrounded the dock, although it wasn't necessarily a crime scene. If there had been a crime, it might have originated elsewhere on the lake. Anywhere else. And perhaps there was nothing criminal about the woman's drowning. Sometimes a death was nothing more than an unfortunate accident. Securing the dock was still proper protocol. It would keep onlookers from gawking at the corpse.

Her father twisted his wedding band around his finger. "They couldn't find any identification on her."

On the lower patio of the Nantucket House, Penn Roberts sat with an elderly man and woman in Adirondack chairs facing the solemn scene unfolding in the backyard. They wore puffy winter coats with fur lined hoods and clasped red mugs between their hands.

"The Roberts don't know her, do they?" Victoria asked, although she'd seen enough to answer her question. The woman from the lake was not someone they were acquainted with, or their reactions would have been entirely different—more grief, tears, and disbelief rather than the concerned curiosity that seemed to keep them out on the patio in the cold.

Her father shook his head. "She's not with them. They told the sheriff they don't have any idea who she might be."

"And she's not a local either, or the sheriff wouldn't have had to ask them. He probably would have recognized her immediately."

She isn't from the peninsula, and she isn't a local. I really need Alex to get a look and see if he recognizes her.

The sheriff pulled off his latex gloves and took out his phone. He stepped away from the corpse, providing a view of the girl.

"We need to get closer." Victoria took her brother's arm. "Come on."

They were almost to the yellow tape when the sheriff pivoted around. "Stop right there." He lowered his phone and glared at Alex. "What part of wait over there didn't make sense to you?"

Alex looked down at the corpse. His skin turned ashen.

"Y'all need to step back." The sheriff's command ended in a fit of coughing. He covered his mouth with the back of his arm until the coughing ended. He cleared his throat a few times, causing a movement of congestion in his chest. "Step away and wait until I'm finished here so I can get your statements."

Victoria gave her brother's arm a little pull to break the spell he seemed to be under. His expression told her everything.

Alex recognized the dead woman.

Chapter 7

The Heslins moved away from the yellow tape surrounding the dock.

Alex stared down at his feet as they walked. Victoria held off on questioning him until they were back at the iron bench and chairs where they had privacy.

"That's her, isn't it?" she whispered, standing in front of the bench. "The girl who was with you last night."

Alex stood behind the chair, gripping the back. "Yeah. She had that dark birthmark above her lip."

Standing close to Alex, Victoria's father ran a hand through his hair. "But it's not Minka?"

"No," Alex said. "Definitely not."

Movement near the front of the house made Victoria turn. A white Mercedes S-class pulled in and parked behind her Suburban. The driver was a male with dark hair.

"I can't believe this." Alex shook his head. "I was just with her. She was alive when she left last night. This is like a bad dream or something."

"Does Alex need a lawyer?" Mr. Heslin kept his eyes on the officers at the dock. "Or would that make him look suspicious?"

"Am I in trouble?" Alex asked.

"I can't answer that without knowing what occurred. You need to focus, Alex. Every detail is important." Victoria moved closer and leaned in, forming a small huddle with her family. "The authorities are going to want to hear everything that happened last night. For starters, who is she and what was she doing at our house?"

"She said her name was Kristen. Kristen with a K."

"Kristen who?"

"I didn't get her last name. She didn't tell me." Alex kicked the toe of his boot into the dirt. "They don't know that anything bad happened to her yet, right?"

Mr. Heslin huffed. "She died, Alex."

Alex held up his palms. "I got that she's dead. I mean…I was simply asking if they determined that she was murdered as opposed to her having an accident."

Victoria studied her brother, analyzing every aspect of his behavior.

Is he acting like anyone would after learning a young woman he recently met has died? Not a good question—everyone responds differently.

"They don't seem to know what took place, yet," Victoria said. "And I saw nothing to definitively rule out an accident. Still, it's suspicious. Why would she have been in the water in the first place? If the sheriff's department staff are any good at their jobs, and it looks like they are, they'll find out for sure." Victoria scanned the lake. Small white caps rolled across the water. With over one hundred miles of meandering shoreline, only a small fraction of it was visible from her vantage point. She wondered if a boat without a driver was drifting somewhere out there.

"Could she have had a medical condition?" her father asked.

56

Victoria shrugged. "That hardly explains how she ended up in the lake, but of course it's a possibility."

"So, how should I handle this?" Alex touched the edge of his cut again. "I guess I need to tell the police I was hanging out with her last night."

"Definitely." Victoria stared deep into her brother's eyes. "Unless..."

"Unless what, Victoria?" Mr. Heslin stared at his daughter.

Victoria wasn't ready to answer. How well did she really know her brother? They spoke every few weeks, but she rarely saw him anymore. She was four years older. Off to college while Alex was still reeling from their mother's unexpected death at the hands of her kidnappers. That could mess a young person up, for sure. People became damaged goods with less reason. Alex had seen a psychiatrist for many years. Victoria assumed the visits were preventive, to help him cope with his loss. Might they have been for something else? Her mind started down the analytical paths she would take if this was her case. She couldn't help herself.

Stop! It wasn't a good time to be treating her brother like a suspect and analyzing his personality. And yet...she had to. She had to think like an agent but act like his sister and support him.

"Alex, did you have anything to do with...?" She couldn't finish her question.

He narrowed his piercing blue eyes. "Did I have anything to do with what?"

Victoria wrapped her fingers around the bench's iron scroll work. She let go as the cold seeped through her gloves and stung her damaged skin. "With whatever happened to her."

Alex winced and jerked his head to the side. Not a yes or a no. "I can't believe you asked me that."

57

That was all she needed to hear. Except...he hadn't actually answered.

Her brother rocked slightly forward and back on his heels. "We talked in the backyard. I came inside right after she left. I saw Dad in the kitchen." He turned to his father. "You were getting a drink of water when I came in."

"That's right." Mr. Heslin stared at his son. "However, you said nothing about the girl being with you."

"You were half asleep. And I wanted to go to bed."

Victoria's nature and her training would drive her to find out what happened with the young woman and to seek justice, if warranted. Yet every bone in her body was now in full protective mode for Alex. Surely he was innocent of any wrongdoing. But would it look that way to others?

If his own sister has even the slightest doubt, so might everyone else.

"What are you thinking?" Alex asked.

"Here, sit down with me." Victoria took a seat on the bench and waited for Alex to join her. "They'll have questions for you as part of their preliminary investigation. They'll want a statement, along with the evidence, so they can create a timeline for her death. Let me ask you a few questions first. The same ones they'll probably ask you."

"Good idea." Alex sat next to her.

Mr. Heslin leaned on the bench behind them.

In the distance, the sheriff and his assistant wrapped the woman with an evidence sheet.

"Let's start from the beginning," Victoria said. "How do you know her?"

"Like I already said a few times now—I don't." Alex clasped and unclasped his hands. "Her name is Kristen. That's all I've got."

"Then tell me how you met. How did Kristen end up in our backyard with you last night?"

"You and dad went to bed early." Alex stared toward the dock as the local authorities slid the wrapped body into the black bag. "Then Minka called. We had a difficult conversation. I drank a few beers and left for a walk to blow off some steam. It was after eleven when I saw Kristen. She was standing in front of Judith's house."

Victoria put her gloved hands under her bottom as a barrier between her and the cold iron bench. "She was just standing there?"

"Yes. All alone. I said hello and introduced myself since I didn't recognize her. I said I was with the two of you and a traveling zoo—something like that. She asked if she could see the donkeys. I put the fire on and we sat there. That was it. About a half hour later, just after a car drove past the house, she said she had to go. She wouldn't let me walk her home. I waved goodbye from the back gate and I went inside."

"What time was that?" Victoria asked as the authorities zipped the bag around the corpse and sealed it.

"I'm not exactly sure. One?"

"Yes. It was shortly after one," Mr. Heslin said.

Victoria twisted around on the bench so she could look at her father. "What were you doing awake at one in the morning?"

"I remembered I had to sign a document—to transfer an investment before the end of the year. I got a drink, scanned the document in my office, and returned to bed. I can check my computer to confirm the time if it's necessary."

The sheriff and his deputy carried the body across the flagstone path to their car. Apparently, the town didn't have medical examiners who could come out to the crime scene.

Not a crime scene, she reminded herself. *No evidence of a crime. Only a suspicious death.*

"She looked young." Mr. Heslin said again, stuffing his hands into his pockets. "How old is she?"

Alex tilted his head and looked up at his father from the bench. "I didn't ask. She didn't say."

"Did she mention college or grad school?" Victoria asked. "Employment anywhere?"

Alex shook his head and stared blankly.

"Then what *did* you talk about?"

"I can't remember."

Because he had too much to drink? Or is he in a bit of shock right now?

"These are the questions they're going to ask you. You need to do better with your answers." Victoria's statement was sharper than intended. Her frustration stemmed from concern, but she had to rein it in. Alex needed her help to analyze his interactions with Kristen and figure out what he might know. "Were you drinking, like more than usual?" Victoria asked. "Taking drugs of any sort?"

Her brother shook his head. "No. I had a few beers. She didn't want anything."

"Okay. Try again to remember your conversation with her."

Alex closed his eyes. "I did most of the talking. She asked me about Colorado. She wanted to hear what it's like there. She asked how long it took to get to the airport. I guess that was strange. Not sure how anyone who lives around here wouldn't know that."

"Did she say where she lives?" Mr. Heslin's face was tight with concern. "Or did you walk her home?"

"I told you I didn't. I offered and she flat out refused. Besides, she was out walking when I met her, so it seemed like a thing she does."

"You sure about not calling an attorney?" Mr. Heslin asked Victoria. "I can call Fenton to come out here, or at least to advise us over the phone."

"Cops read guilt into a request for counsel," she answered. "Alex is a witness like the rest of us. They *might* consider him a person of interest for a bit and do a background check. If we lawyer up now, it makes us look uncooperative. Not to mention, Fenton isn't a criminal attorney."

"And I'm not a criminal," Alex said. "What else are they going to ask?"

"They might ask if you touched her or kissed her. Or had sex with her," Victoria said. "Any reason your prints might be on her body?"

"Wouldn't prints have washed off in the lake?" Alex asked. "Possibly."

"I didn't touch her. She seemed shy. Very shy." His face fell, a mixture of worry and sadness. Victoria understood that same expression could also represent guilt. She silently chided herself for letting that knowledge creep into her thoughts.

"Don't worry." Victoria stood and wrapped her arms around her body. "Tell the truth. Once she's identified, there will most likely be a sad but simple explanation."

Mr. Heslin pulled Victoria close, warming her up. "I'll be right back." He let her go, walked to the dock, and exchanged words with the sheriff that Victoria couldn't hear. The sheriff nodded and her father went inside his boat. He returned a few minutes later, his cheeks red from the chilly wind, and handed Victoria a thick blanket. "Here, put this around you while we wait."

Victoria draped the blanket over her shoulders and pulled it tight against her chest. She tucked her hands and tingling fingers under the folds and was suddenly reminded of being desperately cold and stranded in Greenland.

Interesting how a new problem can quickly make you forget the last one.

Chapter 8

The sheriff signaled Victoria over. She walked to the dock, passing her father on his way back from being questioned. She stopped in front of the sheriff.

"I'd like to ask you a few questions." The sheriff didn't look all that friendly. "Why didn't you leave the body where you found it and call the police right away?"

"I—I—." She averted her gaze, searching for a safe place to focus. She couldn't leave the corpse alone like the plane crash victims in Greenland. All investigative protocol had disappeared there; none of it was possible. But this wasn't remote Greenland. "I didn't want to leave her in the water any longer. Not with the storm coming. The waves were really picking up. She could have ended up anywhere in the lake."

He stared her down but didn't press her further.

"You might want to call in a diver," she said, "if the circumstances of her death warrant one. Do you have a medical examiner here? In the town?"

He scratched at his moustache and scoffed. "Is that what you vacation home owners think? Or is that FBI arrogance talking? This may not be a big city, but we know how to do our jobs."

Victoria was caught off guard by his response. "In a small town, the town physician is often also the coroner."

"We have a medical examiner, so you don't need to be feelin' sorry for us." He handed her a card with his contact information. "In case you think of anything else."

She typed Sheriff Sean Hayes' phone number into her contacts.

He kept her there, saying nothing for several seconds. She could tell he was thinking, trying to be thorough, which she admired, although she did not appreciate his rudeness toward her. Maybe his attitude was the whole small cop versus FBI thing. She'd experienced it before. Or maybe it was personal. In any case, until they discovered what had happened, he was right to take his time and proceed with caution because everything was evidence, no matter how irrelevant it might at first appear.

▼▲▼

When Alex finally got a chance to talk to the sheriff about his encounter with the woman, the sheriff insisted on speaking to him alone.

The owners of the Nantucket House beckoned Victoria and her father to their patio.

"Come in, please," the elderly woman said. Up close, her wrinkles were deep, her glasses thick, and hearing aids filled her ears. Gray strands escaped from her bun, as if she hadn't taken the time to brush her hair first. "And let us get you some coffee."

"Coffee would be wonderful." Victoria moved close to the outdoor heater. "But I'm going to wait out here." She kept her eyes on Alex and the sheriff.

Mr. Heslin joined his daughter, taking a seat near the heater.

When the elderly woman returned with their mugs, tears brimmed her eyes. "Here you are," she said, handing them the coffees. "This should help get you warmed up. It's so sad about the young woman."

"We found her floating in Enticement Cove," Mr. Heslin said, taking a sip of the hot drink. "She hadn't been there long, and she definitely drowned. My daughter is an FBI agent, so she could tell."

"Oh, she's with the FBI," the elderly woman said. "My sister's oldest son was in the FBI. Frank Montgomery. He was in Houston for most of his career, with a few years in Dallas..."

Victoria pressed her warm mug against her cheek, letting the warmth soak into her skin and watching Alex and the sheriff from a distance.

The sheriff had his back to her, but with his arms crossed and his wide stance, his body language was all about power and control.

Alex kept shaking his head.

Victoria wished she could hear their exchange.

The sky had thickened with ominous clouds by the time the sheriff finished talking to Alex and dismissed everyone. The flag snapped furiously at the top of the pole. Whitecaps lapped the shore. It wasn't only rain that would strike at any minute. A storm was brewing.

Victoria and her father met Alex halfway between the dock and the Roberts' patio. Mr. Heslin placed his hand on his son's bicep. "What did the sheriff say to you?"

"He wants all of us to stay put at your lake house. We can't go home until they investigate." Alex looked up at the sky. "I'll tell you the rest when we get back. We need to get out of here."

The lake wasn't a vast ocean, and they didn't have far to go, but Victoria couldn't halt her anxiety about the approaching storm. A month ago, she might not have worried. Now, ever since the plane crash, she wasn't taking any chances with accidents. "Should we ask the Roberts if we can leave the boat at their dock?"

A rumble rolled across the sky.

"The boat will get banged up. I'll take it back." Alex handed Victoria her car keys before he jogged away, saying, "I'll meet you both at the house."

Victoria pulled the blanket tighter around her shoulders and hurried to her Suburban with her father. The white Mercedes with the dark-haired driver was already gone.

Mr. Heslin got in the passenger side. "I should call Fenton now."

Victoria started the car. "Alex didn't do anything wrong. He's a witness. He should be fine as long as he tells the truth."

"Should be fine?"

"He *will* be fine." She flipped the wipers on as fat drops splattered the glass. "The sheriff said something that made me think he's got an aversion to the FBI and outsiders. And that's what he considers me." Victoria shared the sheriff's exact comments.

Mr. Heslin gave a half nod. "If Alex says the girl was alive when she left our yard, and I can back him up because I saw him come in, then that's all that matters."

Victoria wasn't sure she agreed with her father's logic, but she kept silent.

It was pouring when they got back to the house. Victoria grabbed an umbrella and went straight to the patio. Her dogs raced around, tails slicing side to side, pushing each other out of the way to get to her, oblivious to the rain. The donkeys watched, bobbing their heads from the shelter.

Empty bottles sat on the ledge of the firepit near where Alex had been sitting.

Victoria scanned the area for anything the young woman might have left behind. There was nothing she could see. No purse. No phone. And no signs of a struggle. Then she felt awful for considering that there would be. But if the evidence was right there before her, she couldn't ignore it. She closed her eyes and tried to recreate the scene from the previous evening. The young woman's solemn expression was the one thing Victoria remembered most.

She searched for the remote that operated the firepit but couldn't find it. Victoria crouched down next to the control panel on the side of the stone structure. Her head was about level with the overhang around the top edge.

It is possible for someone to scrape their head on this edge if they stand up without moving away first.

With a bit of relief, she straightened from her brief experiment, looking around to see if Alex had returned.

Am I going to be questioning every single thing he tells me?

She gathered the bottles and carried them inside, setting her wet umbrella by the back door. She dumped the empties into the recycling bin under the kitchen sink, where they joined several others.

Does Alex normally drink so much, or is it because of his breakup? Or maybe it isn't much at all if he consumed them over the past two days with Minka.

With the door to the recycling bin still open, Victoria froze, staring down at the empty bottles.

I only have Alex's word that the girl didn't drink anything. What if she did? What if there was something else in that drink? Did I throw away evidence?

She kneaded her fingers in front of the open bin, confused about how to proceed. Her thoughts were broken by a little chirping sound from Myrtle. The fawn-colored greyhound stared up at Victoria, unblinking, then looked at the food bowls.

"Hold on, sweetie, I'll make lunch soon."

Victoria pulled the entire recycling bag from the bin and tucked it in the back of a storage closet, in case the police asked for them.

They wouldn't. They shouldn't. But just in case.

She got the dog food and bowls out and set them on the counter.

She hoped the woman's death was nothing more than a tragic accident. That alone was sad enough. If someone was responsible, that would be worse. And the sheriff might pull Alex into a lengthy case. For everyone's sake, Victoria hoped the investigation would quickly conclude.

The dogs wolfed down their food and Victoria collected their bowls. Alex trudged through the back door, dripping wet.

"I still can't believe this," he said, kicking off his shoes. He set the Tupperware container and his phone onto the counter. "The boat is back up on the lift, by the way."

Normally she would have said, "You sure about that?" and given him a hard time, considering his history with tying up the boat. But they were no longer in teasing mood territory. "Alex. Come in here," she said, putting the bowls in the kitchen sink.

"I need to go lie down." He walked past her toward the stairs. "That was a lot to deal with."

Mr. Heslin came out of his office. "Go talk to your sister. Tell her about your conversation with the sheriff while it's still fresh in your mind."

"Victoria said everything would be fine."

"It will, once they figure out what happened," she said. "However, if the investigation drags on—and I'm hoping it won't, it shouldn't—but if for some reason it does, you might be involved, as a *witness*. They'll look into your background to assess your credibility."

Mr. Heslin sighed as he took a seat in a recliner. "They might ask about his trust fund."

"What would that have to do with anything?" Alex asked.

"Fenton mentioned you recently made another significant withdrawal."

"It is my money, Dad." Alex turned away.

"And as your father, it's my concern that you don't do anything foolish with it."

Alex's shoulders slumped forward, as if he'd already had a long, full day.

It had been a few years since anyone mentioned Alex's trust fund. Victoria wasn't aware of the details and hadn't asked. It wasn't her business. She only knew that her brother had spent a substantial amount of the money their maternal grandfather left them. Not invested, or it wouldn't have been an issue, but spent.

As the family's lawyer, Fenton noted all their significant withdrawals. He didn't require explanations, but he requested them, like with Victoria's recent donation to the animal shelter in Spain that she'd founded in her mother's name.

Their grandfather had given them enough for Victoria to invest in an incredible property in Virginia, to give generously to charitable causes, and to pay Ned a decent salary, when combined with what she made as a special agent.

Alex was a trained emergency medical technician. He loved being part of the ski patrol and keeping people safe on the mountains. In the summers, he worked as a whitewater rafting guide. He didn't make a lot of money doing either job, so Victoria assumed he lived mostly off his trust.

Alex rested his hand on the banister. "No one can prove that I was the last person to see her alive. Can they?"

Victoria stared at her brother and wondered about his question. There were many ways to interpret it. She cleared her throat. "We don't know that you were the last one to see her alive. If she had an accident on her way home, then possibly. If someone did this to her, then obviously you weren't. Right?" She held her breath for his response.

"Right. Unfortunately, people drown," Alex said. "I looked it up before I came in. It's the fifth leading cause of accidental injury, according to the CDC. Ten people every day. That's nine others besides her yesterday."

"Those are averages." Mr. Heslin grunted. "And I imagine they mostly represent people who are swimming, not people found in the water alone with all their clothes on in the winter. Alex, maybe you better not ask or answer questions if the police talk to you again."

Alex dropped his head and gripped the banister. "I told you I was tired." He trudged up the stairs without another word.

There's no way Alex could have hurt her, could he?

The question came before Victoria could stop it. She felt terrible for entertaining it and for doubting her brother, but she had to.

"I'll be in my office." Mr. Heslin slowly lifted himself back up from the recliner and left her alone.

Victoria spotted Alex's phone on the counter. For years, he'd used the same passcode for everything. She'd told him the habit was unwise, but it was possible he hadn't listened.

Creeping into the kitchen, almost on tiptoes, she realized what she was doing and changed to a normal walk. She scooped up his phone and typed his old passcode. It worked. For once, she was grateful Alex hadn't heeded her advice. She found Minka's contact and drop-shared it to her own phone. Then, quickly, she checked his recent calls. He'd called Minka three times last night, all between ten and eleven p.m. Exactly as he'd said. Each call had lasted between five and ten minutes.

Holding her breath, she exited the house onto the patio and called Minka. No one answered. Of course not. No one answered calls from unknown numbers. Victoria could leave a message and wait for a call back. Or...she could use Alex's phone.

She went back inside and again picked up her brother's phone. She retyped Alex's passcode.

This time, she took a moment and scrolled through his photos.

There were pictures of the Colorado ski slopes, but all the rest were of Minka, or Alex and Minka. Hiking, at a restaurant, at a beach, on bikes, sitting on a couch. In every picture with the two of them, Alex was smiling or laughing, close to Minka or touching her. They looked happy and in love.

Still trying to figure out what she would say, Victoria went back outside and made the call.

The phone rang several times. Victoria was about to hang up when Minka answered.

"Hello." It was a matter of fact greeting. No warmth, but no fury.

"Hi. This is Victoria Heslin. Alex's sister. I'm calling from his phone."

"Oh. Hi, Victoria. Um, I'm really sorry about your accident. The plane crash." She sounded sincere. "I'm glad you're back and you're going to be all right. And I'm disappointed that I never got to meet you."

"Yes. So am I. I was really looking forward to spending some time with you. Whatever happened between you and Alex— I'm sorry."

"I'm sorry, too." Minka didn't sound angry. "Um, is Alex all right? Has something happened to him?"

"Alex is fine." She debated telling Minka about the drowned woman before deciding it wasn't necessary. "I guess I wanted to make sure you got back to Colorado okay. We felt terrible that you had to go all the way back to the airport alone and I've been thinking about you and wanted to call." Every word of that was the truth.

There was a pause, undoubtedly because this call was officially weird now. Poor Minka probably had no idea what to think.

Their conversation had brought Victoria relief. What did that relief mean, exactly? That she hadn't completely trusted her own brother and needed to make sure Minka wasn't the dead girl? If so, that wasn't good at all.

Chapter 9

Rain pelted the house for hours, splashing against the windows and keeping the dogs inside. Covered by fleece-lined coats, the donkeys clustered under the shelter.

Victoria curled up in the cushioned window seat with a blanket and her iPad to read her new e-book. This—getting cozy and engrossing herself in a new novel—was exactly how she'd imagined her stay at the lake house. When she reached the bottom of the first page, she had to scroll back again and start from the beginning. She barely remembered what she'd just read or which parts of it mattered. The book was a mystery set in the summer. The characters were on the beach. Only that much had sunk in.

The same questions dominated her thoughts. *Who was Kristen? How had she died?*

After her third time reading the same pages, Victoria pressed the home button on her iPad and swiped her finger upward to close the book.

So much for enjoying a new novel.

She opened her news feed and skimmed over headlines and first paragraphs, skipping from one article to another, unable to focus on anything long.

A sadness she couldn't shake had tainted the lake house trip. If only she was informed on what was happening with the investigation, she might be able to relax. Instead, she wondered what the sheriff had discovered since they found the body.

Switching from the news to her personal email, Victoria found a slew of new messages related to the plane crash. Interview requests were still coming, along with messages from major agents and publishers who wanted to write a book about her ordeal. They were like vultures, wanting to peck off a piece of her to get to the meat of the story. Luckily for the press, two of her fellow survivors wanted to share their haunting experience. They *needed* to share it. So Victoria's contribution wasn't necessary.

She hovered her finger over the delete button for the first email but didn't press it, choosing to ignore the messages for now.

Victoria got up and headed to the kitchen. "I'm going to make those cookies," she said to her dogs. "It's a perfect day for baking."

▼▲▼

Alex came back downstairs in the late afternoon.

"Good timing, Alex." Mr. Heslin gathered the deck of cards from the table. "We just finished a game of Gin Rummy. Want to join us?"

"Sure. It smells awful down here. What burned?"

"Those are your sister's cookies."

"I forgot they were in the oven." Victoria shifted in her seat. "But I'll try again tomorrow."

Alex opened the fridge and stared at the shelves for a few seconds before selecting a pre-made sandwich he'd purchased the previous evening. "Are we still having dinner at Judith's?"

"I hope not," Victoria said as her dad reshuffled. "I don't really want to go."

"Because of the drowning?" Alex asked. "I thought you found dead bodies all the time. Remember that killer—what was it the press called her—The Numbers Killer? Or is it because Phoebe will be there?"

"I just don't feel like going out."

Alex opened his sandwich. "You have to go, Tori. It's you she wants to talk to."

"We all have to go." Mr. Heslin tapped the deck on the table to straighten the cards. "Judith called earlier to make sure we were still coming and I said we were. She told me she'd already prepared most of the food. I didn't see how I could cancel without being rude." Mr. Heslin set the cards down and stood. He pressed his palm against his hip and shifted his weight from side to side. "I brought a few good bottles of wine from home for an occasion such as this."

Alex studied his father. "What's wrong? Why are you moving around like your days are numbered?"

"I slipped. I'm fine. Just stiff." Mr. Heslin sat back down, picked up the cards, and began distributing them. "I think the dinner will be a nice distraction from this morning."

▼▲▼

The Heslins arrived at Judith's house carrying bottles of red and white wine and closed umbrellas. The storm had moved on, leaving the air laden with dampness.

"You look beautiful, Victoria," her father said as they climbed the front steps.

"Thank you." Having brought nothing appropriate to wear to a dinner party, Victoria had chosen dark jeans and a white sweater worn with her running shoes rather than her hiking boots. A little makeup—some color to accentuate her sharper-than-usual cheekbones, a touch of lipstick and eyeliner—went a long way to compensate for being underdressed.

A white Mercedes drove up Judith's driveway and into the garage. Victoria wondered if it was the same vehicle she'd spotted in the morning.

Alex rang the doorbell and stepped back. After several seconds, when he was reaching toward the door again, Judith answered. Her hair was a silvery blonde now, straight and level with her jaw. A scarf completely concealed her neck again.

"Come in." She moved aside, opening the door all the way. "So glad to see you all." She adjusted the corner of her blue-rimmed eyeglasses and softened her voice to a conspiratorial whisper. "You definitely deserve a few drinks after the events of the day. Oh, my."

Victoria wondered what information Judith possessed about the mysterious drowning.

A large, framed poster of Judith's most famous book—*Lucinda's Secrets*—graced the foyer wall. The image depicted the profile of a woman drifting underneath a lake, her long hair floating around her. Dark water half covered the word *Secrets*.

A creepy sensation snaked its way down Victoria's spine. The book's cover had always struck her as spooky, but today it was even more so. Conspicuous similarities existed between the slender woman with long, tangled hair in the picture and the woman they found earlier in the day.

"Did you have a nice Christmas?" Judith asked, leading them through her house.

"We did," Mr. Heslin answered. "It was a quiet one. Victoria and I were in Virginia. Alex was with a friend and her family in Colorado. How about you?"

76

"I spent the week before Christmas in Turks and Caicos." Judith made a gesture with her hand. "Absolutely lovely. I'd do it again in a heartbeat."

In a large room with white walls, white trim, and white furniture, an enormous Christmas tree glistened with white lights and silver ornaments. The back wall of windows offered a view of an illuminated pool appearing to meet the lake beyond.

No one else was around. Victoria experienced a twinge of hope.

Perhaps it's only us and no Phoebe.

"Take a seat." Judith accepted the bottles from her guests. "And thank you for the lovely wine. Now what can I get you to drink? Shall I open one of these?"

"I'll have a beer if it's an option." Alex remained standing near the back windows, looking out at the pool. "Whatever kind you have works for me."

"That sounds good," Mr. Heslin said.

"And for you, Victoria?" Judith pinched the edge of a throw pillow, moving it over a few inches on a loveseat.

"Whatever you're having," Victoria answered.

"I'll be right back. Make yourself at home." Judith strolled from the room, her heels clicking against the wood floors. She returned minutes later with the drinks and a man in his mid-thirties, not much older than Victoria. "Everyone, this is John. And John, these are the Heslins—Tom, Alex, and Victoria. Our families hung out together in summers past."

John had a contemporary look about him, with skinny jeans and a tailored shirt. Not especially handsome, his eyes were a bit too close together on his narrow face, but he kept himself in good shape. Victoria was sure he was the dark-haired man she'd seen in the white Mercedes that morning.

77

"Nice to meet you," John said, draping his arm around Judith and tapping his fingers against her shoulder.

Definitely not Phoebe's husband.

Judith probably made an impressive living from her novels. Wouldn't she be a great catch for anyone who craved a life of luxury? Victoria didn't want to make the obvious cynical assumptions, but she was an excellent judge of character, part of her profiler background, and something wasn't right. She couldn't quite put her finger on it. Perhaps it was the way John avoided eye contact with all of them, or the way he kept fidgeting, now strumming Judith's shoulder.

"Where are you from?" Mr. Heslin asked.

John's hand left Judith's shoulder and disappeared behind his back. "I live outside the city. New York City."

"You two been together long?" Alex asked.

Victoria was grateful for her brother's directness. She was curious as well. Judith seemed happy, but something seemed strange about the two of them together. Something besides the age difference.

"Six months." Judith stared at John like he was a god. "John is in marketing. I hired him to help me with my publicity. That's how we met."

"I was a big fan of her writing," John added. "Still am, of course. Anxiously awaiting a new book, whenever it might come."

Judith's smile disappeared. "Well, let's not talk about that right now. How about the terrible discovery this morning?"

"It is awful." John took a seat. "And it's hard to believe they still haven't identified her."

"Really?" Victoria shifted forward on her large square of sectional. "That is surprising. Someone should have reported her missing by now. Although, if she lives alone, it might be a day or two before friends or family realize she isn't where she should be."

"That's why I've insisted that Phoebe call me every single day, no matter where she is or what she's doing." Judith sat down on the corner of John's chair, pressing against his leg. "Even if it's only a simple text to tell me she's alive and well."

"That's a good habit," Victoria's father agreed.

"So, the young woman definitely doesn't live here full time." Judith kept her voice low, as if she was telling a secret and didn't want anyone eavesdropping. "Because outside the peninsula, it's a small town. Practically incestuous, some people say. Everyone here knows everyone else."

"How did you hear they haven't identified her yet?" Victoria asked.

"Oh, I have my ways." Judith tossed her head back. "Actually, Phoebe told me. She heard when she was in town late this afternoon."

"Hello, Heslins."

Phoebe's greeting, drawn out and dramatic, sent another cold sensation slithering down Victoria's back.

Phoebe sauntered in, her full hips swaying. Lush black hair framed her smooth skin and crimson lips. She wore a plunging V-neck sweater and carried a large glass of red wine. Eyes gleaming, she stopped in the middle of the room. "Wow, Victoria. Look at you. It's been so long. Over ten years."

Phoebe's presence was all it took for troubling memories to come flooding back. Like Phoebe's penchant for playing truth or dare. Lurking barely below the surface, she'd had a bizarre obsession with death. She talked about it, read about it, and seemed enthusiastic for others to face it. Her eyes glistened with anticipation whenever someone opted for a dare. Her voice rose louder than the others, habitually proposing something where death was a distinct possibility.

I dare you to hold her under the water for two minutes and not let her up, no matter what she does. I dare you to let us lock you inside this chest to see how brave you are.

"Nice to see you, Phoebe." Victoria's father rose from his chair. "Tell us what you've been doing with yourself these days."

"Oh, a little of this and that. I'm always so busy." Phoebe tilted her head and jutted one curvy hip to the side.

She's unemployed, thought Victoria, wondering if Phoebe had ever held an actual job.

"It's nice to come to the lake and...do nothing for a bit." Still standing, as if she wasn't sure she would stick around, Phoebe took a few steps toward Victoria. "Although after a few days here, I'm bored as hell already. Everything about Lake Lucinda reminds me of being a teenager again." She stared directly at Victoria. "Don't you agree?"

"I suppose." Victoria took a large gulp of her wine. *And that might be why I'm getting hives from listening to you.*

Phoebe's gaze moved to Victoria's hand and stayed there. Victoria's instinct was to curl her bandaged fingers into her palm, but she couldn't do it while holding her wineglass. She twisted her hand to the side, holding her glass at an uncomfortable angle.

"Is that from the plane crash?" Phoebe asked.

"From frostbite," Victoria said. "Never use a gun with your bare hands in sub-zero temps."

"A gun? Oh, my," Judith exclaimed. "Weren't you in the middle of nowhere? Whatever was the gun for?"

"I shot a bear." Victoria surprised herself by sharing more information than she intended. She hated having all eyes on her and realizing they wanted more. And she had only herself to blame this time.

"They make prosthetics for missing fingers, you know that, don't you?" Phoebe was still peering at Victoria's hands. "I met someone who has one. Sliced his finger clean off in a freak boating accident. If it hadn't disappeared into the ocean, he could have had it sewn back on."

"Yes. I'm familiar with prosthetics."

"And that's all?" Phoebe lowered herself onto the edge of a large white chair identical to the one John and Judith occupied. "I mean, hundreds of people died, and that's all that happened to you? You come home looking slightly anorexic with missing fingertips? Hmm...You must feel like you cheated death in a big way." The corners of Phoebe's red lips twitched.

Victoria experienced the chill again. Phoebe was older and curvier than when they were girls, but her fascination for death hadn't changed. Victoria could handle death. She had more experience with it than anyone in the room, but she wasn't about to share her still-fresh emotions and guilt with Phoebe.

"After your ordeal, it must feel incredible to be alive," John said. "Do you have a whole new appreciation for life?"

Victoria nodded but wasn't really sure if that was true. Not yet. Dr. Monroe, the FBI's psychiatrist, said the experience would take time to process. Victoria might experience guilt, depression, elation, and gratefulness, all at once or in phases. The guilt was real. That she knew. It didn't stem from anything she specifically had or had not done but existed because she had lived through the terrible experience when so many others had not. Survivor guilt, Dr. Monroe called it. And then there was the unexpected episode of PTSD earlier that morning. She wasn't sure where she stood on any of it yet. And now wasn't the time to figure it out. A change of subject was in order. She cleared her throat. "Phoebe, before you came in, we heard the authorities still haven't identified the woman who drowned. Your mother said you told her. How do you know?"

"Oh." Phoebe crossed her legs. She held her wineglass out in front of her. "They sent me to the store to buy rosemary and carrots for our little dinner soiree because *John* forgot to get them." She emphasized his name as if John was a constant source of irritation. "People in the store were talking. I mean, everyone was talking. The drowning was clearly the principal topic on everyone's mind because what else do they have to talk about, right?" She laughed and red wine sloshed against the sides of her glass. "The girl working the register dates a deputy. They don't know who the drowned girl is, but they have a suspect."

"A suspect?" Victoria's hand tightened around the stem of her goblet. "Do they know what happened?"

"They don't." Phoebe's smile dropped, but her eyes betrayed her intense interest. "Not yet."

"Then how can they have a suspect if they don't know what happened?" Victoria said aloud, not intending for anyone to answer. "What do they think the suspect did?"

"I assume, as anyone would, that the suspect played a role in the girl's untimely death. And now, what that really means is that none of us are safe until they find that person, are we?" Phoebe raised her glass to the edge of her lips and stared at each of them. "One of us on the peninsula might be a murderer."

Yes, one of us might.

Alex leaned one shoulder against the patio door and drank heavily from his glass.

John remained silent.

Mr. Heslin frowned. "Let's hope that's not the case."

82

"Oh, but wouldn't that be fabulous for my dear mother? It's exactly what she needs." Phoebe cackled with laughter, and Victoria recoiled from the sound.

The room was silent. Even Alex didn't have a response.

An electronic beep came from the kitchen.

Judith clapped her hands in front of her heart. "That would be the roast. Dinner is ready. That doesn't give us much time to catch up here first, but we can chat at the table and come back here afterward. Everyone, please move to the dining room and have a seat."

Saved by the bell crossed Victoria's mind. Although, there was still a dinner to get through. Who knew what might come up during their meal?

Chapter 10

An elaborate table was set using crystal glassware and layers of white china with silver trim. The design on the salad plates featured prancing reindeer. A large bowl of tossed greens and a tray of roasted vegetables were already on the table.

"We have assigned seats this evening," Phoebe said with unmistakable condescension, making clear it had not been her idea.

Victoria found her name carefully scripted in chalk on a tiny piece of slate, next to Phoebe. John and Judith sat across from her. The Heslin men were at each end of the table. As Phoebe and the guests settled into their places, Judith and John left the dining room and then returned with more dishes. Judith carried a basket of bread and a carving knife. John held a large platter of meat. Victoria wished she could take her portion home for her dogs.

"Judith, everything looks fantastic." Mr. Heslin slid his linen napkin out from a silver bow.

John nudged the salad aside and set the platter on the table. "Cooking is one of Judith's many talents."

Judith moved to John's side. She handed him the knife then squeezed his shoulder, letting her hand trail gently down his arm.

After John carved the roast, they passed the platter around the table. Everyone except Victoria took a generous serving.

"No meat?" Phoebe refilled her wineglass. "Are you still crazy about animals, Victoria? Because I remember you used to talk to your dogs all the time, like they were people." She laughed, and that same hint of cruelty from years ago rang out in her tone.

"She still does. It's very sweet." Alex stuck his fork into the roast and took a bite. "Wow, Judith, this is delicious."

Judith gripped her silverware. "It's a beef tenderloin and I'm so glad you like it, Alex."

"And I remember you used to feed all the mangy, wild animals when you were here," Phoebe said, still focused on Victoria.

Unlike the teasing from her brother, Phoebe's stung purposely. But thanks to her comment, Victoria made a mental note to refill the bowl of dog food she'd left on the front porch for the foxes.

"Hmmm." Phoebe shifted toward the table, her smile tight and her eyes gleaming—a ghoulish expression. "What was it like this morning when you found the woman's body? Did you know immediately that she was dead?"

"Don't ask me." Alex added a piece of warm bread to his plate. "I was in bed."

"It was shocking and sad," Mr. Heslin answered. "Victoria and I were the only ones on the water. It's awful to think the body might still be out there if Victoria hadn't spotted her. She was easy to miss, the way she was drifting under the water."

"Like my character in *Lucinda's Secrets*." Judith bobbed her head. "I'm not sure why, but I've always thought there was something rather romantic about death by drowning. The bodies seem so—peaceful, floating as they do."

Phoebe leaned forward, far enough to expose her cleavage. "When have you ever found a dead body floating in a lake for real?"

"I haven't, thank goodness," Judith answered. "But I did write a book about it, dear. Which involved quite a bit of research."

"You should research this new mysterious woman and her death," John said. "Her story might be another bestseller in the making."

No one responded.

John cleared his throat. "I mean, after some time has passed. You should write about it before someone else does."

Phoebe scoffed. "You trying to get my mother to strike gold again? The royalties aren't quite rolling in like you expected, John?"

Victoria shifted uncomfortably in her seat. She didn't want to witness John's or Judith's reaction, although Judith seemed to accept the comment as if it was nothing unusual.

Mr. Heslin kept his eyes down, having developed a sudden interest in his plate.

"There's not much of a story if it's a tragic accident," Judith said. "But when you find someone in the water with all their winter clothes on, that's not likely, is it, Victoria?"

"It's not." The mention of the young woman's clothes made Victoria think there was something important there, but it eluded her, clouded by her distaste for the overall tone of the conversation. She didn't enjoy speculating over the young woman's demise as part of their dinner entertainment. Dealing with death as part of her career hadn't made her any less sympathetic. She understood the heartrending pain of suddenly

86

losing a loved one. Someone would experience absolute agony upon learning of Kristen's death.

And if anyone was to blame for that death, that person should pay.

Victoria caught John's attention. "I saw you at the Nantucket House this morning. How did you end up there?" She kept her voice intentionally light, not wanting to appear as an investigator trying to determine his motives.

"Oh. I was on my way back from the store," John said, "getting the groceries for tonight—"

"That would be the trip I mentioned where John forgot to buy everything on the list," Phoebe said.

John continued as if he hadn't heard Phoebe. "I saw the police car with its lights flashing. I thought there might have been a robbery." He turned to Alex. "While we're asking each other questions, why did the sheriff want to speak with you, if you were in bed when your father and sister found the body?"

"Because, uh—" Alex glanced at Victoria. His look clearly asked if he should share information or keep a secret.

Victoria shrugged with one shoulder. There was no reason to lie.

"I actually met her the night before. The girl who died."

John let out a sudden cough, deep in his throat. He covered his mouth with his napkin. The coughing continued, his face growing red, his eyes watering.

"Are you okay?" Judith patted his back, her face full of concern.

He twisted away from the table, but the coughing continued.

"Oh, dear." Judith held his glass out to him. "Here, John, take a sip of water."

Victoria pushed her dining chair back, ready to race around the table and do the Heimlich maneuver. Although, as long as he was coughing, he could breathe.

John held up a hand. One more pronounced cough and he turned back around, lowering his napkin from his mouth. "I'm fine now." His face was red as he accepted the water from Judith.

"What were you saying, Alex?" Phoebe asked. "Before John had his near brush with death right here at my mother's exquisitely decorated dining table."

Alex gripped his knife and cut into a slice of tenderloin. "Her name is Kristen."

"But—" Judith straightened, leaning forward in her chair. "I don't understand. I must have missed something. I thought no one knew who she was. You do?"

"No. We only talked."

"Where and how did you meet her?" Phoebe asked, refilling her glass. "Do tell. This is getting interesting."

"Here, actually. On the street right in front of your house." Alex stabbed another forkful of meat.

"Really?" Judith frowned, causing lines to form at the edge of her eyes. "She was outside my house? Whatever for?"

"I'm not sure. She knew you lived here," Alex said. "And that you're an author."

"That doesn't mean anything." John picked up his knife. "Judith is famous. Anyone could learn that she owns this property."

Judith batted her eyelashes at John before her expression turned serious again. "What time was the girl outside?"

"Between eleven and midnight," Alex answered. "I figured she was a guest staying at your house. Someone's friend."

"Not mine," John said rather quickly.

Phoebe stared intently at Alex. "You talked to her in front of our house, and that was it? That's all? You have absolutely nothing significant to share about meeting her the evening of her death—her very suspicious death?"

"Yeah, that's it." Alex stared right back at Phoebe, as if challenging her.

Victoria studied her brother as he took a drink from his glass.

He didn't quite tell the entire story.

"Hmm." Judith leaned back. "A young woman alone at night and she stopped to talk to a complete stranger? That doesn't seem wise at all. It happens all the time in my mystery novels. An instance of poor judgment is almost a necessity for my plotlines to play out. In real life, young women should be more careful."

"Hey," Alex laughed. "It's me she was talking to."

"And we all know what a charmer you are," Phoebe said with a wink. "But charmers can be the most dangerous of all."

Alex cut another slice of tenderloin. "Speaking of being questioned by the sheriff, he acted like he had it out for me."

"I can see that." Phoebe cocked her head. "He used to hate you, Alex."

Alex frowned. "Why?"

"Yes, Phoebe, what reason could the sheriff have for disliking Alex?" Mr. Heslin posed his question as if the mere notion of being against Alex was preposterous.

"No one else here remembers?" Phoebe tilted her head to one side. She looked from Alex to Victoria. "The sheriff we're talking about is Sean Hayes. We hung out with him a few times one summer. He owned that ancient party boat with the slide." She laughed, more derisive than amused. "Anyway, his girlfriend broke up with him to go out with Alex."

Alex lifted his beer, then set it back down hard. "Who?"

"Sofie—Sofie—I can't remember her last name. Blonde hair, tiny waist, and big boobs. Remember her now, Alex?"

"Yes. We went out on our boat a few times. That was all." Alex narrowed his eyes. "That was like, what—twelve years ago? If the sheriff has any sort of life, he shouldn't be holding a grudge about something like that. Seems—impossible."

"Maybe there's another reason he gave you a hard time— something else you did that you failed to remember." Phoebe laughed, her eyes glistening over the rim of her glass. "You never know who might hold a grudge."

"If the sheriff has it out for you, your sister will have to help find the real killer," Judith said. She turned to Victoria. "Won't you?"

"*If* there is one." Victoria twisted her napkin in her lap. "And, unfortunately, I have no jurisdiction here."

"Right, right—of course. We shouldn't be getting ahead of ourselves," Judith said. "We're all hoping it was an accident. No one wants a murderer running loose on the peninsula, do they? But here's something that might be useful. I'm friendly with the medical examiner in town. Monica Stewart. She's a wonderful forensic pathologist. I spent time with her when I was doing research for one of my books and then made a big fuss about her in the acknowledgements. I believe it was for *The Best Husband*. Remember that one, Victoria? You told me you loved it."

"I did." Segments from the book's plot materialized in Victoria's mind. "It's about the woman with amnesia...after an accident...which turns out not to be an accident at all. The man who tried to kill her convinces her he's her husband and fabricates a life they supposedly had." The plot came back to Victoria easily. "It was chilling when we found out not a word of what he told her was true."

Judith clapped her hands. "Yes. Yes. Oh, I love, love, love that you remember!"

Phoebe rolled her eyes.

"Anyway," Judith said, still beaming, "Victoria could call Dr. Stewart to see what she found. I'm assuming she'll be quite accommodating, since you're with the FBI. Her office is next to the sheriff's building. And that would be where the poor girl's body is right now."

Under the table, someone's foot rubbed up against Victoria's. Startled, she pulled it away and scanned faces to identify who had bumped her, Phoebe or John. Neither acknowledged the contact nor met her gaze.

The conversation drifted toward more mundane topics, but Victoria remained tense until they finished eating.

Judith set her napkin on the table. "Let's go into the sitting room, where we're more comfortable. We can have dessert there. Victoria, dear, you must know we're all dying to hear much more about your incredible survival story."

"I'll bring the dishes into the kitchen first." John pushed his chair back.

"You go sit down with our guests, Mother. You've done enough work this evening. I'll get the dessert." Phoebe set her glass on the table, knocking it sideways as she let go. She righted the glass and stared at the red liquid staining the placemat like drops of blood.

Victoria helped stack the dishes for John and Phoebe, then followed Judith into the living room, where she would soon be the center of attention. Not her favorite place to be. "Where is your powder room?" she asked, mostly to postpone the inevitable.

"Same place it's been all these years, dear. Don't you remember?" Judith gestured to an arched doorway on one end of the dining room. "Out that door, walk past the kitchen, and it's the first room on the right."

Victoria left to find it.

Another framed portrait of Judith hung in the hallway. Her author photo from years ago. Victoria studied the familiar image. Back then, when Victoria was a teen, Judith had seemed like an older woman. Not old exactly, but not young. Now, Victoria could see Judith had only been in her forties at the time of the photo. Strange how the years brought perspective.

A soft burst of laughter from down the hall caught Victoria's attention. She walked in that direction.

John stood facing the kitchen island. Walking toward him, Phoebe tottered a bit on her heels.

She's a bit close to him, isn't she?

Phoebe's hand gripped John's behind. He didn't flinch like he should have. He grinned at her over his shoulder.

Victoria blinked, making sure she'd really seen what she thought she saw. She felt a wave of revulsion toward both of them and deep sadness for Judith. Betrayal by a boyfriend was one thing, but by one's own daughter? And yet, knowing Phoebe, Victoria wasn't as surprised as she should have been.

▼▲▼

"It was not a good day, dogs, and I'm glad it's over." Victoria struggled to pull the comforter from under her dogs and up to her neck. Three of them sprawled horizontally across her

92

bed, leaving barely enough room for her hips and shoulders. She wouldn't dream of moving them, so she flipped onto her side. "We got home from Judith's a lot later than I would have liked. The entire dinner was strange."

Myrtle got up, circled in place, around and around and around, then settled back down with a groan, her side pressed firmly against Victoria's.

"I can't stop thinking about the woman we found in the lake. I wish I knew what happened to her. And why it occurred right after she was at our house."

Victoria's peace from the previous day was long gone. When she stopped thinking about the drowned woman, her mind replayed the horrible image of Phoebe and John in the kitchen.

Poor Judith. How could they?

A part of Victoria wanted to tell Judith. She deserved the truth. But it would cause so much pain. Judith would get over John. No matter how much she might like him, he was replaceable. Her only daughter was not.

"Phoebe's more despicable now than when we were younger," Victoria whispered.

A dog grumbled from the floor.

A wave of loneliness spread over Victoria, an empty ache, even though her father and brother were in the house and her animals were usually more than enough company. Suddenly, she wished she was with Ned. She might have been, except for his insistence that she go to the lake with her family and relax. So far, that wasn't going as planned.

The long day had left Victoria exhausted, and yet, she couldn't fall asleep. She scooped her phone off the bedside table and called Ned.

"Hey, there!" he said. "How are things at your lake house?"

"You wouldn't believe the day we had. It was kind of awful. So, first tell me how you're doing."

Ned summarized his follow-up visit with a physician. No complaining, no pity. "Requests for interviews and talk show appearances are still pouring in. Guess it's going to be awhile before we're old news."

Victoria sighed. "I'm glad no one can find me right now." She shared the day's events, starting with the boat ride and her flashback. "It was pretty unnerving. I wasn't expecting it. Has anything like that happened to you since we got back?"

"No, not yet anyway. Don't worry. It's normal. Tell the psychiatrist you spoke with."

"I will." Then she told him about finding the drowning victim. She didn't mention a word about Phoebe. Victoria didn't want to talk about Phoebe and sure didn't want to fall asleep thinking about her.

"It's a good thing you're there to help sort things out." A rustle of movement came from Ned's end of the call. Victoria imagined him walking through his condo.

"That's one way to look at it. As ridiculous as this sounds, right now, I feel like I bring trouble everywhere I go. I promise, I'll never ask you to fly overseas with me again."

"That *is* ridiculous. And it's a shame. Because I'll be ready to go to Spain again soon. I owe the rescue clinic some time."

"That's so kind of you." Victoria's eyes were drooping. She forced them back open. "I think I'm falling asleep. I miss you, Ned."

"I miss you, too, Victoria. Tell all the dogs hello for me."

Her eyes closed as she said goodnight and tossed her phone onto the nightstand. Emotionally drained, she fell fast asleep.

Izzy barked. A sharp warning.

Victoria's eyes flew open. She sat up.

Someone was outside her room.

Alex peeked his head around her partially open door. "Hey, I'm going to borrow your car, all right?"

"Oh. Okay. My keys are in the mudroom hanging on a hook." She picked up her phone to see the time. Almost midnight. "It's late," she grunted. "Where are you going?"

"To the store. Goodnight, Grandma," he said as he closed the door.

She settled her head back down against her pillow.

What stores here are open this late? she thought before drifting back to sleep.

Chapter 11

The smell of bacon wafted from the kitchen. Victoria wouldn't eat any, but it still smelled amazing. The aroma reminded her of family and when there were four of them.

On the other side of her frosty window, the sun rose—a glint of light behind the rain clouds—something she appreciated more than ever after her sunless ordeal in Greenland. Her dogs watched her from their beds, eager for their feeding and ready to jump up at the slightest sign she was about to start the day. For several seconds, she luxuriated under the warm blankets. It seemed like nothing unusual had happened and the lake house was a safe respite from the rest of the world, a place where she could let her guard down.

Then reality returned—the stranger in the lake.

Who was she and what led to her death?

Victoria was up in a flash. She needed to know.

Downstairs, she poured herself a cup of coffee, placed a bagel into the toaster oven, and took a bowl of berries out of the fridge.

Did the medical examiner finish the post-mortem yet?

When her breakfast was ready, she sat in the breakfast nook with her iPad. She opened her browser and typed: *drowning victim, Lake Lucinda, December 27.* She'd previously used her index finger to type on her iPad. Now, with the tip of her index finger missing, she typed with her thumbs and discovered why most people did the same. It would take some getting used to, but it was more efficient.

The only article that came up in her search was a short one, little more than an expanded headline.

Lake Lucinda boaters discovered the body of an adult female in Enticement Cove. Authorities have not identified the drowning victim. An investigation is underway.

Izzy jumped up from the floor, barking. The other dogs followed and ran to the door. Someone or something was outside. Victoria left her iPad on the table while she went to the front of the house.

Through the side windows, a shadow fell across the steps.

She tensed, bracing herself for a visit from the sheriff and his slightly hostile attitude toward her.

If the authorities still haven't identified the young woman, Alex might be their only source of information. That must be why the sheriff is here. So relax. There's no evidence that Alex did anything wrong.

A hard, fast knock started the dogs barking again. Victoria moved them aside and opened the door. It wasn't who she was expecting.

Rather than waiting on the covered porch, George Wilson—from the trailer across the street—stood in the misty rain, several feet from the bottom of the front steps. Dark sunspots covered his skin, as if he'd spent his entire life outside without using sunscreen. A small bulge protruded from one of his cheeks. His olive-colored work pants and corduroy shirt hung loosely on his wiry frame. The red handkerchief around his neck formed a triangle that pointed to his heart. One deeply wrinkled hand with broken capillaries gripped a wrench.

97

"Hi, Mr. Wilson." Victoria leaned against the doorframe and blocked the open doorway with her body so her dogs wouldn't get out. "How are you?"

George grunted. "Good. Your father home?" His voice was gravelly, as if it rarely got used. He shifted his weight from side to side, his watchful eyes looking almost everywhere except Victoria's face.

"Yes. He's here. I believe he's working in his office. I'll go get him. Please come in and get out of the rain."

George leaned toward the bushes and spat. When he straightened, the bulge in his cheek had disappeared. He surprised her by trudging up the steps in his scuffed work boots and coming inside. He hitched his pants up the same way Victoria had been doing lately. She closed the door.

The dogs rushed to surround him in the entryway. A smile appeared on the old man's face as he petted them.

Although George had lived across from the Heslin family's lake house for as long as they had owned it, Victoria knew little about him. She wondered if he'd ever married or had children. She'd previously assumed he hadn't. In fact, when she was trying to determine which house on the peninsula Kristen had come from, it hadn't occurred to Victoria that Kristen might be George's visitor—a relative of his, like his granddaughter. But she wasn't, or George would have said so already.

It was probably weird to ask about his family now. But that wouldn't stop her.

"Do you have family, Mr. Wilson? I can't remember, it's been so long."

"Uh...nope." He answered without looking up from the dogs. He petted Big Ed and Oliver at the same time and Myrtle rubbed against his leg like a cat. "Not anymore." His slight smile disappeared.

Victoria's father came around the corner. "George. Hey. Nice to see you. How are things?"

"Good. I brought the wrench you need." George delivered one last rub to a dog's head, then straightened, holding up the tool. A few drops of rainwater slid down the steel handle and onto the floor. "Want me to look at your pipe?"

"No, no—I wouldn't want to trouble you. It's only a little leak. I can fix it myself with the right tool. I don't know where mine went. Maybe I took it back to Virginia with me."

"I might as well have a look. Seeing I'm here and all."

"I won't refuse your offer, but it's really nothing," Mr. Heslin said. "I assure you."

Victoria was glad he accepted George's offer. Her father was a brilliant business person, but his knowledge might not transfer to fixing leaking pipes, whereas George could supposedly fix anything.

"Can I get you some coffee, first?" Mr. Heslin asked.

"No. I'm good." George glanced up at the wood-beamed ceiling. Maybe he was looking for water spots.

"Okay. Come on." Mr. Heslin extended his arm toward the back of the house. "It's on the dock. I need to grab my coat." After getting his coat from the mudroom, he left the house with George following.

Myrtle whined and poked her nose against the window, smudging the glass.

"What's wrong, Myrtle? You already had your breakfast. It's hours until lunchtime." Victoria rubbed the little greyhound's neck and followed her gaze out the window toward the ground.

99

The bowl Victoria set out earlier for the foxes was partly visible. With so much on her mind, she had forgotten to refill it when they returned from Judith's house.

She unlocked the front door and reached for the bowl.

It was full.

Strange. Then again, she hadn't been to the lake house in years. The foxes needed time to find the food. She hadn't heard them at all last night. Though she'd been so sure they'd already discovered the little stash when she'd heard a shriek two nights ago. The sound had come from close by.

Victoria froze.

Was it a fox she'd heard? The skin on her neck prickled.

She stared out at the woods across the street. Hugging her body and feeling vulnerable, she kept watch, unsure of what she expected to see.

Too much time has passed. You can't be sure of what you heard.

But she was sure.

Leaving the bowl on the porch and locking the front door, she went to the mudroom and shuffled through her coat pockets for Sheriff Hayes' business card. As she entered his number, his name popped up. She'd forgotten she'd already put his contact in her phone.

His phone rang. No one answered. She left a message asking him to call her.

In the kitchen, she opened the refrigerator and peered inside without really seeing the contents. She wasn't hungry, anyway. What she needed didn't reside in the refrigerator or in the cabinets. She needed information. It was getting harder by the minute to hang around the house, patiently waiting.

I've got to find out what the post-mortem exam uncovered.

Calling the medical examiner was worth a shot. After a few seconds on the internet, Victoria had the number for Dr. Monica Stewart's office. She called and again had no luck getting an actual person to answer.

"You've reached the office of Dr. Monica Stewart. Dr. Stewart is out of the office until January third. If this is an urgent matter, please contact Dr. Philip Ross until her return."

Victoria did a quick search on Philip Ross. He was a family physician. His online photo put him solidly over the age of retirement, with slightly rounding shoulders, thinning gray hair, and small spectacles. His office was on the same street as the medical examiner's office. He might be a good general practitioner, but did he know how to conduct a forensic investigation? Would he be able to determine if Kristen's death was an accident or not?

"I'm going out for a bit," Victoria told her dogs, heading back to the mudroom. "I won't be long."

The dogs scrambled up, expecting an outing.

Putting on her coat, Victoria dug into the pockets for her car keys. A used tissue and the receipt from Prince's grocery store were the only items in there. The dogs huddled around her. "Where are my keys, guys? Oliver, where are my keys?"

Oliver's tail swirled in full circles as he looked to the leashes on the wall, then back to Victoria.

"You're not coming with me, sweetie. I'll take you out for a walk later."

Oliver swung his head around and slunk off.

Victoria scanned the hooks in the mudroom, still searching for her keys.

Oh, yeah. Alex borrowed my SUV last night.

She hurried back to the kitchen, spotted her keys inside the key bowl, and scooped them up. The dogs followed her to the mudroom again. "Okay, I'm really leaving this time. You stay here and be good dogs." Before going out the door, she stopped long enough to pat each dog.

As she backed out of the garage, her father and George came into the view of her SUV's back up camera. Her father had his hood up against the falling rain. George's hair was slick and wet.

Victoria stopped her SUV and rolled down her window.

"I'll bring the right tool over later." George shielded his eyes with his arm and walked away, unhurried.

Her father ducked into the garage and out of the rain. "I can come get it now."

"Nah. I'm gonna bring it over to ya as soon as I find it." George stopped next to the tall enclosure surrounding their trash bins. The gate was hanging slightly off, the corner slanting toward the ground. "I'll fix the hinge on this gate here while I'm at it."

"Thanks, George," Mr. Heslin called after him. "I appreciate your help. We can wait until the rain stops."

George raised his wrench overhead as he kept walking.

Mr. Heslin turned his attention to Victoria. "Where are you off to, honey?"

"The medical examiner's office. To see what they've found and ask if they need assistance."

Mr. Heslin patted the top of her door. "Call me if there's anything I can do to help."

"I will. I shouldn't be long. I'm going to try again with the cookies when I get back."

If I can stop thinking about the investigation long enough to focus on something else.

Chapter 12

With the soft swiping of windshield wipers in the background, Victoria's GPS directed her to the Medical Examiner's office. Ruts filled with muddy water pockmarked the roads under the gloomy sky.

A few miles from the peninsula, a massive uprooted tree blocked traffic in both directions. A crew of men with raincoats and hard hats stared at the fallen oak.

Victoria backed up her car until she had more room, then did a three-point turn to get herself in the opposite direction. She found an alternate route on unfamiliar roads lined with small homes. Most needed repairs. Old furniture, appliances, and children's toys were piled high on their decaying porches. The homes' sad conditions were likely the result of the declining mining industry—mostly coal—and the unemployment sweeping the area over the last decade.

Did Kristen live somewhere out here? Probably not, or the sheriff's department would have recognized her. Like Judith said, most everyone here knows everyone else.

The shabby homes were a sharp contrast to the ones on the Lake Lucinda peninsula. Perhaps the sheriff wasn't the only one in the town who had an attitude with the homeowners in the more affluent area.

After several miles and turns, Victoria reached the center of the town.

Her GPS announced, "Your destination is on the right."

Spotting a cinderblock building with a dented sheriff's vehicle in front, Victoria parked. She pulled the hood of her coat over her head before getting out of her car.

The sheriff stood under an awning in front of the entrance. One hand held a Styrofoam cup with a *Joey's Mart* logo while the other held his phone to his ear.

Victoria approached.

He dropped the phone to his side and dipped his head. "Ms. Heslin."

"Hi, Sheriff. Please, call me Victoria. I heard you were having trouble identifying the drowning victim. Is that still the case?"

The sheriff set his cup on the stair ledge. He rubbed his hand across his eyes then stroked his beard.

Victoria stopped a few yards away. "I've worked a lot of homicide cases. I'd be happy to help if I can."

"First off, what makes you think it's a homicide investigation?" His cold had worsened since yesterday, making his voice more nasally, obscuring his southern accent. He sounded like he should be in bed drinking hot soup rather than standing outside on a cold, rainy day.

"I meant *if* it is one."

He stepped out from under the awning and into the rain. They were both getting wet now. "You can't honestly think you should help, do you? First, you moved the body before we got there. And second, your brother is the only person who seems to know Kristen. And when you put those two things together..." He huffed. "I think it's best if you leave."

Something deep inside her steeled—anger, and an overwhelming instinct to protect her brother. "Alex had nothing to do with her death."

"Maybe not." The sheriff picked his cup up from the ledge. "That's yet to be determined. However, you're not the first person to insist their family member couldn't possibly be guilty."

Victoria curbed her frustration as rain pattered her hood and dripped onto her face. "I left a message for you with your office before I came. I heard a scream coming from the woods. From the left of my house, if you're facing the lake. This was after Kristen left our yard. It was 1:30 a.m. I'm absolutely certain of the precise time."

The sheriff frowned. "You just rememberin' today that you heard someone scream, but you're sure about the exact time?"

"Yes." She wasn't accustomed to being patronized. His comments had her a bit rattled and feeling compelled to explain. "Until today, I had reason to believe what I heard was a fox. I'm sure you've heard them. They can sound frightening. Like a woman screaming. Then this morning, I discovered the food I put out for them was untouched. Considering the timing, there's a strong possibility I heard the young woman from the lake, and not a fox."

He stared at her. "I heard you brought a pack of giant dogs to your father's house. You think a fox would go near it?"

"Foxes and dogs sometimes play..." She shook her head. *Why am I explaining something that has absolutely nothing to do with the issue at hand?* "Listen, the currents were strong yesterday, with the storm brewing. Kristen could have gone into the water anywhere and drifted to Enticement Cove. However, since she was

106

at our house during the evening, it seems more likely she entered the lake from somewhere nearby. That's why I think it was her I heard. Did anyone else mention hearing a scream?"

"No. I interviewed everyone on the peninsula. Everyone who's aroun', which doesn't amount to many people compared to the number of homes out there. No one else claimed to have heard anythin' unusual."

Victoria wiped water from her cheeks. "Did you search the woods around the cove?"

"We did."

"And you found nothing? No footprints? No purse or a dropped phone?"

The sheriff kept his expression blank, revealing nothing.

"Look, I have years of experience with not only homicide but also missing person investigations...whatever it is you need. But in order to help, you have to fill me in on the information you have so far. Are the post-mortem results back?"

"Ms. Heslin, your help is not necessary, and you have no jurisdiction here. I already asked you once—nicely—to go. For all I know, you and your brother..." He snorted. "Never mind. Go back to your father's place and do some online shopping, or whatever it is you do in your mansion, and we'll run our investigation."

Victoria scoffed—he had some nerve, and he had her pegged so wrong—but this wasn't about her. She was more interested in the information hidden within his words—*for all I know.*

They still haven't learned what took place or who she was.

The sheriff remained standing with his legs spread, blocking the building's entrance like a bouncer at an exclusive club. He opened his mouth to speak. The door swung open behind

107

him. An old man wearing a suit and bowtie emerged in the doorway. He resembled the online photo of Dr. Philip Ross, who was replacing the medical examiner over the holiday.

Wringing his hands, the elderly man looked directly at the sheriff. "What are you planning to do about this, Hayes? Because I frankly have no idea how to proceed. This is unprecedented."

The sheriff moved in front of the door, turning his back to Victoria. He lowered his voice, but she still heard him say, "Give me a few minutes to deal with this, and then I'll come back inside."

She moved over, trying to see around the sheriff and not really caring if he saw her doing it. "What happened? Is it related to Kristen?"

The doctor retreated out of sight.

The sheriff pulled the door closed and turned back to Victoria.

"Let me talk to your medical examiner." Victoria attempted to walk around him. "I won't touch anything, if that's your concern."

The sheriff moved left, blocking her.

She was not about to do a little dance with him, nor would it be appropriate to force her way past.

Victoria tried to put herself in the sheriff's shoes.

Everyone is a suspect until proven otherwise, until they find the truth.

Could she blame him for trying to do a good job? And *was* she breaching guidelines? If Alex was guilty—absolutely. But he wasn't. He couldn't be. His only involvement was that he met the young woman on the evening she died. Did the sheriff's behavior have anything to do with animosity toward Alex, as Phoebe suggested?

"You should leave, Ms. Heslin. I'll find you if I need you."

Victoria took a deep breath. "I understand." She started toward her car, stopped, and turned. Sheriff Hayes still had his eyes on her. "You've got my number. Good luck." That was all she had left to say. There was nothing passive aggressive in the statement.

She climbed in her SUV and tossed her wet coat onto the passenger seat. Her breath fogged the windshield. She started the car and flicked on the wipers. Through the cleared windshield, the sheriff remained on the steps, phone against his ear again, watching her, his scowl more defined than before.

She gave the sheriff a tight-lipped smile and a wave, as if they'd had a normal, professional encounter. It was important to know when to walk away. The last thing she should do was anger the sheriff further and potentially make the situation more difficult for Alex. Yet she wanted to help. Kristen, if that was indeed her real name, deserved a thorough investigation into her death and justice if she was killed. And yes, Victoria had an ulterior motive. If there was foul play involved, she couldn't let Alex be an easy suspect only because the real one proved too difficult to identify.

Seeing she had little choice, she would give the sheriff the benefit of the doubt, trust in his abilities, and hope he had people to advise him. That being said, she couldn't stop wondering if the sheriff's department was on the right track. Were they making progress? Or were they overlooking pertinent angles of investigation? Fortunately, she knew someone who could help. Her friend and colleague, Sam. One of the best intelligence analysts in her office. She called him as she approached the main street of the town.

"Victoria, how are you?" Sam asked straightaway, his voice full of the good-natured enthusiasm that characterized his personality.

Victoria pictured him with his feet up on his desk, one of few men in the office who wore jeans and hoodies rather than a suit. His reputation as an amazing analyst took precedence over his choice of attire.

"I'm fine. I'm in West Virginia with my dad and brother. My father has a lake house here. And..." She hesitated to tell him what happened because it meant admitting out loud again that death seemed to follow her everywhere. But she could hardly ask for his assistance without telling him the facts. "Yesterday morning, we found a body in the lake near our house."

"Oh, no."

"Yes. A young woman who remains a Jane Doe. The local sheriff's department is blocking me from helping."

"They would be wise to take your help if you're offering. Must be fools."

She elaborated on the sheriff's reasoning by telling Sam the complete story.

"Well, now I can see their hesitation."

"My brother has no idea what happened to her. It's strange and terrible timing that he met her first. If it was a murder, the perpetrator is still out there." She stopped at a four-way stop and checked the car's digital map, making sure she was still heading in the right direction. "I only brought my iPad. I don't have my work computer or my PIV card so I can't access any of our databases. I wasn't planning to do any work while I was here. That's changed."

"Are you sure you can be objective, Victoria?"

"Yes. I'm sure." *I think I'm sure.* "I'll try. In the meantime, is there any way you could look into it? Access their local database and keep me posted?"

Sam didn't answer right away. Someone always needed something from him, and she'd caught him right in the middle of a busy workday. Or maybe he found her request unreasonable. Victoria swallowed. Her mouth suddenly dry.

Coming up on her right was Joey's Mart, the gas station and store whose logo was on the side of the sheriff's coffee cup. A mix of warmth, sugar, and caffeine held a powerful appeal, but chances were good the convenience store wouldn't have lattes. She kept going.

"Sure," Sam finally said.

Did it take him a long time to respond? Or am I being paranoid?

"And can you check on missing persons' reports to match a young woman aged seventeen to twenty-five? She told my brother her name is Kristen. Kristen with a K."

"I can do that for you."

"And one more thing—George Wilson. Can you dig up his background? His address is 1080 Peninsula Point Drive, right across the street from my father." She gave him a second to write it down or type it in. "Actually, just one more thing, and I promise this is the last. John Stein. That's a common name and I don't have an address, but he's in his thirties and he's from New York. Dark hair. He does some sort of marketing or publicity work. Judith McPharland is one of his clients." She stopped for a breath, hoping she hadn't pushed her luck with so many requests, especially since she wasn't officially working the case. "Thank you so much, Sam. If there was an FBI office anywhere around here, I would go in and access the database myself. It's killing me that I don't have the information. I promise I'll make it up to you."

"You have nothing to make up to me, Victoria. When you were missing, I would have done anything to get you back. All of us felt that way. Rivera especially."

"I know. I'm so grateful. We would be frozen forever in the snow if you and Rivera hadn't led the way to finding out what happened with the plane."

After a few pleasantries, Sam said, "I have to go. I'll talk to you later."

On the town's main street, Victoria drove slowly past a hardware store with a giant handmade sign advertising a post-Christmas sale, followed by a bar, a pizza place, an ice cream and fudge shop, and a pharmacy. At the end of the road, there was a new café. New to her, at least. A cute chalkboard sign in the store's window advertised specialty coffees and baked goods.

She smiled. *My kind of place.*

The rain changed to sleet, bits of ice pinging the windshield and sliding down the glass. She pulled into a parking space in front of the shop. There was only one other car nearby, ancient and rusted. Hard to believe it would run, never mind pass an inspection.

Leaving her wet coat on the passenger seat, she dashed to the café with her head down.

A bell chimed above the lavender-painted door when she pushed it open. The décor—a variety of tables, some round, some square, with mismatched chairs—reminded her of a popular café in Georgetown near her college campus and brought back memories of pink-frosted cupcakes and lots of lattes while cramming for tests. People packed the Georgetown café every day of the week. Finding an empty seat there was like winning a small lottery. This café was empty. Victoria stood alone inside the door, dripping water onto the polished concrete floors.

A girl emerged, rushing out through a swinging door behind a counter decorated with evergreen garlands and red bows. Freckles covered her cheeks and a red braid trailed over one shoulder. She wore a small, gold nose ring. Her nametag said Abby. She greeted Victoria with a bright smile, showing teeth with a gap in the center. "Hi! What can I get you?"

The café employee sparked unease in Victoria. Something to do with the stranger in the lake. It wasn't Abby's demeanor; she was full of enthusiasm. Yet there was something there, something significant, barely out of grasp. Victoria couldn't put her finger on it yet.

She scanned the menu and spotted a list of flavored syrups. "I'll have a large hazelnut latte, please."

While waiting for her drink, Victoria closed her eyes and pictured Kristen lying on the dock. Fairly new-looking running shoes. Designer jeans. An expensive sweater.

What is bugging me?

Long, tangled hair. Pale, smooth skin. The scratches on her face. Her slightly parted mouth—that's when it came to her—that was it.

Between parted lips, Kristen's lower teeth had been visible. They weren't perfect. A center tooth crossed toward the next. No dental disaster, but highly unusual for anyone whose family owned a home on the peninsula and could afford the orthodontia for a flawless smile. However, less than perfect teeth were not unusual for the residents in the small town, as the pretty café employee had unknowingly proven.

So what does that mean?

Everything Alex recalled suggested Kristen had walked from somewhere nearby on the peninsula. She'd told Alex that she'd lived there a long time. Now, that story didn't fit. It didn't make sense.

Was there another home like George Wilson's on the peninsula? One that had been there before second-home owners with big budgets took over? Another modest home or a double-wide tucked back into the trees? She'd have to find out, although that didn't fit with Kristen's new, expensive clothes.

Abby set Victoria's coffee on the counter. "Here you go."

"Thank you." Victoria moved to the front of the bakery display case and hovered a finger above the glass in the corner. "I'd like to buy the rest of these pastries, too."

The girl put the pastries in a bag. She handed them to Victoria, who couldn't help noticing the girl's teeth again.

"Please come back." Abby exited the counter area, disappearing through the swinging door.

Victoria left two large bills in the tip jar on the counter.

As she pulled away from her parking space, a silver Range Rover took the spot next to hers. Harrison from the grocery store. He leaned forward and waved. Victoria waved back. She was glad the sweet girl would have another customer.

Chapter 13

Victoria drove back to Lake Lucinda from the café, eager to share the few things she'd learned on her outing.

A surprise waited at her father's house—the sheriff's car parked out front. There may have been other sheriff's department vehicles in the town, but the conspicuous dent told her this one belonged to Sean Hayes.

"He might be interviewing Alex," she muttered to herself. "I shouldn't have stopped for coffee." Except the coffee had been delicious and absolutely perfect when nothing much else was going her way. She hoped the sheriff was only there because he had reconsidered her offer of help.

She parked in the garage, shut off the engine, and leaned sideways to grab her phone. Something metal glinted under the garage lights, between the passenger seat and the center console. Shimmying her hand into the tight space, she trapped the object with her finger and slid it upward. It was the jade necklace Alex had bought for Minka, the same one Minka had been wearing in the photo. The clasp was broken, the tiny metal clamps twisted open.

What caused the necklace to break?

Inside the house, the dogs ran to her, snorting and wagging their tails like mad, shoving each other out of the way to get there first.

Her father sat at the kitchen table with an open book about Presidents in front of him. "The sheriff is here."

Victoria pushed through the excited animals and made her way to the kitchen. "I saw his car out front. Where is he?" She set the bag of pastries down, tossed her keys into the key bowl, and dropped the necklace on the counter next to a pair of headphones. She didn't see Alex. "Is he questioning Alex alone?"

"He asked to see the area where the girl was sitting. That's all. They're outside. They've only been out there a minute."

"He's back because they don't know who Kristen is yet. Alex must be the only person who saw her recently."

"Or the only one admitting it," her father mumbled.

Victoria grabbed a pastry and plunked the bag down beside her father's book. She sat near him by the window where they could see Alex and the sheriff under the covered part of the patio. The sheriff looked around. He wasn't questioning Alex.

Her brother kept covering his mouth with his hand, a habit of his. It was also a telltale sign a person had something to hide. She wished he would stop doing it.

"How did it go at the medical examiner's office?" her father asked, peering into the bag of pastries.

"The sheriff doesn't want my help." She relayed her earlier conversation while keeping an eye on the sheriff.

"Were you out of line?"

"I was just offering a hand."

"Would you let an outsider help with your investigation if they were related to a key witness?"

"Depends on how the investigation was going. It's a little troubling that they don't seem to have information they should have by now."

116

On the patio, the sheriff ambled around the firepit.

With his hand still covering his mouth, Alex gave them a quick look through the window, raising and lowering his brows.

Victoria took glances at her newsfeed so she wasn't overtly watching Alex and the sheriff. She couldn't concentrate on a single article. She doubted her father was processing any of his book either.

Although the plane crash occurred weeks ago, news articles about it still trended. She scrolled past every mention, then looked up again. "They've been out there a long time."

Unable to sit still, she got up and crossed the room to the kitchen. She warmed a cinnamon roll in the microwave, tore off small pieces, and ate them standing up at the counter. The sweet dough felt dry in her mouth. She filled a glass of water and took a sip to get it down, eating a few more bites without really tasting it. The refrigerator clicked on and whirred quietly in the background.

The back door opened and ushered in a rush of cold air. Alex and the sheriff came inside.

"Mr. Heslin." The sheriff touched the brim of his hat. He shifted toward the door as if he was about to leave.

Mr. Heslin set his book down. "Do you know who she is yet?"

"We don't,'" the sheriff answered.

"Have you interviewed everyone on the peninsula?" Mr. Heslin folded his arms across his front. "Did you ask the Roberts if they heard a scream?"

"Yes. We've spoken to everyone staying here. And no one else reported hearing anything unusual."

Victoria frowned. "Everyone at the Roberts house is on the old side—at least one of them wears hearing aids. Perhaps they had already removed them for the night. Or they thought the sound came from an animal, like I originally did."

The sheriff sniffed hard. "Yet that doesn't tell me why your father and brother didn't hear what you think you heard. Strange, isn't it? And Alex said he had just gotten into bed. So, by his own account, he wouldn't have been sleeping very soundly."

Did Alex have so much to drink that he passed out? Has that ever happened to him?

Victoria wasn't sure if the scream she heard made things better or worse for Alex. All she had was the truth. They needed to follow it.

"If Victoria heard a scream, then there was one." Mr. Heslin spoke with the same tone he used to command board meetings. "And to make sure your timeline is correct, the scream happened after the girl left, after I saw Alex go upstairs."

"I might have been brushing my teeth with the water running when the scream occurred." Alex gestured to his headphones on the counter. "Or wearing headphones and listening to music. In fact, I'm sure I was." His gaze moved over slightly, landing on the necklace. He narrowed his eyes.

"There you go." Victoria reached for the headphones and held them up. "That's why Alex didn't hear the scream. One mystery solved."

The sheriff studied Alex a few seconds longer than normal. Then his eyes swept the room. "Are you about to have the house painted?"

"What?" For a second, Victoria had no idea what he was talking about. "Oh, the sheets? No. Those are there to keep the furniture clean. We're not painting." The sheets were doing their job. Muddy prints covered them. She lifted one off the nearest chair so the sheriff could see there wasn't anything hiding underneath.

The sheriff looked out the back windows, his eyes moving from one side of the yard to the other. "I'm going to check out those woods one more time. Enjoy your day." He dipped his head again, walked to the front door, and let himself out.

Alex leaned against the kitchen wall. He rubbed his chin and blew out an audible breath. "My flight back to Colorado is January first. He says I have to stay until...well, he didn't say when."

"I should have called Fenton immediately," Mr. Heslin said.

Victoria shook her head. "If Alex is innocent—"

"*If?*" Alex raised his voice. "What the hell, Tori? Of course I'm innocent."

"Shh." She held up her hand and her gaze shot to the front door, worried the sheriff might overhear them from outside. "Calm down. What I was going to say is that if we brought in an attorney instead of being cooperative, it might not have looked that way. The sheriff was already acting like we think we're above the law. You're a witness of sorts, that's all, not a suspect." Victoria turned to her father. "Go ahead and call Fenton now. I never imagined they still wouldn't have any clues as to what occurred."

"Yeah. Definitely call him." Alex opened the pastry bag and looked inside.

"I want to be very clear that we one hundred percent trust you, Alex." Mr. Heslin shot a quick glance at Victoria, then back to his son. "You may have caused your share of trouble in the past, but you've never lied about any of it. Never denied it. You've faced the consequences head on."

Victoria nodded, leaning on the island across from her brother. "Did the sheriff question you when you were out there?"

Alex pulled a donut from the bag. "He mostly looked around and stared, like a psychic waiting for some message from beyond. He asked a few questions about Kristen. He asked if anything about her or our conversation suggested she was worried about something. And if I had any concerns about her in general."

"That's fine." Victoria clasped her hands, then opened them. "See? He's trying to figure out who she was and what might have been going on with her, since no one else in the area has provided information."

"He also asked me where I was last night."

"Last night?" Mr. Heslin straightened. "What does last night have to do with the girl going into the lake two nights ago? Did he tell you why he was asking?"

"Nope."

"You told him you were with us, right?" Mr. Heslin narrowed his eyes at Alex. "Having dinner at Judith's? And we didn't get back until after eleven."

"Yes. I told him," Alex said.

He also left in my car late last night. And that must be when the necklace ended up in there.

"The sheriff found evidence to show her death wasn't an accident, didn't he?" Alex asked. "That's why he came back, right?"

"I don't know. I wish I did." Victoria hoped Sam would come through for her.

"It's not like this is a big city." Alex finished the donut, grabbed a napkin off the counter, and wiped his hands.

120

"She could be a college girl vacationing with friends who don't realize she's missing yet," Victoria suggested.

"Those don't sound like very good friends," Mr. Heslin said.

"True." Victoria grabbed the empty pastry bag and crumpled it up. "I'm just throwing out ideas. Someone has to be missing Kristen soon. Even if she lived alone. A friend or family member will notice she isn't responding to texts and calls and get worried. Alex, did you see her use her phone when you were with her? To check the time before she left, something like that?"

"The sheriff asked that, too. Not that I can remember. I never saw a phone."

"That's unusual in itself. People can barely stay off their phones for ten minutes nowadays. Especially young people." Victoria ran her tongue over her lip while she thought. "Tomorrow is Monday. If Kristen has a job and fails to show up, someone will notice and eventually report her missing."

"What if you and Dad hadn't spotted her floating in the water?" Alex asked.

"What are you asking?" Mr. Heslin narrowed his eyes at Alex.

"Victoria said a branch snagged the body. What if she'd sunk to the bottom and stayed there? It would almost be like she had never existed at all. Like her death never happened." Alex bent over, his hands on his knees. "I can't believe this. I'm a nice guy who had a chat with a girl. Then, she ends up dead in a lake." He exhaled loudly. "Damn it. I didn't even know her."

Victoria froze. So often, this was when the perpetrator broke down and blurted out that it was an accident, that he hadn't meant for any of it to happen. A small part of her expected a confession of sorts. Dreading one, she held her breath.

121

Alex straightened. "Tori, you have to figure out what happened." Anguish filled his eyes, reminding her of when he was young and needed help with something that really mattered to him, something he couldn't accomplish on his own. His desperate expression grasped at her heartstrings, yet she couldn't think of a particular instance where she might have seen it before. And then she did—when their mother went missing. When their family was helpless and afraid.

"I will." She crossed the room and hugged her brother. He needed her again. He needed her to find out what happened to Kristen so he could move on, free from any worry or guilt or blame. And this time, because of her background and experience, she could help him.

Over her brother's shoulder, she spotted the sheriff through the window. He'd opened an umbrella and walked along the edge of the woods with his head down, stopping every few steps to scan the ground.

"I was looking for this." Alex picked Minka's necklace off the counter. "Where did it come from?"

"It was in my car."

"Oh. Good. Minka yanked it off her neck when she stormed out of here. I went to mail this to her the other night when I borrowed your car. I was going to drop it in a Fed Ex box with a few of her other things, but there weren't any envelopes, and then I must have dropped it."

So that's why he borrowed my car.

Outside, the sheriff trudged methodically toward the dark murky waters of the lake.

She hoped he would find something.

Secrets were hiding on the peninsula. And someone was lying.

Chapter 14

With announcers' voices and the occasional whistle reaching the kitchen from the soccer game her father and brother were watching, Victoria poured kibble into her dogs' dishes. She debated making lunch for herself, but decided against it. A few pieces of the rich cinnamon bun had been filling enough, and she was rarely hungry when she was working a case. Except...she wasn't officially working this case. She only wished she was.

She sat back and turned her iPad on again. A check of her email revealed a new message from Sam. The subject line read: J. Stein and G. Wilson.

Victoria opened the message and devoured the contents—background information on John and George—with a hunger she hadn't possessed for food in days.

John Stein, a self-employed "publicity enhancer," had a record—a sexual assault that occurred eleven years ago. He pleaded innocent, claiming he was drunk and misunderstood the situation, and got off with the slightest of punishments. It might have been an isolated incident. Or was it the only time he got caught? And was he even the right John Stein?

She opened an attachment. The man in the photo was Judith's John. No doubt.

Next came the information on George.

According to Sam's research, George had a daughter. She was in her late fifties now. George must have been quite young when she was born, a mere teenager. He'd never married, but for twenty-one years, he'd voluntarily paid child support to the mother of his child.

That didn't fit with what George told her when she asked if he had family. So why had George lied? What reason could he have for saying he had no family?

In his email, Sam had included the name and phone number for George Wilson's daughter. Victoria didn't waste a minute before calling her.

"Hi," Victoria said when someone picked up the line. "Is this Laura Wilson?"

"Yea, whaddyawant?"

"I'm Victoria Heslin." On the spot, Victoria decided her call might be better coming from a concerned neighbor rather than an FBI agent. "I'm calling about your father, George. I live across the street and—"

"Did he keel over?"

Unless Victoria was mistaken, the question was ringing with anticipation.

"He's fine."

"Oh." The disappointment came across loud and clear. "Then whatever you callin' 'bout, I don't need to hear."

"Wait, um—so, you and your father aren't close?"

Laura let out a mirthless chuckle. "A decent man helps his children when he can, when he has way more than he needs and they don't got much."

Way more than he needs? Is she talking about the same George Wilson from across the street? Recluse George with the quiet and simple life? With the truck that has to be over thirty years old?

"The greedy bastard owns a fancy property worth millions of dollars—you would know that's true if you're really his neighbor. What's he need all that for? What's the use a sittin' on all that money when his only daughter is dirt poor? All he has to do is sell the damn place and help me out with what he gits. Until he does, I told him he has no right to say he has a child anymore."

The woman's attitude shocked Victoria. "You're almost sixty years old. And it's my understanding he paid child support until you were twenty-one."

"And pretty soon I'm gonna be dead without gittin' what I deserve. I have the diabetes and it's bad. What's he waiting for, huh?" Laura exploded with a string of expletives. "Makes me so mad talkin' 'bout it. I could strangle that greedy old man with my bare hands for being so stubborn and selfish."

The call ended abruptly with a slamming sound.

Victoria gaped at her phone. She rarely rushed to judgment without knowing the full story—people and situations often had a way of hiding surprise twists, but she definitely felt sorry for George. No wonder he didn't claim to have a family.

Between Phoebe McPharland and Laura Wilson, I'm a shoo-in for daughter-of-the-year around here.

She set her phone on the kitchen island and went to the cabinet for a glass.

Sam's name lit up on her phone screen. She lunged back over the quartz island to grab it.

"Hey, Sam."

"Hi. Did you see my email?"

125

"I did. Thank you. I'm going a little nuts here. I can't stand being in the dark. The sheriff came to our house and as far as I can tell, the woman from the lake—I've called her Kristen so many times, I'm convinced that's her name—anyway, sounds like they still haven't identified her."

"And now that's going to be more of a challenge."

Victoria clutched the back of a counter stool. "What do you mean?"

"This case is a lot more complicated than I imagined when you told me about it this morning. There's definitely something fishy going on. No pun intended, since the dead woman came out of the lake, and I'm not minimizing the graveness of the situation."

"Sam—"

"Let me start again. There's more to her drowning than a random accident. The local ME's office has quite a predicament."

She gazed at her phone, watching the seconds tick by. Her impatience was getting the best of her. "Spit it out. Please. What did you find?"

Excited shouts came from the family room. Something important happened in the game.

"The young woman's body went missing before the medical examiner did the autopsy."

"What do you mean by missing?"

"Someone broke into the medical examiner's office and took it. If the ME's physical facility is anything like their information systems—only took me a few minutes to gain access—it wasn't hard for someone to do."

Victoria made a fist and pressed it against her lips, struggling to process the unexpected information. "When did that happen?"

"Either last night or early this morning."

She gritted her teeth. "It must have happened last night. That explains why Dr. Ross was wringing his hands in the doorway and asking the sheriff how to proceed."

And—darn it—it explains why the sheriff was sniffing around Alex to see if he had an alibi.

Her heart skipped a beat.

Alex borrowed my car around midnight, after we got home from Judith's house.

"Victoria? Did I lose you?"

"I'm here." An uneasy feeling was growing in the pit of her stomach. Her chest tightened. She didn't want to ask the next question, but it was important. "They must have security cameras, so they have a description of the person who did it, right?"

"Believe it or not, from what I can tell, they don't. I think they must have a small operation there."

Sam's response brought a sense of immediate relief. And for that, she was ashamed. Whoever stole Kristen's body was likely involved in her death. The authorities needed to catch and question that person. No matter who it might be.

Victoria leaned her elbows on the counter. "We have to figure out why someone stole the body. What evidence or secret did they want to keep hidden?"

"You're way better equipped to answer that question, Miss Profiler." He conveyed admiration rather than a smart-aleck response.

She hung her head, thinking about what the theft meant for the investigation. It might have reached a dead end. "They can't obtain any evidence from the body. Nothing at all."

127

"Not necessarily. There is some good news. The ME hadn't started the post-mortem yet, but Sheriff Hayes did everything he could do before the body went missing. He logged all the stats: brown hair, brown eyes, height five-foot seven, weight one-hundred-twenty-four pounds. He got prints, and he sent blood samples to a forensics lab yesterday afternoon for a full workup and a DNA test."

"That's great that he got the blood samples." *Is it great? Why doesn't it feel great? Why am I suddenly so nervous?*

"After someone stole the body, the lab moved the test results to priority."

"Good. But unless they do the test results in house, they will take days or weeks to come back, even when expedited. And the holiday will slow things further. What else did the sheriff record?"

"Let's see...an estimated time of death. With the victim's body temp, taking into consideration the water temperature, they wrote the time of death as two a.m. When you found her, she'd only been dead around seven hours, give or take an hour."

Two a.m. A short time after Alex said she left...but enough time for many things to have happened before she died.

It was the "give or take an hour" that bothered her.

"You still there?" Sam asked. "Did I lose you? Can't tell if one of us is getting bad reception."

"I'm here. I'm so glad the blood sample went out. No one shot or stabbed her. I would have noticed. The water probably washed away any DNA evidence transferred from someone else. The only evidence of what took place might be in her blood. Those test results are critical."

Alex shouted, making Victoria flinch. Someone on the television must have scored.

128

"I also searched for instances of recent and similar deaths in the area," Sam said. "I don't see any, but at some point, every string of serial killings has to start with victim number one. So, you be careful, Victoria. I'll check for additional information later in the day."

"You're the best, Sam. And I will be careful. Thank you."

Victoria went into the family room, petting her dogs as they walked with her. Her father and brother watched soccer players in blue and white jerseys race across a stadium field.

She leaned her hands on the back of the couch. "Alex."

He acknowledged her with a slight twist of his head.

"Where did you go last night when you borrowed my car?" She kept her voice neutral, the same tone she'd use if she was asking him where he put the bag of pretzels they got at the store.

"I told you." Alex turned back to face the game.

Is he buying time while trying to figure out why I'm asking again? Or simply too caught up in the game to answer me?

Alex sprung off the couch, pumping his fist in the air with his eyes on the TV. "Oh, yes! Brilliant stuff!"

"Alex?" she prompted.

He sat back down. "Oh, uh—just to the Fed Ex box near the pizza place. Then I came back because there weren't any mailing envelopes in it."

Mr. Heslin frowned. "You shouldn't have gone out alone, Alex."

"Seriously?" Alex finally took his eyes off the game and gave the conversation his full attention. "I shouldn't have left the house without supervision? No one mentioned to me that I'm supposed to act like I'm already in prison. Victoria is the FBI agent. She gave me her car keys and didn't say anything like, hey,

Alex, don't leave the house or they'll blame you for something else you didn't do." Alex shook his head and blew out a loud breath.

"You're right." Victoria stretched her fingers against the back of the couch. "But there's more to Kristen's drowning than a tragic accident now. I asked a colleague to get me some inside information."

A cloud of darkness crossed her father's face. He muted the television.

Victoria told them about the missing corpse.

Alex pushed himself off the couch. "So that's why the sheriff asked where I was last night. And you, too?" His face fell as he stared at Victoria. "You don't trust me?"

"I needed to know where you went. A body disappearing from the ME's office—that's not normal, obviously. Far from it. It could never happen in most cities. Look, there might be a killer somewhere nearby, covering his or her tracks. Until the whole matter clears up—we need to watch out for you."

"This is nuts!" Alex clasped his hands over his head and dropped his head back. "Why would I take her body? What would I do with it?"

Mr. Heslin focused on Alex. "As far as we know, thanks to the information from Victoria's friend, the authorities have little information and lots of questions. While they find the answers, you might be in a tough spot."

Chapter 15

On the path connecting their neighborhood to the nearby mountain trails, the Heslins walked single file back to the lake house. Weak, late-afternoon sunlight streamed through the trees. The sleet and rain had stopped, leaving behind mushy ground. Victoria's dogs forged ahead with their ears up, unconcerned with the mud.

Walking cleared Victoria's head and helped her think through an investigation. At least, it did when she was alone.

"Hey, why didn't we bring the donkeys and make them carry a picnic or something?" Laughter sparkled in Alex's eyes. "Remind them of their Sherpa days."

Victoria shook her head. "They've never done anything like that, Alex. I told you, they were skin and bones when a rescue group found them on a horrible farm in North Carolina."

Alex shortened his leashes as Big Ed tried to explore something off the side of the trail. "Skin and bones when rescued? Who does that remind you of? Guess you can really empathize with them now, huh?"

"Hmm." She was glad Alex wasn't as upset with her as he'd been earlier in the day. After all he'd been through—Minka leaving, Kristen's mysterious death, doubting suspicions from his own sister—she was grateful his usual, cheerful attitude was making an appearance. He seemed to be in a much better mood than before. Or, he was joking because he was nervous and anxious about the whole situation.

"Kristen might have angered someone after she left our yard." Mr. Heslin kicked a small rock with his boot, sending it sailing into the trees. "A jealous boyfriend."

Ever since they'd found Kristen, Victoria's family had gone round and round discussing scenarios—ideas ranging from a mundane accident to a robbery gone wrong. Victoria's experience taught her all ideas were possible, no matter how far-fetched. Figuring things out was what she did well. Trying not to think about the mysterious situation was the challenge.

She edged around a puddle. Her dogs slogged straight through it, splashing mud onto their long legs. "An investigation would look into family and friends, boyfriends in particular, and create a timeline with the events of her last few days. But that's impossible until they determine her identity. The best sources of information are phone records and computer files—also unavailable."

"So, what are they investigating?" Alex asked.

"The sheriff should visit anyone in the area with a record of violent crimes, and registered sex offenders, although there didn't appear to be signs of sexual assault. Without the medical examination, we'll never know unless the body shows up again."

I wonder if Judith knows about John's sexual assault record. John was there after we pulled Kristen from the lake. He said he'd seen the flashing lights. Was that really the only reason he was there, taking it all in—a normal curiosity?

Images of Phoebe's hand on John's butt replayed in Victoria's mind, making her cringe. She had told no one what she'd seen. She was experienced at being the bearer of unexpected, devastating, life-changing information. The news that someone

132

had murdered or kidnapped or abused a beloved family member. With work, she had no choice in the matter. Now, she could choose to remain silent. Maybe a hand on a butt was no big deal. Judith seemed so happy. Victoria had almost convinced herself that it was none of her business when another wave of uncertainty hit her. If a member of her family was betraying her, would she want to know?

Alex reached overhead to push aside a thin, low-laying branch with his free hand. "You think Kristen ran into psycho Phoebe and accepted one of her messed-up dares?"

Alex was joking about Phoebe and her past predilection for risky games, but was there something to his suggestion?

Phoebe's menacing voice from over a decade ago echoed through Victoria's mind. *I dare you to hold her under the water for two minutes no matter what happens.* What if Phoebe's morbid proclivities had progressed to something beyond games? Improbable, but not impossible. Something unusual had happened and someone was responsible. Even though few people were around the peninsula for the holiday, there were reasons to mistrust every one of them.

Victoria took her eyes off the rocky trail to study her brother. An uncomfortable ripple of doubt thread its way through her thoughts.

I need to do whatever it takes to get rid of it. Alex didn't do this. He couldn't have. Even if it was an accident. And my father hasn't doubted him for a second. So, why do I keep raising these questions? Why do I keep seeing things that appear wrong to my trained eye?

If only Alex hadn't borrowed my car on the same night someone stole the body.

Reaching the paved streets of their neighborhood, Victoria took in the beauty and tranquility that had lured people into purchasing vacation homes they rarely used. The properties relayed the impression of being occupied. Professionally-tended yards. Fresh paint. Cleared roofs. Everything was in tip-top shape, waiting for the owners to return. Most of the properties had Christmas wreaths and boughs of greenery on their doors and gates, though Victoria believed the homes had remained vacant over the holiday.

The notion of empty homes made her think of something. "Have there ever been squatters on the peninsula?"

"I don't think so. Look." Her father gestured to a prominent security company sign in a front yard. "All the homes have security systems and video cameras."

"Do *you* have video surveillance?" Victoria asked.

"No. We have an alarm system. I never bothered having video installed. I didn't see the need with George keeping an eye on the place. He checks on most of these homes when they aren't occupied. Assuming he's doing what we're paying him to do, no one could hide out in any of these homes for long and get away with it."

Victoria studied George's property as they walked past. Ironically, the only home with a full-time resident was the one that looked somewhat abandoned. The rusted car. The old sink. Almost frozen in time. Except...the wheelbarrow and shovel were gone.

"Did George ever come back to fix your leaky pipe?" Victoria asked.

"No." Mr. Heslin said. "I'll wait on him. It's not an emergency."

They reached their driveway. "Can we keep walking a bit more?" Victoria asked. "I want to have a look at the end of the street."

Alex kept walking toward the house with two of her dogs. "I'm going in."

"I've also had enough for one day," Mr. Heslin said.

"If you'll take the rest of the dogs in, I'll take these three and go a bit more. I won't be long."

"See you soon, honey." He kissed the top of her head, then looked up at the horizon, where the last of the day's light was quickly disappearing. "Don't be long and be careful."

Once she was alone, the street was empty, shadowy, and silent.

The first-floor windows of the Nantucket House were brightly lit. Two large Christmas trees now lay discarded at the curb with bits of leftover tinsel hanging off the branches.

Kristen's death had shaken but not devastated the home's inhabitants. Victoria was an excellent judge of recognizing faked distress. Theirs was genuine.

The windows in the next two homes were dark. Both homes had iron fences with heavy gates and security signs. The ownership of both places had changed since she'd last been to the lake.

With no warning, Izzy, Oliver, and Myrtle lunged after two fat squirrels chasing each other. Gasping, Victoria held their leashes tight and leaned back as they pulled her forward. The squirrels raced up a tall oak. The dogs stared up into the treetop, their ears pointed, their lean, muscular bodies tensed.

"That will teach me to pay attention." She shortened their leashes, wrapping length around her palm to avoid her fingers, and tugged the dogs away from the tree.

135

They were in front of Lucinda Lee's former estate by the time the dogs settled down and were walking on loose leashes again. Izzy squatted to relieve herself on the edge of the front yard, outside the massive iron gate.

Victoria studied the property.

Mature elms shielded the property. Through them, Victoria spied a three-tiered fountain taking center stage in the circular driveway. And on a visible section of the house, shades covered the windows.

Maybe to keep onlookers like me from staring inside.

To the right of the main house, the cottage Lucinda Lee had built for overnight guests sat nestled against the woods. The once extravagant estate now seemed modest compared to the newer mansions constructed along the waterfront.

Victoria thought about each of the houses on the peninsula and their owners, the few she knew.

Are any of them capable of murder?

"Hi, again."

A man's voice startled her. She whipped around.

Harrison walked toward her from the woods. "I didn't mean to scare you."

A flush of heat spread over her face. He'd caught her unabashedly staring at his house. Not to mention that her dog had just relieved herself on his grass. Some people wouldn't care. Others would. Which type of person was Harrison?

"Hey, there." She chose not to apologize in case he hadn't seen it happen.

Harrison carried a small pine wreath with a red bow like the one from his car. His hands were dirty, as if he'd been doing yard work without gloves. No wedding band.

"Victoria, right? No, that's not it."

136

"Yes. You got it right. Victoria."

"Oh, good. It feels like I've been following you. First the grocery store, then the café. I suppose it's bound to happen. There's only so many shops in town." Eyeing her dogs, he moved closer.

"Right. That was my first time in that café. I really liked it." Up close, she admired his strong, fresh-shaven jaw and straight nose. His prominent scars made her curious about how he got them. But his blue eyes were red-rimmed and bleary. Hungover? No. She could tell when someone had recently shed tears. Harrison had been crying.

She pulled her thoughts away from his face, feeling as if she'd somehow invaded his privacy. "I noticed your West Virginia license plate. Do you live here year-round?"

"No. But I've been spending more and more time here lately. I met your brother last summer. Other than him, I'm not sure I saw anyone else at your father's house when I was here. It barely gets used."

"That's true." And after the events of the past few days, Victoria wasn't sure she ever wanted to come back. "So where else do you call home?"

"Connecticut. That's where I grew up."

"Oh." She turned toward Harrison's house. "When I was a girl, we believed this house was haunted because it's so secluded. We'd dare each other to run through the yard and do a bunch of odd things to make us even more afraid. This house always had an aura of mystique."

Harrison laughed. "Haunted, huh? Can't say I've noticed any ghosts." He stared at his house, giving her a quick chance to study him further.

"Are you okay?" She asked, concerned, although mostly curious.

Harrison touched the large scar on his cheek, tracing a finger along the raised skin. "I'm dealing with some family stuff right now. My sister is really sick. She has been for some time." A flicker of something—possibly pain—crossed his face and ruffled his rugged charm.

"I'm sorry."

He didn't care or seem embarrassed that I noticed he'd been crying.

"Thank you." Harrison looked down at the wreath in his hand and began pulling off the bow.

Victoria was about to say goodbye when he spoke again. "How is your brother doing? I heard he knows the girl you found in the lake."

Great. Everyone knows.

"He's fine. Concerned about the young woman. As we all are. It's a little troubling for everyone, isn't it? Not knowing who she is or what happened to her."

"Your brother spent time with her and he doesn't know who she is?"

"Alex only talked with her briefly. She was out for a walk. She said her name was Kristen. That's all he knows. I think that's all anyone knows, which is very strange."

Harrison stood only a few feet away. Victoria caught a faint whiff of cologne or aftershave.

"I'm sure someone knows who she is.'" Harrison tucked the bow into his coat pocket, pulled his arm back, and sent the small wreath sailing into the woods like a frisbee. "That's for the birds. It's the one and only decoration I put up for Christmas."

"And you still got us beat in terms of decorating," Victoria said. "Well, I need to get back. Nice to talk to you."

"Nice to see you again, Victoria." Harrison waved. He gave no indication he was about to head back to the woods or toward his house.

With her dogs leading, Victoria walked away. Still no sounds of movement came from behind her. Although she would not turn around and check, she was pretty sure Harrison was watching her go. This would make the second time he had a view of her backside, if he took the opportunity. She wasn't sure how she felt about that.

Chapter 16

Just before lunch, the dogs' ears perked up and their heads swung toward the front of the house.

The doorbell rang.

"Stay. Don't move." Victoria took one more picture of Oliver and Big Ed looking regal on the couch with a view of the lake in the background. "I'll be back, handsome fellows. Hold those poses."

She walked through the kitchen, glancing into the oven on her way to the door. Four baking sheets filled the racks. The cookies were just starting to turn a golden shade of brown. Only a few more minutes.

She expected to see George with her father's tool. She was eager to ask him about the other homeowners in the neighborhood. Instead, Phoebe teetered in high-heel boots at the top of the front steps, peering in through the glass.

Oh, great. What does she want?

Victoria opened the door. The white Mercedes waited at the street. John was in the driver's seat.

"Hello, Victoria. My mother asked me to give this to you after our dinner. Guess I forgot." Bracelets jangled on Phoebe's arm as she handed Victoria a book. "It's her latest. She published it several years ago."

Victoria didn't recognize the title or the cover image, and she had a good memory for those sorts of things. "Oh. That was so nice of her. Please tell her thank you."

Phoebe snorted. "You can tell her yourself. Better do it before you read the book, so you don't have to lie."

Victoria wanted to say goodbye and shut the door. She resisted. Phoebe had spent much more time at Lake Lucinda than Victoria.

She might know things...or be responsible for them.

Still, she wasn't going so far as to invite Phoebe inside. No reason to completely ruin the day. Besides, John was waiting. She'd just ask a few quick questions. "Have you met Harrison Daughton, who lives in Lucinda Lee's old estate?"

Phoebe broke into a huge grin. "You're interested?"

That's what Alex said. Why does everyone think I'm on the prowl?

"I'm simply wondering if he has a family."

"He's single, but I have seen a woman in his car before. More than once. You'll have to ask him yourself, find out who your competition is. He's not my type. Too much of a hermit for me." Phoebe's grin disappeared as she reached out and put her manicured hand on Victoria's arm. The intimidating glint remained in her eyes. "We're all so sorry about your brother."

Victoria cringed inside at Phoebe's touch. "Sorry about what?"

Phoebe lifted her hand away. "Well—Alex is sort of the main suspect now. The only suspect that I'm aware of. Everyone thinks he murdered that girl."

Victoria gripped the side of the door. "Everyone who?"

"You know—" Phoebe gestured, whacking her big hoop earrings. "—the locals."

"Is that so?" Holding her tongue, Victoria looked past Phoebe. From the Mercedes, John stared back at them.

"I can't imagine what Alex is going through," Phoebe continued. "But don't worry. Remember, Lucinda Lee's killer never went to jail. Of course, her death occurred long before any of the CSI-type testing stuff existed. Still, I'm sure your father has a fabulous lawyer or two to sweep things under the rug."

Victoria's jaw clenched as she struggled to maintain her composure. "Alex hasn't done anything wrong, Phoebe. Maybe you could make sure *everyone* knows that, too."

He's not the one with a sexual assault record. He's not the one obsessed with death. And he's not in any position to capitalize on another mysterious murder at Lake Lucinda by writing another bestseller about it. Did you ever think of that, Phoebe?

She didn't actually say those things, but the thoughts echoed in her mind.

"Hmm." Phoebe's tight smile didn't budge. "All of this makes me wonder what we would find below the surface of the lake if we dredged it."

Phoebe's continued presence on the front porch made Victoria's skin crawl. She should have taken the book and said goodbye minutes ago.

Phoebe lowered her gaze to the bowl of dog food a few feet away. She laughed. "Oh, my God. You *are* still trying to feed all the wild animals, aren't you? Why on earth would you want those diseased critters coming up to your door?"

"You wouldn't understand, Phoebe."

"No, I guess I wouldn't." Phoebe laughed again. "We're off now. You take care. Maybe we'll run into each other again in ten more years."

Decorum required Victoria to respond with "Oh, I hope so," or "Be sure to tell me when you visit again." But she couldn't do it. She said goodbye and shut the door before Phoebe was off the porch.

Someone needs to figure out what happened with Kristen once and for all.

Still seething, Victoria opened a cabinet in the mudroom, found the binoculars they used for bird watching, then headed back outside by herself. The sheriff had checked the woods, but she could check them again. She walked in the direction from which she'd heard the screams, scanning the soft ground, the mostly bare trees, the bushes and shrubs.

In a soft muddy area void of pine needles, Victoria spotted a footprint, the back half of a narrow shoe. Several more prints went back and forth through the woods, from the lake to the road. Had the sheriff already seen these? Or had he and his deputies made them? Had he taken shoe prints from all of them to rule out which belonged to the Heslins or George?

No one asked me for my shoe prints yet.

She crossed the street and walked around George's property, near his fence. As if the barbed-wire fence wasn't enough of a warning, she counted three *No Trespassing* signs.

George's broken sink sat alone against the side of the trailer. He still hadn't returned the shovel and wheelbarrow to their long-established places.

Victoria sighed. This wasn't even her case and here she was out searching for evidence, driven to find the truth. She wanted whoever was responsible for Kristen's death brought to justice—since the missing body had all but convinced her the death was no accident. And she needed the rumors about Alex to disappear. The sooner the better.

When she returned, a foul burned smell permeated the house.

I forgot the cookies again!

The kitchen windows were partway open, letting in cold air. The baking sheets sat on top of the counter. The charred cookies resembled small hockey pucks. Even the dogs wouldn't touch them.

Alex and her father sat at the kitchen table.

"She wasn't on drugs," Alex said, speaking to her father. "She was shy. Quiet. If you'd asked me if someone like her was going to go for a midnight swim, I would have said, no. Not her. No way." Alex got out of his seat and went to the sink, taking an empty plate with him.

Victoria wished she'd come home sooner in case she'd missed something important, besides taking the cookies out of the oven. "I'm going into town to get some groceries." She hoped the smell would dissipate by then. "Anyone want anything?"

"Yeah. If they have them, I'll take a few of those same donuts you got the other day," Alex said as he opened the dishwasher.

"Dad?"

"I'm good," he answered.

Victoria grabbed her keys and a cap for her head. "I won't be long."

"Nice job with the cookies." Alex's laugh came from behind her. "If mom can see us, she's getting a real kick out of your baking skills. Third time is the charm."

Victoria drove to the grocery store first, buying meat for her dogs and some food for dinner. Then to the café.

She was the only customer, again. The same girl exited from the door behind the counter, eyes wide with excitement. "Hi. You came back! Um, did you leave that big tip when you were here before?"

"Hmm?" Victoria feigned ignorance.

"Oh. Someone left an excellent tip on the same day that you were here last time. I was sure it was you. Because that's never happened before, and there weren't many other customers. The man with the Range Rover came in after you, but he's a regular, sort of. He's nice and all and he tips, but not that much, even though he must be so rich, because of his car and all."

"Does the man with the Range Rover come in by himself?"

"Usually. I think. He gets a vanilla latte and a large regular coffee and then some of the baked things. Croissants usually. When you were here, he only got the one regular coffee."

"The croissants do look good. I'm going to have the same thing I ordered last time—"

"A large hazelnut latte." Abby looked pleased with herself as she reached for a cup.

"Yes. Good memory. And I'll take four of these donuts, please."

"Sure, thing." Abby started the espresso machine and then crossed to the baked-goods case. "Did you recently move here?"

"No. I'm visiting. My dad has a place on the peninsula."

"Oh." Abby blatantly scanned Victoria, taking in her favorite faded cap, her too-big sweater, her jeans and muddy boots. Victoria didn't look wealthy or glamorous as one might expect from those who owned homes on the peninsula.

"The peninsula is where the mystery girl drowned. I heard a ski patrol guy from Colorado killed her."

Victoria gasped. "Who told you that?" Her question came out sharper than she intended.

Abby's face fell. "I...I'm not sure. Not any particular person. It's just what people are saying." The phone rang on the wall behind the counter. "I have to answer this." She turned her back to Victoria.

With an ache in her heart, Victoria stuck two large bills into the jar again and left with her purchases.

Chapter 17

Wearing a sweatshirt and sweatpants she'd owned since college—still her favorite go-to pants for lounging—Victoria moved Judith's most recent book off her lap. As much as she hated to admit it, Phoebe might have been right. The story wasn't captivating compared to Judith's others. Perhaps that wasn't completely Judith's fault. Victoria's investigative experience caused her to poke holes in the novel's plotline and criticize the protagonist's flagrant disregard for established protocols, rather than just enjoy the story. Thankfully, the average mystery reader was not an FBI agent.

Has the sheriff's department identified Kristen yet? The question wouldn't leave her alone.

She set her feet on the ground and stretched. Myrtle stared at her from a dog bed.

"Afternoon snack time, is it?" In the kitchen, where the smell of burned cookies lingered, Victoria got biscuits for the dogs. As soon as they heard the familiar crinkling of the plastic wrap, they swarmed her, performing tricks—lifting a leg for a shake, spinning, sitting and laying down.

Victoria grabbed carrots from the fridge and went outside to the covered shelter. The female donkeys approached her with their eyes on the carrots. Offering daily treats had done wonders to improve their comfort level. Over the past two months, their bodies and fur had filled in as their wariness around humans decreased.

Oscar was the most hesitant with her, but improving. After feeding him a carrot, she rubbed his nose. He watched her with an air of distrust but didn't back away.

"You were out here the other night," Victoria whispered. "If only you could tell me what transpired with Kristen."

When Victoria's phone rang. Oscar's long ears flattened as he backed away.

"It's all right. It's only a noise." She took her phone out of her pocket. Sam's name lit up on the screen.

"Hey, Sam."

"Hi. I checked on your missing floater today. Some of her lab results are in."

"Already? That's great."

"There was flunitrazepam in her system. Enough to incapacitate her."

Flunitrazepam, also known as Rohypnol—the date rape drug—caused weakness and confusion. Its victims might pass out, have a seizure, or possibly die. Flunitrazepam and swimming were a lethal combination.

Victoria's heart raced. *Did Alex give her the drugs?* She searched for other explanations. *Suicide? Might she have been on her way to commit suicide when she crossed paths with Alex? Perhaps all he did was delay the inevitable? But then why the missing body?*

"And there's still no one looking for her, Sam? I was sure someone would file a missing person's report when the work week started."

148

"It's a holiday week, don't forget. Lots of people are on vacation between Christmas and New Year's. I haven't come across any missing persons reports that match her stats or the name Kristen. At least none where the person has only been recently missing."

"Hmm." Victoria trudged back to the house. "Recently missing, that's a good distinction to make. Perhaps she went missing long before she died. Intentionally trying to hide."

"Because someone was after her."

"Yeah." She walked across the patio. "And he finally found her."

In the background on Sam's end, someone called his name.

"Hey, I'm getting pulled into a meeting," Sam said. "But have you talked to Agent Rivera recently?"

"No. Why?"

"He's working a case with parallels to your recent one in Charlotte. He mentioned that he could use your help. Considering you're already working another murder investigation, I told him it sure seems like you're ready to get back to work." An alarm went off on Sam's desk or on his phone. "Listen, I've got to go, I'll get back to you with anything new."

Victoria was itching to get home to Virginia and to get back to work. She missed Rivera. And Sam. And her boss, Murphy. She was glad to hear they needed her. She also missed Ned. But she couldn't leave Lake Lucinda before discovering what happened to Kristen and vindicating Alex of all suspicions.

If Alex was in any way responsible, he hadn't meant for her to die.

And that's what almost every killer's mother tells authorities, too. And all of them really mean it.

She shuddered, disgusted with herself for distrusting Alex. Until they uncovered the truth, there would always be a tiny little *what if* circling her brain. She hated that little *what if*. It had to go. Kristen's death would not remain an unsolved mystery like Lucinda Lee's. Not if Victoria had anything to say about it.

She marched upstairs to Alex's room and knocked.

No one answered.

After looking down the hall, she opened his door and stepped inside. A flannel shirt lay across the floor, one sleeve stuck inside. A pair of pants peeked out from under the bed next to one thick hiking sock. Maneuvering around more of his clothes, she entered his bathroom.

A black toiletry bag sat open on the quartz counter. An electric razor, toothpaste, and a toothbrush lined either side of the sink. She opened the medicine cabinet behind the mirrored door and quickly scanned the shelves. Dental floss. Ibuprofen. Allergy pills.

I can't believe I'm doing this.

She rifled through the toiletry bag and found hotel sized shampoo and soap bottles, deodorant, a nail clipper, and a comb. Under the cabinet were toilet paper and cleaning supplies.

From behind her, Alex cleared his throat.

Victoria jumped. Her hand flew to her heart.

"I didn't think anyone could sneak up on you, Tori. Looking for something?"

"Uh, yes. I need, um—I need nail clippers."

"In my black bag there."

Was there an edge of disappointment in his voice or did I imagine it?

She opened the bag she'd already looked into.

"Help yourself. And keep it. I've got another." Her brother walked away.

"Hey, Alex." Victoria rotated the nail clippers around. "My friend Sam called me again. Kristen's lab test results came back."

"And?"

"She had Rohypnol in her system." She studied Alex for any sign of a reaction. Surprise? Guilt? Shame? "You know what that is?"

Alex's expression gave nothing away. "Yeah. Roofies. Why would she take those? And when?"

"If they were in her system when she was here, you would have noticed. She would have been pretty loopy. Trouble keeping her eyes open. Slurring her words."

"There was none of that. Definitely not. She was sober. And like I told you, she didn't eat or drink anything while she was here. I'm sure of it. She could have taken the pills on her own. An accidental overdose? A suicide?"

"I had the same thought. Did she seem suicidal?" Victoria asked.

"I don't know. It's not like I've ever spent time with someone right before they killed themselves. She didn't seem depressed or despondent to me. I guess she was a little strange."

"Now you're saying she's a little strange?" Victoria had to rein in her frustration. "You didn't say anything about that before. What did you remember?"

"I'm not sure. Nothing in particular. I'm probably way over analyzing the whole encounter."

People did exactly that as time passed. It couldn't be helped. They started to remember things that didn't happen. Filled in the gaps with information and events that hadn't occurred. With each passing day, they became less reliable as witnesses. Not to mention that Alex had been drinking when he was with Kristen.

Feeling guilty, Victoria returned to her room with the clippers she didn't need, sat in the chair overlooking the backyard, and got to work trimming her already short nails.

Were you really expecting to find a bottle of roofies in his bathroom? What if you had? Had you thought of how you would handle that?

She knew exactly what to do as an agent, but not as his sister.

Thank God I didn't find anything.

But something else had bothered her since Sam told her about the drug. Something on the edge of her consciousness.

She dropped the clippers on her bedside table and crossed to the book shelf. She trailed her finger across the top of her books, stopping on her copy of *Lucinda's Secrets,* and slid it from the shelf. So many years had passed since she read the novel. In the intervening years, details from hundreds of mystery stories had blended in her mind with information from her FBI profiling studies and her own case work. But she still remembered the gist of Judith's bestselling novel. The book's chapters alternated between Lucinda Lee's death in the past and a present-day copy-cat killer, developing parallels between the cases.

Victoria opened the book. The title page was autographed in loopy black script.

My dearest Victoria, an avid reader after my own heart and one of my favorite fans. Love, Judith McPharland.

Victoria flipped through the pages, skimming over the story, searching for key words. She sat down to read the last chapter carefully.

In summary, Lucinda Lee's killer was arrested. The detective found drugs in the suspect's car—a prescription bottle originally containing ten sedative pills. Only five remained. The detective determined five of those pills was enough to incapacitate someone, making it near impossible to swim to shore.

Judith hadn't used the phrase *date rape drug* but she'd described a pharmaceutical that might cause the same effect as the drug found in Kristen's system. The concept wasn't shocking or revolutionary. Just a coincidence. Or was it?

Judith's fictionalized account of Lucinda Lee's tragic story catapulted her into the realm of household author names, making her a big success. Phoebe's recent comments suggested Judith's success had dwindled. And the latest book...suffice it to say it wasn't Victoria's favorite.

Victoria fired up her iPad and searched the internet for Judith's name and a list of her books.

Judith's last book—the one Victoria was currently reading, or trying to read, anyway—was published over six years ago.

Victoria kept searching for articles about Judith McPharland. Then she found it. An article that only deepened her sadness for Judith.

Celebrity author, Judith McPharland, accused of personally purchasing tens of thousands of her latest book in order to hit the top sales charts after the book flops.

She was only accused. Didn't mean she had done the deed.

But the next article confirmed the former's allegation.

NYT bestselling author secretly purchases over one hundred thousand copies of her own book from stores after its sales succumbed to terrible editorial and reader reviews.

"Oh, no. Poor Judith." A few more articles seemed to suggest that for a time, she'd been the laughingstock of the publishing world.

The book trouble occurred six years ago. Had Judith recovered professionally? Would a new mysterious drowning at Lake Lucinda ramp up sales of her former bestseller? Or give her a sensational new story to capitalize on? Was either idea a credible motive for murder?

People did terrible, unthinkable things when they were desperate. And it wasn't only Judith who benefitted from her fame and writing success. There was also Phoebe, and now John.

John thought Kristen's death presented an opportunity. He'd encouraged Judith to start researching and writing. And he'd been at the Nantucket House when they found the body. Was he simply taking advantage of an unfortunate event? Or was there more to it than he let on?

After returning *Lucinda's Secrets* to the shelf with the other signed McPharland novels, Victoria sat down and closed her eyes, her head full of new and troubling ideas to consider.

Chapter 18

Mr. Heslin and Alex sat on the couch with their feet on the ottoman, watching basketball. Victoria made herself comfortable beside them. Out of loyalty, she was having another go at Judith's novel.

The program cut to a commercial. Alex muted the television and turned to face his sister. "I just remembered that Kristen showed me a ring and asked if I thought it was real. I guess I thought she was flirting with me. It was on her pinky finger."

Victoria experienced a flash of annoyance that Alex was just mentioning this now. "I looked over her hands when she was lying on the sail." She pictured Kristen's waxy white skin. "She wasn't wearing any jewelry."

"It was a pink stone," Alex said. "So small it looked like a child's toy ring. I must have laughed at it, thought she was joking. She didn't like my response.

"Was she wondering if she could sell the ring?" Mr. Heslin said. "Perhaps she needed money."

Alex shrugged. "The ring wasn't worth stealing, I'm sure of that. If someone stole it from her, they know little about jewelry."

"Anything else you're just remembering?" Victoria barely disguised a hint of sarcasm. The stress of the past few days had all of them on edge.

Alex huffed. "No."

The dogs jumped up, sending their beds sliding across the floor, and ran to the front door.

"That must be George." Standing, Mr. Heslin pressed his hand against his hip and headed to the front of the house. His footsteps moved across the floors then stopped. "It's not George. The sheriff is back."

Alex got up. "What does he want now?"

"He's walking up the path to the house," Mr. Heslin said. "And he's not alone."

"Unless he's here to tell us what happened to Kristen, no more letting him question Alex without an attorney." Victoria hurried to the front window and looked out. The sheriff was approaching with the assistant deputy and a woman. Both wore sheriff's department uniforms.

Mr. Heslin opened the door before the authorities reached it.

The sheriff handed over a large envelope. "I have a warrant to search your home."

Victoria hurried over. "A warrant? What evidence could you possibly have to get a warrant? Where's the affidavit?"

"As I'm sure you know," the sheriff answered, "I don't have to answer your question or show you the affidavit. And as you also know, I wouldn't have been granted one if there wasn't probable cause for a search."

Unless you've got a corrupt judge who also hates outsiders.

"Enough is enough," Mr. Heslin turned away from the door. "I'm calling my attorney."

"Yes. You should." The sheriff took a folded tissue from his pocket and wiped his nose. "In the meantime, you all have to go outside and wait on the street until we're finished. We'll give you a list of whatever we take from the house."

The assistant deputy and the woman entered the house, scanning the large rooms. The sheriff stayed in the entry, making clear the Heslins weren't leaving his sight until they were off the premises.

Victoria reined in the anger boiling inside her. "I need a few minutes to get my dogs out."

The sheriff glanced down at the dogs who were watching him from Victoria's side.

Izzy let out several sharp barks.

"Make it quick, Ms. Heslin."

The woman opened a kitchen drawer and unloaded the contents. Silverware hit the countertop with the jarring clank of metal on stone. Similar sounds came from the office, where the assistant deputy had gone.

"How long is your search going to take? Or can you not tell us that either?" Victoria looked to the kitchen, wondering if she could grab dog food and bowls.

"I don't expect we'll be here long," the sheriff answered.

"Because—" Victoria asked, "—you know what you're looking for?"

The sheriff stared at her. "I need all of you to leave the property."

"I need to get the leashes. My father and Alex are coming to help me." Victoria marched to the mudroom with her family.

The sheriff followed them.

Victoria pulled the dogs' leashes off the hooks. "Yes, sweeties, you're getting an unexpected outing." Her tone changed from sharp to sweet when she spoke to them.

Outside, the Heslins walked the dogs to the end of the driveway.

Her father called their attorney.

"Can you hold these, Alex?" Victoria handed him the leashes. "I'm calling Sam in case he knows what led to this." She was glad when he answered her call immediately. "The sheriff has a warrant to search our lake house. What happened?"

"There's nothing about it documented in the investigation. I'm looking at it right now."

"He said something that made me think he knows exactly what he's hoping to find. Or was he lying? Does this town have a corrupt judge who granted a warrant with nothing to back it up?"

"I don't know, Victoria. I will tell you if I find out. I promise. Hang in there. You've survived worse. Much worse."

Victoria ended the call. With Alex, she walked her dogs up the street and then back, not wanting to venture far from the house, mostly hovering around the driveway.

The sheriff came outside, walked around the side of the house, and disappeared behind the fence that surrounded the garbage bins. Minutes passed before he reappeared and signaled for the Heslins.

They met the sheriff outside the garage. He held up a clear evidence bag with a pill bottle inside. Most of the bottle's label had been torn off.

"What's that?" Mr. Heslin moved closer, squinting at the bag and its contents.

"We'll have to see." The sheriff slid the evidence bag into his coat pocket.

Victoria crossed her arms. "So, that's what you were looking for?"

"It's not mine," Alex said.

"Nor is it mine." Mr. Heslin turned to Victoria.

Victoria frowned, shaking her head. "It's definitely not mine. Doesn't it strike you as a little convenient that it's there, Sheriff?"

"It was in your trash." The sheriff took a few steps closer to Mr. Heslin. "You might want to tell your attorney about this so he can start thinking up a way to refute it."

"Anyone could have put it there!" Alex shouted, his eyes blazing. "The bins are outdoors on the side of the house. You could have put it there now. And you don't even know what it is!"

"He's right," Victoria said. "You come here with a warrant, which I have no idea how you obtained, and then you conveniently find something in the trash outside our house that might implicate my brother. Anyone can see how suspicious that is."

"Why would you say it implicates your brother?" the sheriff asked. "I never said anything about what this is, who it belongs to, or which of you put it there."

Alex gave his sister a sideways glance then shifted his focus back to the sheriff with a look that revealed the anger crackling in his bones. "Of course it's me you're trying to frame. I'm the only one who met her. Believe me, if I gave someone drugs or was using drugs, I would not go and stick the bottle in my own trash bin."

"It was pretty well hidden in there," the female officer said.

"Then whoever framed me wanted you to have to dig deep into our trash." Alex threw his hands up. "Test the bottle for prints, why don't you? You won't find mine on that bottle because I've never touched it before. Whoever killed that woman is out there and they're messing with me." Alex glared at the sheriff. "Is it you? Seems like you've had it out for me since the beginning."

The sheriff shook his head. "I'm just doing my job. And I'm not a dirty cop." He pulled out his handcuffs and walked toward Alex.

Alex tensed, muscles bulging in his neck. He glared at the sheriff, but he put out his hands.

"Don't say anything until Fenton comes," Mr. Heslin said.

Victoria seethed with anger toward the sheriff. She was also angry at herself.

Was it Rohypnol?

Anyone could have planted the bottle, including the sheriff. Yet—as much as she hated to admit it—she should have looked through the trash long before the authorities arrived.

But what would I have done if I found it?

Had she been too much of a trusting sister rather than a good agent?

"Here's a list of what we're taking." The sheriff handed Mr. Heslin a piece of paper.

Mr. Heslin read over the short list. "What's this?" He looked up at his son, his confusion evident.

"What now?" The look on Alex's face said he'd had enough.

"One item on this list is a diamond ring in a black velvet box. And it came from a nightstand in the second bedroom on the right. That's your bedroom, Alex."

"Yeah, well." Alex shrugged. "That's mine."

Victoria and her father stared at Alex.

He was going to propose to Minka. The recent withdrawal from his trust must have been for the ring.

The unexpected bombshell meant the last few days had been worse than she imagined for her brother. "Oh, Alex. I'm so sorry!"

Alex hung his head.

Chapter 19

Victoria returned the key bowl to its rightful place under the last pendant light. She scanned the main floor again, searching for anything else she could do to erase all reminders of the sheriff's search. Since the sheriff left with her brother, she'd already straightened the drawers and returned everything downstairs to their original places—the same places they had occupied since her mother first put them there.

A sharp growl from her stomach reminded her she hadn't eaten since lunch. She hoped her father had grabbed something healthy for himself at the sheriff's office.

She opened the fridge. The dogs ran over, slamming into each other to get to her first.

"You had your dinner hours ago, darlings."

She took out an apple and a chunk of cheddar cheese to eat with crackers.

As she nibbled half-heartedly on her food, all she wanted to do was go to sleep and wake up to a better day. She still hadn't heard from her father about what was going on with Alex.

Samuelson, the criminal attorney Fenton recommended, had arrived a few hours ago. He supposedly had clout in the area thanks to growing up in the nearest city, but he didn't live there anymore and it had taken him over three hours to drive the distance. Anything he accomplished would have to occur after normal business hours, so Victoria worried he might not have accomplished anything at all.

Going crazy waiting, she called her father.

He answered on the second ring. "Hi, honey." He sounded tired.

She put her phone on speaker and set it on the kitchen island. "Are you coming home soon?"

"Yes, I should be back soon. Samuelson will drop me off."

"What about Alex?"

Her father sighed. "He'll get out tomorrow. He has to stay one night. There's a report to complete in the morning when the courthouse opens. Fortunately for him, for all of us, there's not enough evidence to proceed."

"I know there isn't." She was still fuming about the search. "That's good news. I'll see you soon. I love you."

"I love you, too. Keep the doors locked and the alarm on."

"I will."

She trudged upstairs and into Alex's bedroom with her dogs following. Izzy jumped onto Alex's bed and settled down with her head on her paws.

Victoria closed the drawer of the bedside table, thinking about the diamond ring the authorities had found there.

Poor Alex. All his joking with me when we first arrived, he must have been so hurt and didn't want to show it. I wish I had known.

She picked a shirt off his floor and hung it in the closet. Her brother's space had been messy to begin with, so it was hard to tell exactly what part of the disarray the authorities caused. About to make his bed and pick up the rest of his clothes, she changed her mind, letting them stay as they were. Alex could put his room back together when he got back, if that's what he wanted to do. If she went around organizing things he didn't want organized, he might feel more violated than he already did.

She walked down the long hallway, past the balcony with its bird's-eye view of the empty residence, to her own room. The well-built home was silent. No moan or creaks, only the dogs' short nails tapping on the hardwood floors behind her.

Collapsing into the corner recliner, she suddenly felt very alone. She shouldn't have, considering she was usually alone in her own large house. But that was different. She usually worked long hours and needed to be alone to recharge her energy. And between the dogs and the tasks the house required each day, there was never a moment of downtime to think about being lonely. Here, the absence of her loved ones in a place where she'd never been alone was noticeable.

As she took in the moonlit view out the back windows, the sheriff's words echoed in her head—'go do some online shopping or whatever it is you do.'

Her family should have been insulated by their wealth and influence, but the worst of things had happened. Their wealth had been the main reason her mother was kidnapped and died. Her mother's death had fueled Victoria's decision to join the FBI, where she'd faced one horrific event after another.

Then the plane crash. A one-in-twenty-million type of incident for a commercial plane. Although, if she hadn't been in first-class, she wouldn't have survived.

Was a complete stranger's death going to be the next tragedy to consume her family?

Izzy and Myrtle jumped up from their beds, startling Victoria from her thoughts. They raced from the room, their paws slipping and sliding across the wood.

She heard a sound. Low-pitched voices. Outside but coming from near the house.

Victoria bolted after her dogs, who were barking as they barreled down the stairs so fast their legs barely touched the steps. When she reached the bottom, her dogs barked at the front windows, their bodies tense and alert. Any trespassers who weren't a little afraid of the noise seven large dogs made at once were braver than they should be.

She peered through the window into the darkness.

Seeing nothing, she headed toward the switch panel for the exterior lights.

Something smashed against the window. The sudden thud made her flinch and duck out of instinct.

"What the heck was that?"

She rushed away from the windows and hit the switch for the floodlights.

The area around the house lit up, bushes and walkways coming into focus. And in the center of her view, dark, thick fluid dripped down the glass panes.

Two men raced across the front yard, away from the house.

On the street, a truck's motor roared to life. Its lights flashed on—headlights and three big round lights on a running board atop the roof.

Victoria burst out of the house. "Hey! Stop!"

The two intruders clamored into the waiting truck and slammed the doors as the vehicle sped away, tires screeching on the pavement.

Pulling her phone from her pocket, Victoria sprinted after them, trying to get a photo of the license plate. She stopped at the edge of the woods, her chest heaving. The truck had too much of a head start. She'd never had a chance.

She stormed back to the house, peering into the darkness in every direction.

What was that about?

As her adrenaline dissipated, fear took over and she sprinted to the backyard. Her animals were vulnerable. They would eat nearly anything given to them and would escape if someone left the gate open.

Behind the house, the gate was closed. The donkeys were on the other side of the yard. Her dogs were still in the house.

She returned to the front. The wind howled past, cutting through her sweatshirt and carrying a foul scent that hadn't been there earlier in the day.

Victoria went to the windows. Below the center pane, between two boxwoods, a lumpy object lay in the mulch. She guided her phone's flashlight over the ground, revealing dark fur, blood, and guts. She wasn't sure what sort of animal it was, something small like a racoon or opossum.

That damn well better be roadkill and not some sort of sacrifice for their stupid prank.

Her eyes drifted further down the path that led from the front door to the driveway. The intruders had come from that direction.

Were they the ones who put the empty pill bottle in our trash? Did they plant additional evidence? Now I really wish Dad had video monitoring installed.

Staying alert for movement and shadows, she followed the path, wary of what she might find.

There, under the spotlights at the corner of the garage, something dark covered the ground.

She got closer.

A single word came into focus, scrawled across the path. KILLER.

Her mouth fell open as she stared and then looked around again, suddenly feeling vulnerable.

Trembling with anger, she snapped a blurry photo of the defiled path. She took a deep breath and tried again, holding her hands steady, then called the sheriff's office to report the incident.

Chapter 20

After a quick morning workout, Victoria came inside to find her father leaning against the counter in front of the coffee machine, clasping a mug that said, *I'd rather be sailing*. She remembered buying it for him as a Christmas gift ages ago. She didn't see or hear any sign of her brother. "Is Alex home?"

"Yes. He went up to bed. I doubt he got any sleep in his jail cell."

Victoria sighed as she grabbed a bottle of water from the fridge. Her father was upset, understandably, about Alex being taken away. But it could have been so much worse. Alex was alone in a single, temperature-controlled cell, not a maximum-security prison. He might have been bored and uncomfortable relative to his normal accommodations, but he was never in any danger.

Mr. Heslin turned his mug around in his hands. The other side said, *But caffeine first*.

Victoria opened the cabinet and grabbed a coffee cup. "So, what did the attorney tell you?"

"Samuelson found out how that warrant came to be. The sheriff told him he received an anonymous tip about the drugs."

"An anonymous tip?" She huffed. "Seriously? I mean, come on. No one knows who Kristen is, or so they say. No one saw or heard anything happen the night she died. Then someone calls in an anonymous tip? There's the real suspect."

"That's essentially what Samuelson told them. He did well. The charges will be dropped. For now."

"Good. Listen, Dad, I'm sorry I told you not to call an attorney earlier. In small towns, that usually sends the wrong message to local law enforcement. I didn't think we had any reason to lawyer up and look suspicious. I thought cooperating was the way to go and in the best interest of getting to the truth. Alex should have been considered a witness. There wasn't evidence he was anything more, until someone planted that pill bottle. I never imagined all of this would get so complicated."

"Neither did I. It's okay. One of my first orders of business today is getting a video surveillance system installed. If we had one, we might see exactly how that bottle ended up in the trash and who was here last night. Maybe that message was just a few punks screwing with us, like the sheriff suggested. Maybe not." Mr. Heslin walked away from the kitchen and over to one of the front windows.

Victoria stood beside him and followed his gaze across the street. Behind the barbed-wire fence and gate, the back corner of George's truck was visible at the end of his driveway, the rest of it obscured by trees.

"I keep finding myself wondering if it was George," her father said. "I hate to say it because I've trusted the man for years. He's been in and out of our house fixing things since we moved here. And yet, I think it was him."

"You know him better than I do." She wrapped her elbow around her father's arm and leaned against him. "What do you think he did, exactly? Kill Kristen and try to frame Alex?"

Her father lay his hand over her arm and stared out through the glass window Victoria had recently scrubbed clean. "I guess that is what I'm saying. The person who called in the tip must be responsible for Kristen's death. The sheriff said the tip was anonymous. But Samuelson said the tip had to be from a credible, trusted source for them to have obtained the warrant."

Victoria huffed. "Assuming the sheriff followed the guidelines and didn't make up the tip or that he didn't plant that bottle himself."

"You have a point. If the tip and search *were* legitimate, anyone the authorities know and trust is likely to be a local. And George is the only local here. The only one who has lived here for years."

And yet...Phoebe and Judith seemed to know some locals, too.

"Remember George was near the trash the other day, saying he would fix the hinge on the gate?" her father said. "And what makes him look more suspicious to me is that, as far as I can tell, he's as good as gone. Convenient timing for someone who rarely leaves his place."

"Not answering you isn't the same as disappearing. I can see his truck." Victoria thread her arm back through her father's and moved closer to the window, checking for any other sign that George might be around. "I'm not dismissing him as a suspect, but what motive would George have for framing Alex?"

"Based on what you heard in town, and from Phoebe, everyone seems to think Alex is involved. So, if George killed Kristen and is now trying to cast suspicion elsewhere, why not choose the person everyone else is already blaming?"

The red flash in the woods after we brought Kristen's body ashore. George's red bandana.

The sense that someone had been watching them had only grown stronger. And George wasn't the only one who wore red. It could have been anyone. Victoria's intuition wasn't infallible, but

170

relative to the others who were currently visiting Lake Lucinda, George wasn't the person who struck her as the most suspicious. Odd, and a bit of a recluse—yes. *And perhaps someone could say the same about me.* But the one she most suspected—no.

And yet—why hadn't he returned her father's calls or come back to help him with the leak? Her father paid George well for his time. Strange that George would jeopardize that relationship. Unless something more important was keeping him away.

Did George see something that night? Did he see Alex and Kristen together? Is that why he's avoiding us now? If so, he didn't show any signs of distrusting us when he was here a few days ago.

"We need to talk to George," Victoria said. "As soon as he reappears."

Her phone vibrated in her sweater pocket. She took it out and read the screen. "It's Sam." She set her water on the entryway console table and answered as her phone buzzed a second time.

"Hey," Sam said. "How are you doing there? What's happened since the search?"

"My brother spent the night locked up in a cell." Victoria told Sam about the bottle of pills and the anonymous tip. "I don't know who is responsible." An image of curvy hips, a creamy white sweater, and Phoebe's creepy grin flashed into Victoria's mind, even though they had just been discussing George as the perpetrator. "But I intend to find out. Thank goodness my father got a capable attorney to show up or Alex might still be there now. I'm realizing how unfair it is to people who don't have that privilege, but he's my brother and he's innocent."

"This is the last thing you need going on right now. You're supposed to be recovering out there, aren't you? Hardly relaxing to have your own brother carted off to jail for something he didn't do."

"Exactly! Sam, thank you for believing me. For believing in him. I'm starting to think this entire town has jumped on the Alex-is-guilty bandwagon. I really appreciate your help."

"You still aren't getting any information from the local authorities, are you?"

"No, and I don't see how that's going to happen now unless I can bring them concrete evidence on the guilty party."

"I have something that might help," Sam said. "The victim's DNA results. The lab they used pushed the analysis through to help identify the girl. The results didn't match anything in the law enforcement or military databases. That's okay because there are lots of people taking DNA tests these days for the fun of it. I found a partial match."

"You found a match in one of those genetic ancestry services?"

"The databases are supposed to be confidential. I don't want to get anyone in trouble. Particularly not you and not me. Anyhow, the victim's DNA partially matches a woman named Gloria Bozeman. She's seventy-six years old and lives in Pittsburgh. There aren't enough commonalities to be a parent or sibling, but enough for a close relative. I sent you her address and phone number."

"This is great, Sam. Do you think the local sheriff's department will find this information on its own?"

"Not likely. There's a reason I get paid the big bucks, right?"

"If this connection pans out, I'll have to tell the sheriff, but I don't have to say how I got the information."

"Good luck," Sam said.

Victoria said goodbye, excited to see what the DNA connection might reveal.

Under normal circumstances, typing in the name of your average, seventy-six-year-old non-celebrity brings up little in the way of interesting search results. A few links if the person has social media accounts, some charity donations, a mention of their former employment. Gloria Bozeman was not the average seventy-six-year-old. A search for her name returned pages of article links.

"What have we got here?" Victoria scanned the headings.

Gloria Bozeman: Where's My Daughter?

Without A Trace; Gloria Bozeman's Puzzling Story.

Will We Ever Learn What Happened to Mallory and Kristen Bozeman?

Victoria read the name Kristen Bozeman and her pulse quickened. Another mystery. But was it related to Kristen's death?

After skimming the headings, she clicked on one of the most recent news articles from the Pittsburgh Times.

Eight Years Ago, Gloria Bozeman's Only Daughter and Granddaughter Went Missing in New York City.

Victoria leaned forward, gripping the edge of the table. She read the article and then the next, absorbing every word of every relevant story she could find.

News of the missing mother and child had captured the public's interest, though only for a short time. Mallory Bozeman was an adult woman, a single mother with a few minor arrests and a history of packing up her suitcase and taking risks to pursue her dreams. Therefore, the nature of her disappearance was a matter of conflicted opinion and never unequivocally attributed to foul play. Before Mallory left her mother's house for a temp job in New York City, the two women had argued. According to one news story, their screaming match was loud enough for neighbors to

173

overhear before they witnessed Mallory storming away with her young daughter in tow.

Victoria clicked through the images of Mallory Bozeman. Tall and slim. Attractive even with heavy makeup. Holding a cigarette in several photographs.

Mallory was twenty-seven when she disappeared. Her daughter, Kristen, was nine years old. No one ever heard from them again.

Pressing her lips together, Victoria leaned closer to her screen. "I need to find photos of Kristen Bozeman."

Similar to the images of her mother, the online photos of Kristen were small and grainy. The first was of a young girl with long legs and straight, dark hair. She was grinning, with one arm around a Shetland pony.

Victoria enlarged the digital photo on her screen.

Kristen Bozeman could have been almost any cute girl with long eyelashes and a slightly upturned nose, except for one thing: in the exact place it needed to be, above the girl's right lip, there was a beauty mark, as if someone had taken a brown magic marker and pressed the tip against her skin. The similarities were plain to see. Although the images were of a child, Kristen Bozeman bore an uncanny resemblance to Kristen from the lake.

Today, the ten-year-old girl who disappeared would have been nineteen. The drowning victim looked a bit older. Alex also thought she was older, but it was possible she was only nineteen.

Victoria had to share the news. "Dad! Alex!"

Her father left his office and came into the kitchen, carrying papers in one hand. "What is it?"

"Kristen disappeared from Pennsylvania with her mother. Nine years ago!"

Mr. Heslin frowned. "I'm not following you."

"My colleague matched Kristen's DNA to a woman who has to be her grandmother. I did some research. Kristen disappeared nine years ago, along with her mother."

"She's been missing for all those years?" Mr. Heslin leaned closer to Victoria's screen from over her shoulder. "What was she doing here?"

Victoria enlarged the picture of Mallory. Victoria might as well have been looking at the young woman she had seen on the patio. They had the same hair color, the same high cheekbones, the same delicate neck.

Mr. Heslin set his papers down on the table and drummed his fingers over them. "This certainly complicates things. Kristen and her mother must have been living somewhere in the area. Do you think the townspeople knew and aren't saying?"

"I'm not sure."

Could Mallory and Kristen be part of a witness protection program? No. People in witness protection began new lives with new identities. No one here seemed to know Kristen at all. And where was Mallory? Why hadn't she come forward to claim her daughter?

"None of what you found explains what happened to Kristen, does it?" Victoria's father asked.

"No. But determining who she is will help the investigation." Victoria got up from the table and hurried up the stairs. "Alex!" She knocked on his closed bedroom door. "Alex, are you in there?" When no one answered, she pushed the door open. The room was empty. The bathroom was also empty.

From the bedroom window, she scanned the dock. There was no one there.

"Where the heck is he?"

175

She ran back down the stairs. Sensing her excitement, her dogs followed her into the mudroom, tails twirling in circles and smacking the walls.

Victoria opened the door to an empty garage. No sign of her SUV. "You've got to be kidding me." She removed her phone from her pocket. In her haste, the device slid through the space where the top of her middle and ring fingers used to be and smacked the floor. She scooped it up from under her dogs' legs and called Alex.

He didn't answer.

Her father was in his office, his face inches away from his computer screen. "I'm reading an article about the disappearance now. Hard to believe all this. First, she disappears. Then apparently, years later, she drowns. Then her body is stolen. It's like she's cursed or something. What next?"

"Yeah, it's crazy. And I'm a little worried about what comes next. Do you know where Alex is?"

Mr. Heslin shook his head, staring at his screen.

"I want to tell him what I discovered, and then we should talk to the sheriff in person, although I'd rather talk to Gloria Bozeman first. Oh, and I have to tell Sam." Victoria returned to the kitchen table. So many things were happening at once, moving the investigation forward. She controlled much of the information at this point, but hadn't decided what to do with it yet.

She sent Sam an email with what she had found and requested the police case files from the Bozeman's disappearance.

An electronic whirr signaled the garage door opening.

Victoria rushed to the mudroom and whipped open the door to the garage. As her SUV pulled in, she waited with her hands on her hips.

Alex waved at her from the driver's seat. The engine made clicking noises, cooling down, as he got out of the car. "What's up?"

"Where were you?"

"At the post office." Alex edged past her and into the house.

"What were you doing at the post office?" Mr. Heslin stood behind Victoria, blocking the doorway into the kitchen. "I have stamps in my office. And more importantly, you shouldn't be leaving the house."

"Didn't we just have this same discussion? I can leave the house. I wasn't arrested. I'm not on probation. Although I don't doubt Sean Hayes is watching me right now, like George used to do. Look, I needed to get out of here or I was going to go crazy. I did an errand for God's sake. I mailed Minka's necklace and a few other things she left behind. What's the big deal?" He stuffed his hand into his pocket and pulled out a small paper. "Here you go, Tori. A receipt from the U.S. Post Office. Happy?" His voice was heavy with sarcasm. "And your car is fine. Not a scratch. I even moved your seat back to its position."

"It has nothing to do with borrowing my car, Alex."

Then what is it? Why am I so concerned? Because I still think he might be out hiding evidence?

She took a deep breath. "We found something huge. Something about Kristen. Come in Dad's office and take a look."

Alex and Victoria followed their father to his desk where he angled his laptop to the side for Alex.

Alex read, furrowing his brow. "That photo sure looks like it could be her."

"It certainly does," Victoria said.

177

"See that—there you go." Alex folded his arms across his chest. "Kristen had some dark secrets going way back and none of them have anything to do with us. That should get the sheriff off my back for good, right?"

"I think it should," Mr. Heslin said.

"Can you find out where she's been hiding all this time?" Alex asked, removing his coat. "And where her mother is?"

"That's what I intend to do." Victoria gripped her phone as she dialed the number for Gloria Bozeman—the woman she now believed was Kristen's grandmother. "She might be the key to understanding everything."

Alex draped his coat over his arm. "Let's hope so, because right now, she seems like the only key."

The call connected. It rang and rang. The entire family stared at Victoria's phone.

Pick up. Pick up. Pick up.

A voicemail service clicked on.

Victoria left a message that included her FBI identification number and a phone number for verifying it. She leaned on her father's desk, hoping Gloria would return her call as soon as possible. Until then, she planned to read everything she could find on Kristen Bozeman and her mother. She hoped to uncover something that would pull all the strange, convoluted pieces together in a way that made sense of everything.

It would help if I could officially work the case.

Chapter 21

From the dock, Victoria watched the sun set behind the mountains, creating an exquisite display of pink, orange, and violet across the sky. Mist rolled gently across the surface of the quiet lake. There were no boats and no other people. Two loons, a female and a darker male, glided across the water, their upper bodies peacefully still while their little feet were paddling unseen below.

Victoria leaned against the railing and checked for a call from Gloria Bozeman, even though it was impossible to have missed one when she hadn't let her phone out of her sight since she'd left a message.

Kristen's past disappearance in one state, combined with her recent death and her body going missing in another, was more than enough criminal activity to warrant the FBI's involvement. Victoria just hoped her boss would also see it that way.

She called Murphy, half expecting him to be unavailable because of the holiday.

Murphy answered.

"Hello, Victoria. It's nice to hear from you, but you need to talk fast. The last bowl game is about to start. My Bulldogs are playing and I don't want to miss the kickoff—hey, that's my good luck chair, Tommy. Get up. I have to sit there when my team plays. They're counting on me."

"This won't take long." Victoria paced on the dock, needing to move while she spoke. She got right to the point, summarizing everything that happened since they found Kristen's body in the lake, and everything they had learned since. "Kristen Bozeman's story begins with an unsolved disappearance. Her mother's situation is still unknown. All of it must somehow relate to the events here. Can we reopen the investigation?"

The loons came closer. Victoria studied the tiny white stripes in their gray feathers as she waited for Murphy to respond.

"You piqued my interest and made a great case for our involvement. You're in a position to get almost whatever you want, being the media darling of the moment. But I can't give you that case. Nor should you be working on it. Not with your brother involved."

Victoria's jaw clenched. "Alex isn't a suspect. He met her the night she drowned. It's a coincidence. That's all it is. Whatever happened to Kristen started nine years ago."

"We don't know that. And you can't be certain the child who disappeared is your floater based on a partial DNA match that has yet to be confirmed."

"I'll have a better chance of finding out if I'm working in an official capacity."

"Sorry, Victoria. You understand how this works. Having you involved would be a mistake that could backfire on all of us."

"You best get off that phone or these wings are going in the trash." Murphy's wife, Celia, spoke so loudly and clearly that it sounded like she was on the phone with them.

"I'm almost done," Murphy said.

Static and muffled voices came over the line. Victoria wished she *had* offered to call back when his football game ended.

"Listen, Victoria—" The background noise had disappeared. "I'm glad you called. I was going to reach out to you in a few days. Officially. If you're ready to start work again, I'm good with that. Your psychiatric wellness tests came back and you're cleared to return whenever you want. There are still a few physical tests you need to pass, but those shouldn't be a problem, right?"

"Right," she said, bending and straightening her trigger finger. "I can shoot with either hand." *And I better start running again tomorrow.*

"The bottom line is that we need you and if you're ready to come back, it's all approved. But you won't be assigned to the investigation there."

"I intended to come home right after New Year's. I can't now. I can't leave until this case settles."

"Really? You're willing to be away from your house and all your animals for as long as it takes?"

"They're all with me."

"Figures. Anyway...I understand. Family is family. If you need to be there to support your brother...just tell me when you're ready to come back. Or if there's anything we can do to help— other than putting you on that specific case. We're here for you."

"What about giving the Bozeman case to someone else in our office?" Victoria scrunched her face like she was bracing for a blow, afraid of getting another no for an answer. "Like Rivera?"

"Not Rivera. Listen, I'll look into it and see what we can do. I want to help. The sooner the case resolves, the better things will be for your family. I get that."

"Thanks, Murphy."

"In the meantime, you have to tell the local sheriff what you found."

181

"I will. So, are you going out later tonight or staying in?"

"We've got people here now. Obviously. A house full of rabid Georgia fans and one poor misguided soul who went to 'Bama. All I want to do is watch my game. How about you?"

"I hadn't thought about it until now. We're not exactly in a celebratory mood here."

"Understandable. Well, Happy New Year's Eve, Victoria."

"Thanks, Murphy. Same to you. Enjoy your night."

As she put her phone down, it pinged and a burst of light flashed on the screen. A voicemail from Rivera. Somehow, she had missed the call. She called him back and this time, it was his phone that went to voicemail.

She checked again to see if Gloria had called, then returned to the house.

Chapter 22

Resting on one end of the sectional, Victoria scrolled through movie options on the TV. "I can't decide on anything. At this rate, I'm going to be flipping through these all night." She tossed the remote across the couch to her father and joined him in staring into the fireplace. Orange and blue flames danced along the fake logs and cast shadows on the carved wood bookshelves. Focusing on the simple fire helped her relax, but not enough to take her mind off all that had happened at the lake.

Gloria Bozeman hadn't called back. And it was unlikely she would now that it was getting late. Outside the tall windows, the sky was a deep black.

"Wake up everybody!" Alex sauntered into the family room carrying a bottle of Dom Perignon. He lifted the green bottle and grinned. "We're going to open this at midnight, so don't fall asleep now. I'm not letting this bottle go to waste."

Victoria checked the time and groaned. "It's only ten. I doubt I'm going to make it to midnight."

Alex ruffled her hair. "Yes, you will. I'll make sure of it."

Mr. Heslin reached for the champagne. "Let me see that bottle."

Alex handed it to his father, who turned it over in his hands. "This is a rare, special bottle. It's very expensive."

Alex shrugged.

Oh. The special champagne was to celebrate his engagement!

Victoria felt sad for her brother all over again.

A loud whistle followed by a sound like crackling gunfire made the dogs' heads and ears pop up all over the room. Myrtle jumped from the floor and ran up the stairs.

Across the lake, an explosion of color cascaded down from the sky.

"Oh, no. Darn it!" Victoria scrambled off the couch and hurried after her terrified dog. "Fireworks? And way before it's midnight! Myrtle is going to find the deepest, darkest closet and hide in there until morning."

Three of her dogs were already panting and pacing. The others were still on their beds, unaffected by the sounds, watching the reactions of the scared ones with mild interest.

Victoria followed Myrtle up the stairs, "I have medication and thunder shirts to help calm them, but I didn't think to bring either."

Victoria had dreaded fireworks since she was a little girl. The loud noises forced the family's greyhounds to cower and tremble in the bathrooms and closets. Now, the fireworks terrified her own dogs. Not all of them, thankfully, but it only took one to make her feel stressed and helpless. The fourth of July week was the worst of the year at her house. Once the fireworks started, she was miserable until they ended. When would they stop? How many? How long? How much could the poor dogs endure before they lost their little minds? She could only sit with them and wish the noise would end sooner rather than later.

Through the back windows, a buzzing ball of white light flared into the sky on the other side of the lake. With a giant boom that echoed across the water, it exploded into snake-like hissing prisms of orange and green.

A donkey let out a terrified noise. Hooves crashed against the side of the shelter.

"Um, I think your donkeys are scared, too," Alex said, going to the back window.

Victoria was halfway up the stairs. She turned and shuffled back down, her frustration and anger building. "I don't know if they've ever heard fireworks. I have no idea how they're going to react."

"You go check on them." Alex headed toward the stairs. "I can sit with Myrtle and tell her the world isn't ending. Rub her belly or something."

"Thank you, Alex, I would appreciate that." Victoria rushed to the mudroom and grabbed her coat. One good thing about rain was it prevented fireworks displays. If only it had kept raining right through New Year's Eve. Instead, the sky was dark and cloudless, the perfect backdrop for the colorful lights.

Another loud braying sound came from the backyard.

"Do you want to bring them into the garage?" her father asked. "Would that help? It's sort of like a giant closet."

"If they're afraid, that might help." She jammed her feet into her boots. "I'm not sure. I have to go out there."

Her father was already putting on his own coat. "I'll open the garage door and wait for you to bring them in, if you need to."

Victoria hurried through the house, out the patio door, and into the yard. Another set of lights soared into the sky, fizzling and cracking, going out with an ear-splitting boom and a giant burst of white, circular light.

185

The donkeys huddled together, nostrils flaring. The spotlights revealed the whites of their terrified eyes. Oscar pawed the ground with his hooves. He reared up and came down hard against the shelter wall.

"It's okay, Oscar. It's okay, boy." Victoria kept her voice calm and soothing as she grabbed their leads. "Those are just loud noises. They aren't going to hurt you." She reached for his halter.

Before she could grab him, he reared away, narrowly missing her chest with his flying hooves.

She let him go to deal with the girls first. "Come on, babies." They stamped and snorted, their ears flattened to their heads. With quick movements, she snapped leads to their halters. "Follow me. I'm just going to put you in the garage where you'll feel safer. No windows. Less noise." She led them through the gate and around the side of the house.

Inside the garage, her father was waiting. He took the leads she handed him.

"Thank you, Dad. I'll be right back with Oscar. Hold them on a short lead. They're afraid and might try to bolt."

"I've got them. You just get the big fellow."

"I'll be right back." Victoria jogged back to the yard. She had her hand on the side gate when another round of fireworks exploded in the sky with a bang-bang-bang-bang, as if the lake house was in the center of a battlefield.

She watched in horror, paralyzed, as Oscar ran straight at the wooden fence.

Is he going to jump it? He can't clear that height!

The fence could keep dogs inside, but not withstand a charging donkey. It might break, or it might not. She wasn't sure which would be worse for Oscar.

The donkey surged forward, snorting and braying. He showed no signs of slowing. Without hesitating, he smashed chest first into the rails, shattering the wood beams. He burst through and raced away into the night.

"No!" she shouted after him, her heart pounding. She squinted to see him in the darkness but he had already disappeared. A sense of fear and helplessness overwhelmed her.

She shouted to her father, telling him what had happened. "Shut the dog door so the dogs can't get out. I'm going after Oscar." She sounded breathless because she was so afraid of what might happen. She had no idea what Oscar would do, and neither did he. He might keep galloping forward until he exhausted himself. Or try to find something safe and familiar, like an open barn type structure. But there wasn't anything like that on the peninsula. Fences surrounded most yards. There was only the road. And the woods. And the lake.

Worst-case scenarios appeared in her mind before she could stop them.

It's safer here than being near a highway. And at least there aren't many cars. Just stay calm.

But her heart was pounding, and she thought she might throw up.

There were no streetlights on the peninsula. With most of the homes unoccupied, inky darkness enveloped the roads. If anyone was out driving, would they see a terrified donkey racing into the street before it was too late?

Victoria made a split-second decision. She ran back to the shelter and grabbed the blanket Oscar had been wearing earlier. Then she raced back to her house for Izzy. Her little Spanish greyhound wasn't afraid of the fireworks and was perhaps her only dog who *might* consistently come when called.

Victoria attached a blue light-up collar around Izzy's neck. She let Izzy smell Oscar's scent on the blanket. Then, hoping she wasn't going to regret her next move, Victoria grabbed her phone and rushed outside with Izzy.

"Go find Oscar. Go find Oscar."

Izzy understood the command. She'd been trained to hunt for scents and certain objects, but she'd never been asked to track another animal before.

Victoria jogged down the street in the direction Oscar had taken. Izzy trotted at her side.

"Oscar!" Victoria called, knowing she was probably wasting her breath. The donkeys were just starting to trust her and associate her with comfort and food. She had a lot of work to do before they might come when called. And Oscar wasn't going to listen to her when he was terrified. If he was even in the vicinity to hear.

She pressed the button on the side of her phone and said, "Flashlight on."

Nothing happened.

She tried again. "Flashlight on. Flashlight on." She wanted to throw it into the woods.

A circle of light appeared and her phone responded, "The flashlight is on."

Victoria aimed the light over the soft ground, looking for hoofmarks. Oscar had taken off down the driveway and might have stuck to the road. He had a tiny bell on his halter, in case something like this ever happened. With the fireworks still going off, and the speed at which he'd been running...no way would she hear it.

Please don't run into the road, Oscar. Please don't get hit by a car.

188

Izzy alerted, raising her head and tail before bolting off. Her blue light sailed through the darkness a few feet off the ground like a high-speed demon. Victoria sprinted after the light, following it down the road and into the natural area alongside George's fence. The soft ground sucked at her boots. Splashes of mud flew up around her. No lights came from George's home. The windows were black.

Izzy scuttled into the woods, the unfenced area of George's property.

Victoria had to slow down, holding her arms outstretched to protect her face. Snarled branches snatched at her pants and snapped around her shoulders as she pushed forward. Her flashlight illuminated thick roots and mounds of wet, decaying leaves. She alternated her focus between the blue light ahead and the ground. Head up, head down. Head up, head down. An earthy, damp smell surrounded her. She didn't think Oscar had come through that way, yet she continued to follow her dog, hoping Izzy smelled or sensed something Victoria could not.

Something crunched and snapped behind her. Not loud enough to be Oscar. She stopped moving to listen. Another noisy round of fireworks prevented her from hearing it again.

Is someone else in the woods?

A shadow moved in the distance, blurring into the trees until Victoria wasn't sure if it was real.

George probably wouldn't take kindly to someone creeping around next to his house at night. And Alex seemed to think George perpetually kept watch for anything unusual. She was trespassing and hoped George wouldn't come out with a shotgun.

What if he thinks Oscar is a wild animal and shoots him? Or what if he shoots me?

That thought made her forget all else.

189

"Hello! Mr. Wilson? It's Victoria Heslin from across the street. My donkey got loose."

No answer.

"Mr. Wilson! I'm just in your woods because I'm trying to find my donkey!"

Ahead of her, the blue light stopped moving.

Taking tentative steps and stopping to listen between fireworks, Victoria caught up to her dog. In a slight clearing between giant oaks, Izzy had her nose to the ground in a mound of loose dirt. She dug fast and frantic with her front paws, sending pine needles and dirt spraying out to the sides.

"What are you doing? What about finding Oscar? I don't think he came through here." Victoria moved her light over the area, peering into the dark woods. "And I know he's not underground."

The fireworks quieted. Another rustle of branches.

Izzy popped her head up and listened, then barked.

Someone was following Victoria through the shadows.

"Hello?" A prickle of fear slid up her neck.

A beam of bright light flipped on, blinding her.

Izzy's barks came faster.

"Victoria? Is that you?" It wasn't George's voice.

Victoria shielded her eyes and looked away. A bright spot remained in her vision where the light had been. Another blast of fireworks lit up the surroundings and offered a chance to see who was coming toward her.

It was Harrison.

"Victoria, hey, sorry about the light." He diverted it to the ground. "I just wanted to make sure everything was all right. Was that you yelling?"

"Yes."

Without moving from her digging spot, Izzy barked again. Harrison came closer. "What are you doing out here?"

"My donkey ran off because of the fireworks. I'm trying to find him." She was about to ask the same of him, although whatever his excuse might be, it couldn't have been any stranger than her own, when Izzy snarled with excitement.

Both Victoria's and Harrison's lights moved over to illuminate the dog. She plunged her nose back into the dirt and resumed digging. With a grunt, Izzy grasped a piece of cloth between her teeth and yanked it sideways, wrenching it from the ground.

"What do you have there?" Victoria asked.

Izzy dropped the fabric and returned to the hole she'd made, her snout disappearing into the fresh dirt. She grasped something else and pulled again. The item was stuck under the ground. Izzy changed her grip and jumped to the side, jerking at the object with all her might until it emerged.

Izzy lay down and stared at her find. Dropping her chin onto her legs, she whimpered.

"What is it?" Victoria crouched for a better look, then recoiled, jumping up and almost tripping and falling over Harrison.

The dog's collar cast an ethereal blue light over a grimy hand emerging from the dirt.

Chapter 23

The fireworks ended, leaving only the stars sparkling in the night sky, until flashing blue lights arrived on Peninsula Point Drive.

Sheriff Sean Hayes arrived first, followed by two other law enforcement vehicles. They parked, forming a barricade on George's driveway, just outside his gate.

Victoria was standing in a depression on the edge of the woods, with Izzy on a leash, when the sheriff stared down at her, making him seem taller than he already was. "You've found another body, Ms. Heslin."

"Not necessarily, but definitely a human hand."

It has to be the missing corpse.

Since she wasn't supposed to know someone stole Kristen's body, she kept her opinion to herself.

With Harrison leading everyone in a single-file procession, they tramped back through the woods. The path was more discernible and worn from foot traffic and snapped branches than when she first made her way through.

"I'm surprised you exercised restraint this time and didn't dig the site up before we got here," the sheriff said from ahead of her.

"Maybe because she helped bury it," his deputy muttered from the end of the line.

"Hey!" Harrison stopped walking and turned around. He was just as tall as the sheriff and had more muscle. "That was uncalled for." He sounded like a wealthy and upstanding citizen, unaccustomed to being treated in any other way. And right then, his offended reaction was just what Victoria needed.

"It's okay," Victoria told him. "I'm getting used to it." She would tolerate the sheriff's behavior toward her so as not to escalate their already tense relationship, but it was nice to have Harrison there reminding her the authorities' subtle accusations were unprofessional.

"Just move along." The sheriff lifted his chin and gestured with his hand.

Harrison huffed before he continued marching forward. At the clearing, he moved to the far side, allowing the authorities to crowd around the discovery. The dirty hand stretched from the fresh earth like a Halloween decoration that should be surrounded by fake tombstones.

Izzy barked and pulled toward the hand. Victoria held her back.

The sheriff focused on Harrison and Victoria and pointed to the edge of the woods. "Wait for me back at the road near our cars. Both of you. Don't go anywhere else."

Frowning, Harrison led the way.

Victoria stopped walking first and turned around.

"Over here," Harrison called from the paved road several yards away. "So you're not standing in the mud."

"I'm good where I am." Victoria wanted to be as close to the scene as possible.

Harrison returned to her side, breathing white puffs into the frosty air. "At their current rate of finding a dead body every few days, the local authorities are going to be experts at handling homicides."

"That all depends on how they handle them." She crouched down, wrapping her arms around her dog for warmth.

Harrison snorted. "Good point. I wonder if this situation combined with the drowning will tank our property values."

She knew he was joking. People joked when they were nervous or uncomfortable.

"They shouldn't be speaking to you that way," he said. "I don't like it at all. I imagine it's because of your brother."

She nodded and peered through the branches. Flashlight beams trailed slowly over the ground and trees. Sean instructed his deputies to return to their cars for floodlights and shovels.

"So…your donkey is back at your house now?" Harrison asked.

"Yes, according to my father. Oscar must have circled back and gone right into his shelter."

"Good. I hope you didn't have important plans for the night." Harrison shifted around and rubbed his boots across the ground. Behind him, metal clanked together in bags as the deputies unloaded equipment from their cars.

"Me? No. I was staying in with my father and brother."

"Are you and your brother close?" Harrison asked. "Because if you are, this must be difficult. I suppose it's difficult no matter what."

"I don't see Alex often. He lives in Colorado, but we're close. And yes, when people suspect someone you love of doing something they didn't do, it's difficult."

The sheriff waited in the clearing, looking around, as if he was listening to the trees and the wind. Then he studied George's mobile home.

George might be in there watching us right now.

New Year's Eve celebrations hadn't stopped a few people from congregating nearby. One of the deputies returned to the cars and stood by the road, preventing anyone from walking beyond the sheriff's vehicles. In the lulls of silence between Sean and his deputies' conversations, Victoria was aware of the onlookers' presence, whispering and chatting on the street, conveying a combination of horror and curiosity. She recognized the Roberts. In their world, death probably occurred quietly in hospitals and nursing homes, not outside in the middle of the night. Not on the peninsula anyway.

Maybe the others, whom Victoria couldn't see, had followed the flashing lights into the neighborhood just for something to do.

Ring in the new year with a dead body on Lake Lucinda!

If Phoebe was still in town, she'd have plenty of material to keep her warped mind occupied. And Judith now had more dark details to inspire her next book, if she chose to write one.

Most of the onlookers would just be curious. Some would be concerned and want to help. One of them might be guilty. Guilty people liked to return to the scene of the crime and witness firsthand the havoc wreaked by their actions.

"Victoria."

Her father's voice broke through her thoughts. She turned to see the deputy letting him cross the line of vehicles. He carried a heavy coat and gloves. "I couldn't find the coat you asked for but this is a warm one."

She took the coat he offered, one her mother used to wear on winter walks. "Is Oscar okay? Did you check him for injuries?"

"He seems fine. I sprayed his chest with the antibiotic. His cuts aren't deep. How are you doing?" He helped her put the coat over her own lighter one.

"But the fence..."

"Alex patched up the fence enough to keep the animals in until the morning, when I can find someone to repair it properly." Her father stared into the woods. "Nothing like this has ever happened here before. Well, except for whatever happened to Lucinda Lee decades ago. I don't know what's going on with this place now."

The sheriff stomped through the woods and shouted at the onlookers, making a point of looking directly at Victoria's father. "Go back to your homes. This is a crime scene."

"Gladly," Harrison said. "You know where to find us."

"Not you." The sheriff pointed a finger at Harrison. "You and Ms. Heslin need to wait."

Victoria's father stepped forward. "Why would that be necessary? My daughter should go home."

"No, Dad. It's okay." Victoria locked eyes with her father, imploring him not to push the issue. "I'll be there soon." There was no way she was leaving if she didn't have to. She needed to know for sure what or who was buried in the woods.

Harrison held out a hand for Victoria's father. "I'm Harrison Daughton. We haven't met yet. I live at the end of your street. I'll watch over your daughter, make sure nothing happens."

Victoria thought her father smirked, but she couldn't be sure. Perhaps Harrison's comment amused him. It sounded rather chivalrous and romantic, except for the circumstances. Or it might have been because Harrison made it sound like Victoria needed

196

someone to watch over her, even though she was a special agent. Either way, she had more important things to worry about than the intent of the comment.

"Thank you, Harrison," Mr. Heslin said. "This is ridiculous, the two of you having to stand out here, but my daughter doesn't seem to mind." He turned back to Victoria. "I'll take Izzy home. Call me if you need anything else. And I've already called Samuelson to let him know something else has happened. In case it's related."

"I'll be fine." She handed him Izzy's leash.

Her father left along with the others who were standing on the other side of the sheriff's cars. There had been nothing for them to see, and the temperature had dropped to near freezing.

Victoria contracted and relaxed her fingers inside her gloves, doing her physical therapy exercises while she waited. A phantom itch pulsated from her missing fingertips, intensifying with the cold.

The sheriff and his team were patient and meticulous in unearthing the body, stopping to document something, then starting again, so the minutes ticked by slowly. Cameras flashed, documenting the scene.

"I agree with your father. This is ridiculous." Harrison moved side to side and stamped his boots around. "We should just go home. They know where to find us. This is some sort of power trip, telling us to stay here."

Victoria shuffled her feet in place and stuck her gloved hands under her armpits. She kept her eyes on the lit clearing through the trees. "I want to wait. Pretend you're outside in Times Square waiting for the ball to drop. That crowd has been there for hours and it's much colder."

He chuckled. "I guess that's one way to look at it."
Harrison rubbed his own arms and made small talk, presumably to pass the time. To her surprise, he didn't ask her anything about Flight 745. Maybe he didn't know who she was, or maybe he was politely pretending he didn't. If he didn't know who she was, then he also didn't know she was an FBI agent. The way he'd promised her father to look after her seemed to support that fact.

Victoria's phone rang at precisely five minutes before midnight. It was Ned.

"Happy New Year—almost." Ned's voice was positive and energetic. Loud music and voices came from the background. "What are you doing?"

She sighed, happy to hear from him and glad he was out having fun. "You wouldn't believe it if I told you." There wasn't a speck of humor in her tone.

From the clearing, Deputy Bob called out, "Oh, no. Not who I thought it would be. Hoo, boy!"

Ned said something else that didn't register because of the party sounds around him and because Victoria was straining to make out what the authorities were saying.

"Ned, I have to go. I'll call you back later." She hung up as she crept through the woods to get closer, not caring if the sheriff or deputies saw her.

"That's George Wilson," one of the law enforcement officers said, leaning against his shovel. "I recognize him for sure."

George? Not Kristen? Oh, no. Poor George!

Deputy Bob let out a low whistle. "Ooh, this is bad, boys. This is bad. We gotta stop whatever is going on here."

The sheriff crouched down near the body, turning George's head to the side with gloved hands. "Looks like someone killed him with a blow to the back of his head."

Unearthed, the corpse now lay beside the ditch under the bright lights. George died wearing the same olive-colored work pants and corduroy shirt he'd worn when he came to the Heslins' house three days ago. His outfit could help establish the day of his death, unless he was the sort of person who wore the same clothes day after day. His eyes were wide open and so was his dirt-filled mouth, as if he was about to speak. Whatever it was he wanted to say, it was too late for anyone to hear it now.

Harrison followed Victoria and stood beside her, gaping. "What the hell? This is—this is awful."

Bob covered George with a sheet. One of the other deputies helped him slide the corpse into a body bag and then onto a stretcher.

"Come back at first light so we can search the woods again," the sheriff said as the deputies hoisted the stretcher up. "Until then, Bob is going to stay and guard the area."

"Well, George is no longer a suspect." Bob stood with his legs apart, his hand already resting on the gun in his holster. He scanned the area as if he expected the killer to come charging out of the woods brandishing a weapon, then rested his gaze on Victoria.

Peeling off his gloves, the sheriff walked toward Victoria and Harrison. He stopped in front of Victoria, rubbing a hand over the back of his neck. "So, you found another dead body near your father's house because you were following your dog to find your donkey." Repeating what he already knew in his exasperated tone showed he found her explanation unbelievable.

Harrison moved closer to her side and placed his hand on her shoulder. Wearing a thick coat, she could barely feel the weight of his touch but knew it was there.

A protective gesture.

Normally she would have moved away from his hand, but she didn't. The situation they faced was probably disturbing for Harrison. His gesture might have been more to comfort himself than her. Victoria wasn't intimidated by the sheriff, but she appreciated having someone on her side. Maybe it was the early hour, or because they'd been standing outside for so long, growing numb in the cold, or that she was still worried about Oscar's injuries, but now that they knew who was buried in the ground, Victoria suddenly just wanted to go home.

"The dirt is fresh and George Wilson hasn't been dead more than a few days." The sheriff's heavy-lidded eyes reflected the late hour, but his voice was deep and smooth, all traces of his cold gone. He settled his gaze on Victoria. "I don't need you to tell me that someone murdered Wilson. I know bodies don't bury themselves. Seeing he lives across from your father's house, had you seen George recently?"

"I've seen him twice since I arrived here last Saturday. The last time was three days ago. He came over to help my father with something. He was supposed to come back with a wrench, but he never did. I don't think his truck has left his yard since then."

"I saw him that same day." Harrison's hand still rested on Victoria's shoulder. "I was leaving the neighborhood. George was crossing the street from his side to the Heslins'. He was carrying a long tool, a hammer or wrench." Harrison sighed. "Look, can we go home now? It's been a long night. You know where to find us if you have more questions."

"I'm sure there will be more questions." The sheriff turned to Harrison. "And I don't think Ms. Heslin needs anyone worrying about her. She's as tough as they come." Then he walked away.

His comment should have been a compliment, but it sounded like an insult.

"Happy New Year," Victoria muttered.

Harrison frowned at the sheriff's back. "Come on. I'll walk you home."

She didn't argue. Exhausted, she trudged out of the woods with him. This case was getting worse, not better.

And the only person who seemed innocent now was George.

Chapter 24

Victoria punched in the alarm code and entered the house. Its warmth enveloped her, a welcome sensation. A lit Christmas citrus candle in the kitchen smelled wonderful, so much better than burned cookies.

Her father came out of his office. "Are you okay?"

"I'm fine." She removed her gloves and coat.

"Was it Kristen's body?"

"It wasn't Kristen." She softened her expression, hating to tell her father the news. "It was George."

Mr. Heslin's mouth dropped open. His hand went to his forehead. "George is dead? Someone *killed* George? What is going on around here?"

She put her hand on his arm and just stood there, letting him process the news. "I didn't get to see his body up close, but from what I heard, he'd been hit in the back of the head with something."

"But they don't know who did it?"

"I don't think so. They didn't rush off to arrest anyone. They'll be looking for more evidence today, once the sun comes up." She walked to the mudroom and hung up her coat. "Someone might be covering their tracks. And I thought I saw George in the woods near the Nantucket House when we pulled Kristen out of the water. He may have seen what happened to her."

Mr. Heslin slumped down onto the mudroom bench. "And someone wanted him silenced."

She sat next to her father, pulled her boots off, and tucked them in one of the mudroom cubbies. "What if George is the person who harmed Kristen and someone who cares about her wanted him punished?"

"In either scenario, there's a killer in our midst."

"Sounds like one of Judith's novels." Victoria pushed her hair away from her face and then put her hands into her pockets. "I hate that it's happening here and it's not fiction."

Mr. Heslin stood back up. "Alex went to bed. I told him he should get some sleep, since we have no idea what's coming next."

"Okay. I'm going upstairs to change my clothes. I'll be right back."

She changed into sweatpants, a sweatshirt and thick socks. As warmth returned to her body, the painful tingling in her fingers intensified. In her bathroom mirror, her reflection looked gaunt and pale, her skin almost as white as her pearls, the dark circles under her eyes more pronounced. There was a headache building behind her temples. She washed her face and then shook two Ibuprofen from a bottle and washed them down with a glass of water.

When she returned downstairs, her father was near the stove top, his hand on the kettle. "I've already got hot water ready for you. Would herbal tea or mint hot chocolate help?"

"Hot chocolate would be great. I'll make it."

She glanced at the microwave's digital time display. It was after 1 a.m. A new year. She hoped it would be so much better than the last, but it was already off to a bad start. The champagne sat on the counter, unopened. "I'm pretty wired," she said. "I don't think I'm going to fall asleep anytime soon. You go ahead."

"I will. Wake me if you find out anything new." He placed his hand on her shoulder. "This is not at all what I had in mind for you when I asked you to come to the lake. I thought I could give you peace and quiet here."

"We'll get through this." She kissed his cheek.

"I'm not sure it's safe for us to stay here anymore."

"Don't worry." Her words belied her own concern. She wished she'd brought her gun. "But I think you should go home. I'll stay here with Alex until this is all...sorted through."

"While I appreciate you wanting to keep your old man safe, there's absolutely no way that I would leave the two of you."

"You're hardly an old man, Dad."

He pulled her in for a hug. "Goodnight. I love you," he said before heading to the master bedroom and leaving her alone.

Victoria made hot chocolate, switched on the gas fireplace, and sat down on the couch with her phone and iPad.

Two murders. They had to be related.

Is George dead because of what he knew or because of what he had done?

Or is a serial killer passing through our midst?

On the surface, the drowning of the young woman and the violent murder and burial of an old man didn't share a common signature or modus operandi. But not all serial killers had them.

Who might the next victim be?

Questions circled through her mind. Where had Alex been after George left their house? As soon as she could account for her brother's whereabouts, she'd feel better and more confident if the sheriff returned with questions. George lived so close. It would only require minutes for someone who lived nearby to kill him. About an hour to bury him in the woods.

Don't go there. Alex couldn't. He wouldn't. Why am I even thinking about it?

Because that's what I'm trained to do.

She needed to look elsewhere.

Every fiber of Victoria's body began to slacken and grow drowsy as she warmed by the fire. She rolled her neck back and forth in languid movements. Falling asleep might not be as difficult as she'd imagined. Yawning, she rested her hand on her pearls.

I need to call Ned back. He might be worried.

It was too late to call, unless he was still at a party. She doubted that. More likely he was already home sleeping so he could get a tough workout in bright and early. They had that in common. She texted him instead, typing and then deleting her message again and again. There was no good way to send a message saying she had found another body, not without leaving the impression that things at the lake were totally out of control.

She ended up with: *Something happened. I'm okay. My family is okay. I'll call you tomorrow. Happy New Year.*

She set her phone and iPad beside her on the couch, suddenly too tired to do more research.

The dogs barked and ran to the back windows.

Victoria groaned. "Shush. It's just the donkeys."

Their barking intensified.

What now?

Victoria pushed herself up from her chair. Her reflection stared back at her from the window. She killed the family room lights, plunging most of the main floor into darkness, so she could see outside and no one could see in.

The donkeys stood together, ears up, alert to something on the side of the house toward the woods.

Alert again, Victoria's heart beat strong and fast. Was someone out there behind the house? Who would be passing by the backyard at this hour?

She resisted the urge to rush out outside for a confrontation. She didn't have her weapon and if she scared off the intruder, she might never learn what he or she intended to do.

Is it the same group who left the roadkill and the message on the front walk? Or whoever framed Alex and killed Kristen and George?

The barking continued. Her dogs raced toward the dog door.

"No. Stay!"

One by one, the dogs plunged through the door and into the backyard.

Whoever was out there would be foolish to stick around with large, barking dogs charging at them. She had to make a move before the intruder disappeared. Without stopping for shoes, she quickly disabled the alarm system, grabbed a steel poker from the decorative fireplace set, and bolted out the back door.

Leaves and branches rustled as someone crashed through the brush and into the woods. The intruder had a big head start.

She raced across the yard. "Stop!"

She fumbled with the gate latch, opened and closed it behind her, and ran toward the woods. Her feet got soaked in a puddle and slid in the mud. The rustling continued and she forged ahead, wondering if it would be best to swing the poker or use it like a sword, if it came to that.

The woods seemed to close in on her, cutting into her arms and legs, pulling at her hair and scraping her face as she plunged through them. She stumbled over a large tree root and crashed to the ground. Just as quickly, she scrambled up and kept moving, guided through the dark by the sounds ahead of her. When she was almost through the woods and into the neighbor's property, heavy footsteps pounded across wood. A motor started up. Before she was out of the woods, she heard a boat speeding away.

She emerged into the Roberts' backyard and sprinted toward the dock. The sound of the engine grew weaker.

She stopped and squinted into the darkness, gulping for breath. The wind blew her tangled hair into her eyes. Her feet were suddenly freezing, her toes numbing fast. She stuffed her mud-caked, scraped hands under her arms to keep them warm.

Small waves lapped the shore from the boat's wake as the intruder escaped into the night.

Chapter 25

The weather was crisp and clear in the morning, a good day for boating. But Victoria had no desire to go out on the lake again. And since her father didn't mention it, he must have felt the same. He had to be sad and concerned about George's death.

And George's daughter, who wanted money from his property, will she be upset? Will she regret asking if George was dead just days ago?

Victoria put on her coat and wrapped a tartan print scarf around her neck. She grabbed her dogs' leashes and her phone. She had two missed calls from Rivera. She stuck her headphones into her ears and called him back. He picked up on the first ring.

"Hey," Rivera said. "Great to hear from you."

"Hi. How are you?" She gathered the dogs and clipped leashes onto their collars.

"I'm good. I heard what's going on there. Sam's been updating me. Any news?"

"Like who is killing people on the peninsula and who framed my brother?" She dug her short nails into her clenched fist. It would be funny if it wasn't so terrible. As she finished getting ready and entered the garage, she filled him in on the previous evening.

"Should I come out there this weekend? See if I can assist the sheriff?"

Rivera sounded hopeful, as if he genuinely wanted her to take him up on his offer.

Her father's words came back to her. *Rivera would do anything for you.* And now here he was, offering to drive out to the West Virginia mountains because once again, through no fault of her own, disaster had struck. As much as her family needed an expert investigator on the scene, she couldn't ask him to come all the way there. And as soon as the sheriff found out Rivera and Victoria were colleagues; any cooperation might end.

"Um, I don't know." She slid on her gloves before opening the door from the garage to the driveway. Chilly air rushed inside. "You could help more by getting me some info. Wish I could access our databases right now."

"Tell me what you need and I'll get it for you."

"I could really use the case files from Mallory and Kristen Bozeman's investigation. They're nine years old. It's possible that no one scanned them. They could be gathering dust in a box somewhere in Pittsburgh."

She stepped outside to see Harrison at the top of her driveway. He waved as she approached.

Her dogs surged forward, interested in meeting someone new.

Victoria stopped several yards from where Harrison waited. She held up a finger for him as she spoke into her phone. "Rivera, there's someone here who needs to talk to me. Can I call you back?"

"Sure. Call me back and tell me what you need. I'll—just call me back when you can. I'll be waiting."

"Thanks." She ended the call, feeling a little guilty about his offer to help—even though she wanted to accept it—without understanding why. Rivera was her colleague and whatever was making her feel strange while talking to him needed to stop. She blamed her discomfort on her father and his less than subtle suggestions about Rivera and Ned.

"Hey," Harrison said. "How are you doing?"

"I'm tired. How are you?" She wouldn't tell him about the intruder in her yard, not until she knew if Harrison owned a boat or not. He probably did. Everyone on the peninsula had boats. And right now, she couldn't trust any of them.

Harrison touched the deep scar where it ran over his chin. "I'm tired, too. Last night was unreal. Like something out of a movie. I still can hardly believe it. And I can hardly believe we waited outside in the cold for over two hours on New Year's Eve." He shook his head. "Would you mind some company on your walk?"

"Sure. I should warn you, our walks have almost as much stopping and sniffing as walking."

"That's fine. I'm in no rush. After last night, I've been a little worried about you. Wondering if it was all bothering you the same way it bothered me. I wanted to check on you, but I don't have your phone number. I was thinking about ringing your doorbell. Glad I caught you coming out."

Victoria started down the street and Harrison fell into step beside her.

She hoped he didn't think their walk was any sort of date.

And yet...Harrison was handsome and easy to talk to. Quiet. Reserved. And someone she had literally met at the grocery store. *Nothing to lose.* All that aside, she honestly wasn't interested. That's what she was telling herself, anyway.

210

"Look," Victoria met his eyes, "there's something I haven't told you. You never asked what I did for a living."

"Oh." He arched his eyebrows. "My apologies. What do you do?"

"I'm an FBI agent."

He laughed. "You're joking."

She didn't crack a smile. Harrison's disappeared.

"I'm not joking. I work out of the D.C. office. I was a profiler and now I'm a special agent."

"Oh."

Victoria couldn't help thinking it was odd but refreshing that someone knew nothing about her family—not about their past tragedies, not that she was an heiress, or that she was on Flight 745 when it crashed. Her recent avoidance of the press had paid off in preserving her privacy.

"So, in your line of work, you deal with...that sort of...you deal with murders occasionally?"

"Yes. That isn't always the case with agents, depending on what they work on, but for me, it's been more of the norm. There's no shortage of killers out there." She lowered her voice. "No matter where I go."

"I have to say, I'm a little embarrassed now. Here I was worried about you and how you would handle the shock of finding a dead person." Harrison stared up at the snow-laced mountain tops. "So, if I may ask, based on your experience and expertise, what do you think is going on? What happened to the girl who drowned in the lake? And to George?"

The dogs stopped to sniff and mark the tall brick column at the end of the next driveway.

"I'm not sure yet. With two deaths and someone trying to frame my brother, there's plenty of evidence to lead the way. Someone just needs to uncover it." She didn't mention the missing corpse. The public didn't know and wouldn't hear it from her.

Near the end of the street, a massive Tudor mansion, big enough to function as a dormitory, spanned from one side of the large lot to the other, completely blocking all views of the lake. Behind the giant panes of glass along the first floor, long draperies shifted. The shadow of a figure moved away from the window.

Victoria stopped and stared at the house. "Do you know who owns this place?"

"Yes. The owner is a linebacker for the Steelers." Harrison feigned throwing a football over his shoulder and jogged a few steps. When he returned, he was walking closer to her than when they started out. "He and his wife bought this place. One of his teammates owns the house next to mine."

"Does the couple who lives here have a daughter?"

"I don't think so."

Victoria angled away, putting a few more feet between them to reclaim her personal space. "When my brother got his license, he came here with friends without telling my parents. You know the drill. Each of his friends says they're sleeping over at someone else's house for the weekend. They would have gotten away with it except that George called my Dad. He didn't know it was Alex at the house."

"George told on your brother? Do you think Alex had a grudge against him?"

Wind whooshed past, blowing Victoria's scarf behind her. "What? No. Alex wouldn't...he was just a kid. That was a decade ago. I brought it up because maybe Kristen was staying in her parents' house alone, with or without their knowledge."

Although, if Kristen's family lived here, why did she have less than perfect teeth?

"If this couple has a daughter, she would be a toddler. They're young. Can't be more than mid-twenties."

Victoria looked at the beautiful house again. A large hawk swooped into the giant elm on one side of the front yard. "I thought I saw someone watching from behind that window."

Harrison pivoted on one foot and walked backwards, checking out the property as they passed. "Might be a cleaning person. The sheriff would have called all the homeowners to make sure none were missing a daughter, even if they weren't here, right?"

"Yes. He should have." Victoria sighed as they rounded the corner to Judith's street. "He probably has. He's being thorough. It's just so unusual that hardly anyone on the peninsula knows each other. It's pretty easy for anyone to be hiding secrets...don't you think?" She let her question hang there, in case Harrison felt compelled to share something about himself or anyone else.

"It's not strange. People come here to get away from their real lives. For privacy and seclusion." Harrison gestured toward Judith's house in the distance. "Speaking of killers and neighbors—Judith McPharland, the author, lives up there."

"Yes. I know Judith."

Harrison separated from Victoria to avoid a fallen branch. "I've bought several of her books as gifts for my niece to read. She likes mystery novels. My grandfather's firm used to do some work for her."

"What sort of work?"

"Marketing, publicity, those sorts of things."

"Oh. I think she has just one person helping her now." *Has the sheriff looked into John Stein?*

213

"I don't believe she's written anything new in years. She must have retired."

"Hmm." Although Victoria would never suggest this out loud to Harrison, she couldn't help but wonder again what the recent murders might mean for the author's career. Would Judith leverage the recent mysterious deaths to launch another bestseller?

The dogs switched places and Victoria swiveled around to uncross their leashes. "Judith has a daughter my age. We hung out a bit when we were younger. She thinks the sheriff has it out for my brother because of something that happened when they were teenagers."

"Do you think that's a possibility?"

"As you saw last night, Sheriff Hayes doesn't seem to care much for me. He definitely seems to have a chip on his shoulder. Would he take it as far as to frame my brother?" She shrugged. "That I don't know."

"I don't know the sheriff, and I don't have other experiences with law enforcement to use as a comparison. Like I said, last night was not a normal evening for me." They walked a few strides in silence until he chuckled. "I've met Judith's daughter. Penelope?"

"Phoebe."

"Right. I'm not the best with names. She hit on me at the store, in the parking lot." He laughed. "You might think I'm full of myself and I imagined it—but there was no imagining this. She came on strong."

Why am I not surprised to hear that? "You didn't imagine it. Oh, look." Victoria stopped and pointed to a herd of deer gathered on the side of Judith's yard. "They're so beautiful."

The dogs stood at attention, riveted by the deer. The herd stared back.

"They look a lot like your dogs," Harrison said.

Big Ed barked. The deer gracefully bounced off and disappeared into the woods.

"Anyway," Victoria said, walking again, "Phoebe mentioned seeing you drive by with a woman in your car. So, you're not always out here all by yourself, are you?"

"That would be my niece. She comes with me occasionally. I told you, my sister has been sick."

"I remember you saying. When was your niece last here?"

The front door to Judith's house swung open. "Victoria! Victoria!" Judith shouted as she stumbled outside barefoot.

If the author hadn't emerged from her own house, Victoria wouldn't have recognized her. She wasn't wearing makeup or a wig. Her hair was thin and gray.

"Wait, dear! Wait up! Please! I want to talk to you." Judith slurred her words. It was obvious she'd been drinking heavily.

Victoria wanted to escort the author back inside. But Judith tripped over a garden stone and fell forward with a giant *oof.* She stayed on the ground, moaning.

Harrison was at her side first, helping her up.

Judith started laughing as she brushed debris from her yoga pants and velvet hoodie. "Well, I'll be. Who put that in my way?"

Harrison put one arm around her waist and one under her arm. "Come on back inside and sit down."

"Thank you." She stared at Harrison. "You're just about the same age as my boyfriend was when he left us, aren't you?"

When he left us?

An odd choice of words, especially for someone who wrote books for a living, someone who chose her words carefully. There was an ominous tone to Judith's question that made it sound more like John had died than driven home.

Harrison answered. "I don't know, ma'am."

No. Don't call her ma'am. It will make her feel old.

But the damage was done.

Judith burst out crying.

Harrison gave Victoria a blank look and silently mouthed, "What did I do?"

Victoria just shook her head as she handed Harrison her dogs' leashes. "I'll be right back." She led Judith back toward her house.

Reeking of alcohol, Judith leaned heavily against Victoria. Harrison followed behind them.

"Is Phoebe inside?" Victoria asked.

"They're gone." Judith stopped crying and straightened, her voice taking on a chilling tone. "They're both gone now. They got what they deserved."

A jolt of alarm shot through Victoria. "Where did they go, Judith?"

A shadow passed over Judith's face as she lowered herself onto the front porch loveseat. "I don't want to talk about them." Her voice had a clarity it didn't have only moments ago. She wiped under her eyes with the back of her hand. "I came outside because I wanted to talk to you, dear. You've been such a sweet girl. Such a nice girl. I wish your mother could see you now. She'd be so proud of you. You'd never hurt her."

"Thank you, Judith. I really appreciate you saying that." Victoria thought Phoebe and John might have left the peninsula when Phoebe dropped off Judith's novel, but now Victoria wasn't as sure.

Are there fresh burial mounds somewhere in Judith's woods also?

Victoria could guess what precipitated Judith's breakdown. She wanted to say, *it's not you; your daughter is a bit of a monster and has been since she was a child,* but that probably wasn't what Judith needed to hear, nor would it help her feel better.

She placed her hand on Judith's arm. "Let's get you inside and I can make you some coffee."

"No. I'm just going to sit here awhile. I'm going to be all right." Judith dropped her head to her chest. "I always am."

With growing alarm, Victoria stepped away from Judith and looked in through the open front door. A large potted plant lay on its side, dirt spilling across the foyer's marble floor. Victoria didn't see anyone else inside. "Um, I'll bring my dogs home and then come back here and sit with you for a bit. I'll bring your latest book so I can finish it."

Judith looked up and smiled through her tears. The effect, combined with her almost unrecognizable look, was a little frightening. "Ever since I learned you joined the FBI, I thought it might have something to do with my books. You seemed to love them. You appreciated the way my detectives pieced the clues together, found the criminals, and brought them to justice."

"Yes, I did." Victoria stepped further back and took a quick look through another window. "I've so enjoyed reading your books, Judith."

"And now you're going to find the real killer, aren't you? You'll find out who did it, no matter who it turns out to be?"

Again, Judith's choice of words was a bit strange. Victoria met Harrison's eyes then turned back to Judith. "Yes, Judith. I'm definitely interested in helping the authorities."

Judith shook a trembling finger. "Fine, then. Fine. Go do it. No matter who."

Chapter 26

The road climbed steeper in a sharp curve, switched back, rose and curved again. Victoria leaned forward, hugging the center line with her SUV. The only thing separating them from a perilous drop over the side of the mountain was a small metal guardrail.

She'd always hated traveling on Red Spruce Knob, especially at night.

"You think you can drive any slower?" Alex joked. The sweet and smoky smell of Bubba's Barbecue filled the car. He opened one of the to-go containers and took out a rib. "I'm so darn hungry."

"Hey, grab a napkin, will you?" Victoria couldn't relate to his appetite. She'd lost hers the day they found Kristen, once they established the connection to Alex, and it hadn't returned. She needed to force herself to eat because she still had weight to gain back after losing so many pounds in Greenland. The spate of murderous activity around Lake Lucinda wasn't helping.

"There might be someone staying in the Steeler player's house," she said, her eyes glued to the solid center line. "I saw someone looking out from behind the curtains when I was walking the dogs."

"Could be maintenance or cleaning people." Alex bit into a rib.

"I'm going over in the morning. I need to be sure there's no one there."

"A few hours ago, you thought Judith might have done something to Phoebe and John."

"Not really. But I might still be entertaining the remote possibility if Phoebe hadn't posted a selfie with her dinner entrée. I could see John's hand on the edge of the shot."

"And now you think someone squatting in the empty home of an NFL player could be responsible?"

"I don't know who I think it is, or if we've even met the perpetrator yet." Victoria slowed further as a car approached from the opposite direction. "I ran into Harrison again when I was walking the dogs."

"You two bonded, eh?" Alex reached into the bag and came out with a wad of napkins. "You better be careful. Everyone wants to be friends with a celebrity."

"I'm not a celebrity. And the nice thing is that he doesn't seem to know anything about us or about me being in the plane crash."

"Then he doesn't have a television or watch the news."

"Maybe he doesn't. I don't think the sheriff knows either. He's definitely not impressed."

Alex wiped his fingers on a napkin and then balled it up. "All I know is, I don't trust anyone until this whole mess is figured out."

Alex wasn't aware of the message left in front of the lake house. Victoria had cleaned everything up to shield him from the grief it would cause him. He didn't know about Phoebe's comments or the girl in the café who said everyone thought Alex was guilty of *something*. But Harrison had said nothing to indicate he blamed Alex. He was waiting for the truth to come out. Victoria didn't fully trust him, or anyone else, but she could at least appreciate that much about him.

A small pickup truck approached, speeding around the narrow curve. Victoria's muscles instinctively tensed from her shoulders to her knuckles. She leaned forward, tightening her grip around the wheel.

The truck shot past them.

Her phone vibrated against the center console.

"It's Dad." Alex pressed the button to accept the call.

"I just found something," Mr. Heslin said. "A phone message from George. He must have left it shortly before his death. I'm going to call the sheriff, but I wanted to tell you first."

Victoria rounded the tight curve. Another vehicle was coming toward them. A large delivery truck. She tried not to tense again.

The truck's high beams flashed on, blinding her.

A jolt of fear erupted in her chest. "What the heck!" She dropped her gaze, straining to see the edges of the road.

"Idiot!" Alex shouted at the windshield.

"What's going on there?" Mr. Heslin's voice strained with concern.

The truck moved right, straddling both lanes. There wasn't enough room for her SUV to pass.

Alex grabbed for the door handle. "The guy must be hammered!"

Victoria jammed her hand against the horn and kept it there. Heat rushed to her face, making her skin tingle with adrenaline. Her heart rate spiked. "Move, move, move!"

"Alex!" her father yelled. "What's going on?"

The truck kept coming, barreling toward them at an angle. She could steer into the side of the mountain or go plummeting over the edge. She chose the mountain, jerking the wheel hard to the left and squeezing her eyes shut. The truck slammed the rear fender of her SUV with a ferocious crunch, sending her vehicle spinning. The SUV careened around in the road, hurtling toward the edge and the steep drop just beyond.

"What's happening?" Mr. Heslin shouted. "Are you all right?"

The ear-piercing sound of the guardrail shearing off accompanied their panicked screams.

The SUV plunged over the side of the mountain.

▼▲▼

Victoria had to force her eyes open. It took seconds for her throbbing head to clear.

Then she remembered.

She was still in her seat, hanging upside down, anchored by her seatbelt. Her head pounded like it was going to burst. Alex remained strapped in beside her, also upside down.

Thank God he'd been wearing his seatbelt.

But he wasn't moving. Blood dripped off his forehead and formed a puddle on the roof of the car below them.

Reaching for him sent a sharp pain shooting down her side.

She kept reaching, needing to find a pulse. She couldn't get to him.

Her seatbelt wouldn't unlatch with her entire body weight pressing against it.

Sucking in her breath and pulling her abdominal muscles toward her back, she yanked the seatbelt open and fell head first.

Another spike of pain burst from her side and spiraled through her body. She gasped and fought a wave of nausea.

With an ominous, slow creak, the car lurched to one side.

Victoria froze and held her breath, afraid to move a muscle. Were they in jeopardy of falling further? How much time did they have?

Get your wits about you and figure out the best course of action.

A lightning bolt of pain erupted inside her skull. She fought against the yellowish grayness creeping into her vision from behind her eyes.

Did anyone know we drove off the mountain?

Panic welled inside her chest. She could hardly breathe. Her heart beat wildly. Suddenly she was back inside the mangled wreckage of Flight 745. Waiting and waiting for help that never came.

She clenched her jaw and tried to break through the flashback.

It's not real. It's not real.

Sweat mixed with blood and dripped from her face.

But this is real. I crashed. Alex and I crashed.

A dizzy sensation mounted right along with her fear, rendering her helpless.

Not now! Pull it together!

"Victoria! Alex! Can you hear me?"

It was her father's voice coming from somewhere in the car.

"Dad! I can hear you. Where are you?"

"Oh, thank God! Thank God! I'm still on the phone, we're still connected. I called 911. What about your brother?"

223

"I don't know." Her vision was fading. "I can't stay awake."

"Hold on. Just hold on. Help is on the way."

Where have I heard that before?

The sarcastic thought appeared despite her fear and pain. She prayed help really would come this time.

"Can you tell where you are?" her father asked. "Where your car crashed?"

"Yes." Her head spun. "Somewhere off the side of Red Spruce Knob."

Above her, Alex moaned.

"Alex is alive. Hurry. I don't think we should move but...I'm...I'm not...sure." Her words became slow and slurred. A ringing sound filled her ears. She pitched forward, vomiting on the roof of the car.

"Hang in there," her father pleaded. "You're going to be all right. Please, hang in there."

Dizzy and sweating, she struggled to answer him. "I will, but I'm going...to..."

▼▲▼

"Victoria! Alex!"

An echoing voice fought with the powerful urge to remain unconscious.

"Victoria! Alex!"

A man's voice. That drawl—so familiar. Why?

Was the voice even real?

"Victoria! Alex!"

It was real.

She moaned. "Here." Her voice came out a weak croak.

He won't hear me.

She tried again. "Here. We're here. Help!"

Someone rustled and crashed through brush, snapping and cracking as he came closer.

"Help." She moaned. "We're here."

But Alex isn't answering.

In the few seconds of quiet, she heard wheezy and shallow breaths come from beside her.

Oh, thank God.

Darkness closed in like an angry fist. She resisted, needing to call out again and wanting to help Alex, but the pull was too strong. She fell deeper, back into a soundless, sightless place with no dreams and no pain.

Chapter 27

Victoria blinked, struggling to open her swollen eyes and then to keep them open. The lights were too bright. Allowing one eye to stay closed, she took in the small room. The bed with metal rails. Tubes and wires. Machines beeping.

A man stood over her bed. Lean and strong. Athletic posture. Short dark hair with neat sideburns and skin several shades darker than her own.

"Rivera?"

He nodded and his face slowly came into focus.

"Where am I? Am I still in the George Washington Hospital?"

Did I just escape the plane crash? Was everything that I thought happened next only a dream?

"Easy there, Tori. You're at West Virginia Memorial Hospital now."

Moving her head, she felt constricting material around her forehead and temples. Bandages. She remembered the crash. An image of Alex, upside down and bleeding, jolted her alert. "Where's my brother?"

"He's in a room down the hall and he's okay. Your father is with him. You Heslins seem to have nine lives, but you're going to scare the rest of us to death."

She pressed her fists into the bed to sit up straighter. An excruciating pain shot through her head. "I have a concussion." It wasn't a question.

"You sure do."

She closed her eyes. Floaters drifted around behind her eyelids like tiny spiked snowflakes. After a few seconds she braved the lights again, opening the one eye that didn't feel as puffed up as the other. "What are you doing here?"

"I came to help you." Rivera crossed his arms. "You're welcome."

"But...I told you not to come."

"And yet here I am. Even though you never called me back. Seems my job is finding you and helping people fix you up. I'm not saying I mind, but I didn't think I'd be doing it again so soon. I'm not here five minutes and you drive off a cliff. If you're trying to avoid me, don't be so drastic. I can take a subtler hint."

She smiled. "Really? That's what you think? You know that's not what happened."

"Then tell me what did happen—if you can."

She leaned forward and groaned from the discomfort it caused. "Alex and I went out to pick up dinner." The sound of the guardrail shredding and tearing replayed in her mind, making her shudder. "A truck ran us off the road."

"We know that much. We haven't found the truck or its driver yet."

"What?" She scrambled to sit up. "You mean he crashed too and he's still somewhere on the side of the mountain? Why can't they find him? What if—"

"No. He's not waiting for a rescue. A family witnessed your SUV going over the side of the road and called emergency services before your father did. They were behind the truck and watched it cross from its own lane into the center. They claim the driver never used his brakes. There should be skid marks all over the road, and there aren't any. After you drove over the side, the truck didn't stop. The driver kept going."

Victoria snorted. "Whoever hit us must have been drunk or texting. Didn't want to go to jail for manslaughter."

"I don't think so. People further down the road saw the same truck driving at a normal speed within its lanes. The driver showed no signs of impairment." Rivera leaned closer. "Your collision wasn't an accident, Victoria."

She clutched the side of the narrow bed. The information sank in like salt on a wound. Fear for her family fueled her anger. Her clenched jaw intensified her headache.

"The sheriff found you and Alex. Now he's looking for the truck." Rivera clasped his hands together, staring down at her.

"You met him already?"

"Yes. You've been sleeping for longer than you realize. Three months. It's March."

Her mouth fell open. "Three months?"

The corners of his mouth twitched and then curled up. "Just kidding. It's the morning after your crash. The sheriff and I developed a good working relationship between the time he pulled you off the mountain and now. I think you'll find him to be far more accommodating than he was before."

"Really? But how? What did you—"

Someone cleared his throat. Victoria turned, ever so slowly.

Her father stood in the doorway, looking tired but smiling. "You're awake."

"Yeah. I'm awake." She closed her eyes. "But I'd rather go back to sleep and wake up feeling human again. How is Alex?"

"Bruised like he lost a cage match and he has a minor fracture. So far, that's all. It's a miracle. I don't know if you remember this, but I was on the phone with you during the accident. I think the ordeal shortened my life a few years." He came closer to her bed, twisting his wedding band. "I don't like this new habit of you ending up in the hospital." He took her hand and squeezed it. "This trip keeps getting worse, doesn't it? It's hard to believe the intent was for you to relax and recover."

Rivera chuckled. "Yeah. If she did her work as an agent as effectively as she relaxed on her vacations, she would have been fired a long time ago."

Victoria started to shake her head, already forgetting the immediate discomfort it brought her, and stopped right away. She let her eyes close and then moaned because it seemed the perfect expression of how she was feeling. "Where's my SUV now?"

Someone picked up her hand. Startled by the touch, she opened her eyes, thinking it was Rivera.

Her father squeezed and gazed down at her. "It's totaled. You'll need a new one to get home to Virginia."

She swallowed and realized she desperately needed a glass of water.

A phone buzzed. Her father held one up. "This is yours. The sheriff pulled it from the wreck. I'm surprised it still works." He looked down at the screen. "It's Ned."

"Let it go to voicemail. I'll call him back. I'm completely embarrassed to tell him about the crash. Like I've become some disaster-prone death magnet."

"Don't say that." Rivera's voice was soft. "It's not true."

The phone kept ringing, Her father set the device on the bedside table.

"Oh. I just remembered. You had something to tell us right before we crashed, Dad, something you were going to tell the sheriff. What was it?"

"Ah. Turns out I had voicemail messages on the landline," Mr. Heslin said as the vibrating phone rattled the metal table. "The most recent was from George, just after leaving our house the other day. He said the owner of Lucinda Lee's place had an emergency and George had to help him first. Said he was going over there and would come back to our place as soon as he finished. So, what does that tell you?"

What does it tell me?

Victoria's brain wasn't functioning at full speed at the moment.

Her father continued. "It sounds like your friend Harrison might have been the last person to see George before he died. And the last person who saw George on the day he died is probably the person who killed him."

Harrison killed George?

"Not necessarily, Mr. Heslin." Rivera spoke with the calmness and respect he showed most everyone. "As far as we know, Alex was the last person to see Kristen alive. That doesn't make him guilty."

I knew there was a reason I loved Rivera.

The instinctive thought came quickly and startled her.

Chapter 28

Wearing jeans and a sweater, Victoria sat with her legs crossed on the hospital bed, impatient to leave. Rivera was busy with his laptop in the corner chair.

"Knock, knock." A woman wearing teal-colored scrubs entered the room, her arms surrounding a giant arrangement of colorful flowers that obscured her face. "I'll set these down over here for you."

Rivera pulled his feet out of the way, making room for her to pass.

"They sure are beautiful." The woman pushed aside two folded towels and lowered the vase gently onto the table in front of the window. "I see flowers coming through here every day, but I don't think I've ever seen such a fancy bouquet before."

"Thank you for delivering them," Victoria said. "They're really...um, big."

"Yes, they are." She rotated the vase half way around. "There you go, I'll leave you two alone now." The woman stared at Victoria for what seemed like longer than normal, smiling, before she left the room.

"They must be from my father. Who else knows I'm here?"

"We're about to find out." Rivera tore open the sealed envelope and read it out loud.

"Dear, Victoria. Get well soon. Best wishes and all my love—Judith McPharland."

"Oh. Very sweet of her. She lives down the street."

"I know exactly who she is."

Victoria uncrossed her legs and shifted them off the side of the hospital bed. She sat still, assessing how much she ached. In slow motion, she reached behind her head to adjust her ponytail. "Wow. Even this hurts."

"You think? I wonder why." Rivera huffed as he scooted the chair closer to her. "It hasn't been twenty-four hours since your accident. You got pretty banged up. And head injuries are serious."

Victoria didn't need anyone to tell her about the dangers of head injuries. Not after one of the flight attendants died from a head injury before their rescue from Greenland. The experience had humbled her to the threat of unseen trauma and made her more wary. But she'd had two CT scans of her brain since she arrived last night, and there was no bleeding. "There's no reason for me to stay longer than I have to. I want to get out of here. Can you hand me my phone?"

Rivera slid her phone off the bedside table and handed it to her. He held on to it a second longer than necessary. Their fingers touched and a shiver coursed gently through her, closely followed by a rush of confusion. She looked up and their eyes met. When she turned away, images flashed through her mind. Rivera outside a hotel in North Carolina. Ned entering her house after a run. Harrison helping Judith to her feet on her front path. Victoria wasn't ready to think about what any of it meant. Not now, with a bruised brain. She needed all her concentration on the Lake Lucinda murders.

Focus.

Who had tried to kill them? Was the killer trying to make sure Alex couldn't defend himself against murder accusations? Or were she and her brother victims of misguided vigilante justice— someone trying to punish them for something they believed Alex had done?

She lowered her gaze to her phone. The screen was shattered, but it still worked. "I've got to figure out what's going on before something bad happens to someone else."

"And you don't have to do it alone," Rivera said.

"Thanks. I need to speak with Gloria Bozeman. I think she's Kristen's grandmother." Victoria scrolled through her recently called numbers, narrowing her eyes to read through the spiderweb of cracks on her screen.

The call went through and a woman answered, greeting Victoria with a flat tone and a raspy, smoker's voice.

Victoria put her phone on speaker so Rivera could hear. "Hello. Is this Gloria Bozeman?"

"Yes." Gloria's voice was sharp. "Who is this?"

Victoria looked at Rivera and widened her eyes. The agents had spent so much time working together previously, that's all it took for her to communicate she was feeling hopeful.

"My name is Victoria Heslin. I'm with the FBI. I left you a message a few days ago about your missing granddaughter."

A chorus of electronic alarms sounded in the corridor. A woman shouted, "Get the attending!"

Victoria was grateful Alex's room wasn't near her own. Someone was in trouble, but this time, it wasn't her brother. She turned the speakerphone function off and focused on Gloria. "I left you my agent identification number previously."

Hospital staff rushed past the open doorway and into the room across the hall. "Code blue. Code blue," a woman shouted.

Victoria cupped her hand around the phone as she pressed it against her ear. "I—uh—you can look me up and call me back if you like."

Rivera closed the door, muffling the noise coming from the corridor.

"I don't need to look you up." Gloria grunted. "I already did when you called me the first time. Where are you? It sounds like you're on your way to a fire."

"I apologize for the noise. I'm in a hospital. I'm looking into reopening your family's case and wanted to make sure we had all the information."

"Oh. I've answered questions for dozens of officers and agents. Kristen isn't missing, she's dead."

"She is? I—uh—it was my understanding she hadn't been located." *Did I miss something?* "Have any of the other law enforcement officers provided you with evidence showing Mallory and Kristen died?"

"No evidence you can see or touch," Gloria said. "I know because I'm her mother. My Mallory wasn't perfect. She was a good woman who made bad choices with men. She seemed to be attracted to drunks. Still, she always called to tell me where she was. And when things didn't work out, she came back home. Every time. And if things had worked out for her, like if she met a man who was gonna take care of her for good, she would'a told me that, too. So that's how I know they're dead."

Gloria seemed to speak without stopping for a breath, as if she'd given the same explanation many times over the years.

Victoria switched her phone to her other ear because her arm was sore and already getting tired from holding it. "Mallory

234

had been working in New York City for a week when she disappeared?"

"That's right. She was doing temp work for a big company called D&S Public Relations."

D&S sounds familiar. Where have I heard it before? Victoria wasn't sure—*damn concussion.* "Who was caring for Kristen while your daughter worked?"

"She had a friend near the city who had a child and worked nights. They were gonna trade off the child care duties. I didn't want her dragging my granddaughter from one short-lived dream to the next. I told her to leave Kristen with me, but she—she—" Her voice choked up before she finished. "Kristen was a beautiful girl. You wouldn't believe how beautiful. There was something really, really special about her. Everyone said so. And now they're both gone. I'll never see them again."

"I'm sorry." Victoria's head was throbbing. The smell of the flowers was overpowering the room. She wanted another way, beyond the partial DNA match, of confirming Kristen from the lake was the little girl who had disappeared. Something more than seeing a photo with a startling resemblance. "Kristen had a beauty mark on her upper lip. Did she have any other identifying characteristics? Another birthmark? Or a piece of jewelry she wore?"

"I gave her a ring for her eighth birthday. Rose quartz. Her birthstone. I bought it at the jewelers in the mall. The band was 14-karat gold. Mallory told me not to give it to her, said Kristen was going to lose it. Kristen loved that ring." Gloria's voice softened as she spoke. "She wore it every day."

A child's pink ring. Kristen from the lake absolutely is— absolutely was—Kristen Bozeman.

"Thank you, this is helpful information." Victoria nodded at Rivera, eager to tell him she'd found another connection. She ended the conversation without saying much more. She didn't have enough solid information to provide Gloria Bozeman closure. And...it wasn't Victoria's case. Setting her phone down, she leaned back against the pillows and closed her eyes, aware of Rivera watching her. "Lot of commotion out in the hallway. Is everything okay?"

After all the frenetic activity in the corridor, the hospital suddenly seemed eerily quiet.

"Someone having a much worse day than you." His voice was soft, coming from closer than before. "What did you find out?"

"It's her. Kristen from the lake is the Kristen who disappeared nine years ago." Victoria suddenly felt drained. "The question is, where has she been all these years? If we can figure that out, I'm sure it will lead us to what happened to Kristen and George." She opened one eye and looked at Rivera. "Can you log into your computer for me?"

"Sure. Pirate lady." He took a seat in the only chair and slid his computer from his bag. "But you're supposed to be relaxing."

"I'm not very good at that. I'll never go anywhere without my work laptop again. It's driving me crazy not to have access to the FBI's databases."

Rivera opened his computer. "Someone on the peninsula must have seen Kristen. Who has the most reason to lie?"

A memory appeared, striking a nerve—a much younger Phoebe and a rock connecting with an innocent goose. Victoria shuddered. "There isn't always a reason."

"You've been here all week looking around the area. What does your gut tell you?"

236

A knock came from the doorway. Dr. Yang entered with a chart under her arm. No white coat. No scrubs. Petite and stylishly put together in business casual clothes, she wore a pink purse slung over one arm. Her eyes moved to the phone in Victoria's hand. "Not a good idea for at least a few days. Talking is okay, but staring at a little screen, or any screen, is not recommended. You want to stimulate your brain as little as possible."

Victoria set the phone on the bedside table.

The doctor widened her eyes at the flowers. "Quite a display you've got there." She returned her focus to Victoria's chart. "One last check and if all is well, I'm ready to discharge you. It looks like you're ready to go."

"Thank you." Victoria wrapped her arms around her waist. "No offense, but yes, I want out of here."

Holding his laptop, Rivera stood up. "Should I leave while you do this?"

The doctor looked at Victoria for an answer.

"He can stay." Victoria scooted back to the center of the hospital bed.

"I'm honored." Rivera smirked and sat back down.

The doctor flicked a pen light on. "Close your right eye, please, and follow this light." She leaned closer, peering into Victoria's eyes. "Do you still have a headache?"

"Yes."

"The pain should dissipate over the next week. If it gets worse, you need to call your personal doctor. And as I said, stay away from bright lights and computer screens. No television. Give your brain a chance to rest." Dr. Yang wrote a few notes on the chart and then tucked it back under her arm. "Do you have someone who can monitor you for the next several days?"

"Yes." Rivera sounded confident. "She's got her family, and she's got me."

His comment surprised Victoria. *I have him? What does that mean?*

Chapter 29

Mr. Heslin started a fire inside the family room's giant stone fireplace. Flames blazed, bouncing warm light off the wide-planked wooden floors, the overhead beams, and the window glass.

Rivera dimmed the overhead lights. "For Victoria's concussion," he said before taking a seat across from Mr. Heslin around the coffee table.

"Thanks," Victoria said, able to see them clearly from the kitchen. The men were more familiar with each other than she had realized. They had bonded over common concerns—first to find Victoria and her plane while she was in Greenland, then the car crash, and now to find the killer stalking Lake Lucinda. People enjoyed having Rivera around, and her family was no exception. He was a likable guy with a great attitude. A lot like Alex, when she thought about it, but with a work ethic to match her own. Perhaps her father had kept bringing up Rivera's name as a romantic possibility due to wishful thinking.

Rivera stared at the painting over the mantle. "Wow, sir. Your wife was stunning. And Victoria looks so much like her."

"Yes." Mr. Heslin gazed at his wife's image. "True on both counts."

I don't look much like her now, thanks to whoever ran me off the road.

Moving with an uncharacteristic stiffness, Victoria crumpled one empty pizza box into the recycling bin and placed a full one into the fridge. Rivera had claimed the pizza tasted great, and it was one of the most popular establishments in the small town, but Victoria could barely taste it and had a hard time forcing herself to eat a second slice. With Alex still in the hospital, two pizzas had been more food than they needed.

Mr. Heslin settled back in the leather arm chair. "Rivera, I sure am glad you're here to help figure all of this out."

"Your help is critical, too, Dad," Victoria said. "You know the people on the peninsula better than I do."

"Which isn't saying much." Her father huffed. "That's exactly what the problem is." He leaned forward slightly with his hands on his thighs, facing Rivera. "No one lives here year-round. George was the exception. The houses sell every few years. Bigger ones go up and those sit empty, too. Few of us interact. Judith McPharland is the only person left with whom I have any history. Maybe it's time to sell this place."

"You might not get a good price if there are two unsolved murders in the neighborhood," Victoria said, echoing Harrison's comment from the other night. "Let's get through this first. And can I make coffee for anyone?"

"I'm good, thanks." Rivera sniffed a few times. "Stop waiting on us and sit down."

Mr. Heslin crossed his legs. "The future of this place is one reason I wanted both of my children to visit now. To see if one of them wanted to keep the house. Leaving it in a trust for both of them could get complicated. They're very different people. If one of them were to want it and the other didn't, well—that would make it a simple decision. Now, with the way the locals treated Alex, I doubt he'll ever want to come back."

"Like I said, let's discuss the house when it makes more sense to do so." Victoria returned to the family room carrying a box of tissues. "I don't want to talk about anything that implies you're no longer around." She tossed the tissues to Rivera. "Here you go. I figured you might need these."

"Thanks." Rivera pulled several tissues from the box and blew his nose. From the sound of things, the tissues had arrived just in time.

"You have a cold, huh?" Mr. Heslin uncrossed his legs and rubbed his hip.

"No. Nothing contagious." Rivera pulled another tissue from the box. "Allergies."

Mr. Heslin stood and moved his lower body in small circles, leaning toward his right side, like a constrained hula dance without the hoop. "What are you allergic to?"

"Dogs."

Her father sat back down, his brow furrowed and his lips pressed together. "Oh." He met Victoria's eyes and said, "Hmm. Too bad."

Victoria prayed her father wouldn't elaborate on his thinking. "Let's get back to work, why don't we." She pulled the dog sheet off the couch and settled into one corner, tucking her legs beneath her.

Big Ed wandered over, focused on Rivera. Victoria shot one arm out across the dog's chest, blocking him from visiting the agent and exacerbating his allergies. "Sorry, big guy, this is as far as you go." She rubbed the dog's head as a compromise.

Rivera cleared his throat with a few coughs. "Back to the investigation. Victoria can call the shots—she usually does anyway—and I'll do the research." He smiled as he reached for his laptop. "But we can't let you overdo it. We want your brain back in tip-top shape as soon as possible. Maybe keep your eyes closed."

"I will...later," Victoria answered, stroking Big Ed's neck. "So, here's what we know so far. Kristen's mother, Mallory Bozeman, was staying at a friend's apartment outside the city. She was doing temp work with D&S Public Relations." Victoria shot up from the couch, startling her dog. "Oh, my gosh. I think I remembered why the name of the firm is so familiar. I have to get something from upstairs."

"You stay put. I'll get it for you." Her father pushed himself up. "What do you need?"

"A book from my bedroom." She plopped back down. "It's on the night table. *Lucinda's Secrets.*"

The dogs lifted their heads, watching Mr. Heslin leave the room and go upstairs, then dropped their heads back down.

Rivera wrinkled his nose as he watched Oliver stand and stretch, walk around and around in tight circles, and then settle back into the same curled-ball shape he'd come out of, tucking his long snout under his front leg with a loud sigh. Rivera laughed. "That was ...interesting." He turned to Victoria. "Are you going to tell me what it is you suddenly remembered?"

"Wait until my father comes back. I want to make sure I'm right before I tell you." She grabbed the throw blanket from the back of the couch and draped it around her shoulders. "But while we're waiting, have I mentioned my father isn't the only one who is glad you came?"

"You have, but I don't mind hearing it again." Rivera tilted his head and smiled.

Her father barely made a sound coming down the stairs and across the room in his socks. He handed Victoria the book.

She flipped through the first few pages.

There it is.

In the list of acknowledgements. Representation by D&S Public Relations.

Another connection.

Victoria handed the book to her father. "Check this out. Judith uses the same firm for her publicity, or at least she used to. The same firm Mallory Bozeman worked at, the place where she was last seen."

"I'm familiar with the company." Mr. Heslin held Judith's novel, studying the front pages. "They're a huge firm. They represent thousands of celebrities. Hundreds of millions in revenue."

"I know," Victoria said. "It might be nothing. Half the people who own homes on the peninsula are from the New York City area. John Stein was also living in the city. But we never rule out related pieces of information. It's all potentially significant until we're sure it isn't." She bent over and cradled her head in her hands, wishing her headache would ease up.

"You okay?" Rivera asked.

"I've been better."

"Let me get you a drink." Rivera headed into the kitchen. "Anyway, it's time for you to take more medicine."

Mr. Heslin moved to his daughter and leaned over. "You didn't tell me that one was allergic to dogs. That changes things. And here he is keeping track of when you need to take your medicine. Even I didn't think to do that."

"Dad." She shot him a look meant to quiet him. He was speaking in a lowered voice, but if he thought he was whispering, he was wrong. "Enough. You're going to make all of us very uncomfortable." She hoped Rivera hadn't overheard.

"But you don't mind me asking him to stay here, do you?" He whispered this time.

"No," she whispered back, monitoring Rivera in the kitchen. "Of course not. Where else would he stay?"

"I feel bad for him. He cares about you. It's obvious." His whisper got a bit louder as he continued.

Victoria shot her father a warning look, not wanting to discuss this with Rivera in the next room.

She didn't know what to do. Her attraction to Rivera was undeniable. And not merely a physical attraction. The ease he had with her father, the way he effortlessly fit in at the house, and how he was so willing and capable of caring for her made him seem sexier than ever. His presence was comforting in several ways.

Victoria didn't want to lead him on without knowing where things stood with Ned. She'd called Ned when she got back from the hospital and told him about the car crash. He'd sounded so worried, even though both she and Alex were going to be okay.

I dislike being torn between the two of them.

She wanted them both in her life.

Her father's comments on the boat had forced her to think about it. And like he said, if she didn't decide soon, she might not have a choice.

Rivera returned with her drink and a bottle of prescription pain pills. He picked up his computer again and sat down near Victoria on the couch.

Victoria took a pill with a sip of water. Feeling a little anxious, she waited for Rivera to log in, again wishing she had her own FBI computer so they could get twice as much work done. Dr. Yang had told her to avoid the stimulation...but this was important. "Let's see what we can find on each of the neighbors," she said.

"Starting with Harrison Daughton." *Did I choose him first because I want to rule him out first?*

Closing her eyes, she sipped her water and listened to the soft touch of Rivera's fingers on his keyboard. She resisted the urge to ask if he had found anything yet.

Rivera cleared his throat, coughed, and cleared his throat again. "I've got a few things on Harrison Daughton IV. He owns two multi-million-dollar properties, the house here and one in Connecticut. There's no record of any employment. He's an extremely lucky man with a large inheritance...uh—"

He's just remembered his audience.

"—or he's, uh, doing something under the table. And there's no criminal record. Not so much as a parking ticket. Unfortunately, the most significant event in his life appears to be a car crash when he was a teenager. He was sixteen. And he was the driver. His sister and his parents died in the crash."

"That must be where he got his scars." Victoria scooted closer to Rivera, looking over his shoulder at images on the screen. "Wait. Stop. Go back to the last page and the picture of the little girl."

"You're not supposed to be looking at computer screens."

Ignoring Rivera's comment, she leaned closer, her shoulder touching the back of his. "There. Look. Who is that?"

Rivera enlarged the text under the image. "Harrison's sister, Katherine. From the dates—the picture was taken a few weeks before she died. She was only eleven years old. They were out celebrating her birthday when the accident occurred."

"Hold on. Keep that picture up while I find something." Victoria scooped her iPad off the table. After pressing the home screen to wake it up, she bit on her bottom lip, talking to herself. "Now where did I find it? Where was it?" Her concentration came at a price—a sharp ache behind her eyes. "I think this is it." She clicked on an article and found the image of Kristen Bozeman and the Shetland pony. Returning to Rivera, she held her iPad next to his computer screen. "Look at Kristen Bozeman before she disappeared and Katherine Daughton before she died. Don't they look eerily similar? The hair. The narrow face. The long legs. They were both very pretty girls."

Rivera touched the edge of Victoria's iPad, steadying it. "They really look alike."

"I've got to see this." Mr. Heslin walked behind the couch, frowning as his eyes moved between the screens. "You're right. They could be twins. Except for that birthmark, it would be hard to tell them apart."

"Find out about the rest of Harrison's family." Victoria closed her eyes briefly and rubbed her temples, waiting for the pain pills to kick in. "He has at least one other sister and a niece."

After a few minutes, Rivera leaned back from his screen. "I'm not finding any other family members. Harrison's entire family died in the car accident. He was the sole heir of his family's fortunes."

"But—that's not possible." Victoria rubbed the base of her neck. "Harrison told me his sister was sick. He helps with his niece. And Phoebe has seen the niece with him. If his only sibling died in a car crash when she was eleven, how could he have a sister and a niece?"

"There are other possibilities." Mr. Heslin leaned against the back of the couch. "He might have married. The sister he mentioned might be a sister-in-law."

"Hmm. Let me check." Rivera opened a new database and searched for information.

Victoria waited impatiently, petting her dogs with her eyes closed until Rivera said, "There are no records of a marriage on file for him."

"Then who is the niece?" Mr. Heslin asked. "Could it be Kristen? Was he pretending Kristen was his niece? Who would do that?"

Victoria kneaded her fingers and made one of them crack. "Kidnappers do it all the time. They pretend the person they kidnapped is a family member."

"But Kristen isn't a child anymore," Mr. Heslin said. "I mean, she wasn't a child when she died."

"Right." Victoria tapped her foot on the floor. They were at least moving forward with a hypothesis—however vague—the notion of a relationship between Harrison and Kristen. Now they needed to test the idea until they could prove or disprove it. "Rivera, I need you to call Phoebe and see if she can give you a description for the woman she saw in Harrison's SUV."

Rivera tilted his head to the side. "Wouldn't she respond better to questions from someone she knows?"

"She's someone I'd rather not talk to," Victoria said. "She sends my blood pressure through the roof. Tell her you're with the FBI and don't mention me or my family. Ask her to give you a description of the woman she saw. The approximate age. Anything she can remember to rule out or confirm Kristen as Harrison's companion."

Rivera called Phoebe and put his phone on speaker. "Miss McPharland, this is Agent Rivera of the FBI."

"What do you want?" Phoebe came across curt and dismissive. "Do I have to talk to you?"

"It will be easier for you than having to report to one of our offices," Rivera said. "This should only take a few minutes of our time."

Phoebe sighed loudly. "What did you say your name was?"

"Agent Dante Rivera from the FBI's D.C offices."

"Hold on, Agent Rivera. I'm looking you up on the internet."

While they waited for Phoebe, Rivera went back to searching one of the FBI's databases on his laptop.

"Oh." Phoebe's voice took on a new, focused tone. "Dante Rivera. Is this you? This picture in the navy suit. Because if it is, you're hotter than any FBI agent I've ever seen."

Mr. Heslin shook his head and lifted his eyes to the ceiling.

"If you're on the FBI's home page and the picture has my name below it, then you're looking at me," Rivera answered, staring at something on his screen.

"Then I'd be more than happy to help you with whatever it is you may need." Phoebe's attitude had completely changed from arrogant and hostile to overly flirtatious.

Victoria moved her lips in silence. "I told you." She hadn't actually warned him, but it had to be clear to all of them that Rivera would get more out of Phoebe than Victoria might have.

"I appreciate your offer to help, ma'am. I have some questions for you about Harrison Daughton, who lives near your mother's lake house."

"Hmm. Agent Rivera, you know a lot about me already, don't you? Is it possible you know what I'm wearing right now, or is that something you'd like me to tell you?" She laughed, deep and throaty. "Now why are you asking me about Harrison?"

"I'm asking as part of an ongoing investigation," Rivera said. "That's all I can tell you."

"Listen, Agent Rivera," she said, her voice enticing, "I'm all for giving, as long as the person I'm with is giving it as good."

Mr. Heslin placed his hands over his eyes and shook his head again.

Rivera seemed unphased. "Have you ever seen Harrison Daughton entering or leaving the Lake Lucinda area with a female in his vehicle?"

"You want to get right to the questions, do you? Oh, you're no fun, Agent. I understand your questions pertain to the recent deaths on the peninsula and whoever killed those poor souls. So, now Harrison is the person of interest and you think I might have relevant information."

"We'd like to rule out as many people as possible. Have you seen him with a female in his vehicle?" Rivera repeated.

"I have. A few times. I saw him with a woman in his Range Rover the day after Christmas. Harrison wasn't a priest, apparently, but neither was he much of a partier. If you want my opinion, he's simply too nice and too boring to have killed anyone."

"Ask Phoebe to describe her," Victoria mouthed.

Rivera nodded. "Can you describe the woman he was with?"

Phoebe sighed and seemed to give up on the game she was trying to play, as if she suddenly realized she had other things to do and wanted to get off the phone. "She was Caucasian, age twenty to thirty—approximately, had brown hair—I think. Harrison was with the same woman every time—I'm pretty sure. Now if you want to hear where I might direct my searching if I were you, I'd start with the Heslin family—"

Mr. Heslin jumped up, winced, and pressed his hand against his hip. "That little—" he hissed. "Of all the—"

Victoria shook her head, which sparked a flash of nausea.

Right when I thought Phoebe couldn't get any worse, she did.

"Thank you for your time." Rivera ended the call, but not before anger disturbed his otherwise calm expression.

"It's not much to go on." Victoria inhaled to compose herself, "But it leaves open the possibility that Harrison's companion was Kristen."

Rivera was still looking at his computer screen.

"What is it?" Victoria asked. "You found something else, didn't you?"

"Yes." Rivera's voice rose and his irritated eyes lit up. "I was searching the history of D&S Public Relations. Get this— D&S stands for Daughton & Son. The firm was founded by Edward Daughton. Harrison's grandfather. Harrison inherited the company after his father's death and didn't sell it until a few years ago."

Victoria pressed her hands against her cheeks, thinking. "Harrison might have been at the firm's NY office when Mallory Bozeman was working there. He might have seen Kristen with her mother."

"So, where is Kristen's mother now?" Mr. Heslin asked. "Where have either of them been all these years?"

No one answered. A few seconds passed. Mr. Heslin stood and walked out of the family room.

Victoria got off the couch, dropping her blanket onto the seat behind her. She paced in front of the fireplace, then stopped in front of Rivera. "Get Harrison's address in Connecticut. Then call his neighbors. We need to find out who else knows about Kristen."

"I think you forgot to say please," Mr. Heslin called from the kitchen.

"Please. I'd do it myself if I had my laptop—"

"And if you didn't have a concussion," Rivera finished. "And after this, you should get some sleep."

A few minutes later, the room was quiet when Rivera connected with Gladys Herman, the elderly woman who lived next to Harrison's estate in Connecticut. After Rivera introduced himself as a federal agent, provided his identification number, and apologized for the late hour, he put the phone on speaker so they could all hear what Gladys had to say.

"Harrison is a private man and a wonderful neighbor." Gladys spoke with a relaxed affectation that came from having lots of money and no worries. She also seemed to have no reservations about sharing information over the phone with a stranger. "He's the best kind of neighbor. Rarely is he around, and he keeps his property well maintained. We use the same yard service as he does, weekly throughout the year."

"Have you ever seen him with anyone else?" Rivera asked. "A woman? Someone who might be his niece?"

"As I said, he's hardly ever around, and my husband and I travel abroad often, but I have seen his niece here and there over the years. He's been helping his sister with her child for as long as I can remember."

Victoria felt a chill and a strange fluttery sensation when Gladys mentioned Harrison's sister and niece.

"Can you describe her?" Rivera asked. "What she looks like now?"

251

"I can try. For one, she's no longer a child, she's a young woman. I'd say she's a little taller than average. Long legs. Straight brown hair. A lovely young lady. Beautiful, really. Quite shy. Never speaks unless spoken to. And then she's exceptionally polite."

Rivera slid a tissue from his pocket and quickly blew his nose. "Have you ever met Harrison's sister? The mother of the niece he cares for."

"Now that you mention it, no. I don't think I have. Not that I can recall. Harrison would be the one picking up his niece and bringing her to his house. His sister is quite ill."

"Did he tell you what sort of sickness his sister has?"

"No. Something serious. It's never come up and I've never asked. It's none of my business. Now, I don't want to give you the impression that Harrison and I are well acquainted. We've spoken a handful of times. He gave me a lift once when I was in a bind. I don't take taxis or Ubers. Not at my age. I see Harrison in passing, occasionally, if he drives past my house when I'm in the front gardens."

"You said he picks his niece up from his sister's house. Do you know where she lives?"

Gladys inhaled deeply, loud enough for Victoria to hear. "I believe somewhere in West Virginia. In the mountains. Though I'm not sure why West Virginia comes to mind. Harrison's license plates are from there. Perhaps I've simply imagined he's from there and goes back to help his sister out. Sometimes he's gone for weeks, possibly months at a time. So very kind of him, don't you agree? He's a good man. I imagine he wouldn't still be single at his age if he didn't have his sister to take care of and her daughter to help raise. Few women will put up with another woman coming first."

Listening to Gladys talk about the nonexistent sister made Victoria feel like she was living in a Twilight Zone episode. She let her mouth fall open to express her disbelief. Her father's expression returned the sentiment.

"Is Harrison all right?" Gladys asked. "Has something happened to him?"

"He's all right, and I'd appreciate if you don't tell him we spoke." Rivera thanked Gladys and said goodbye.

"This is creeping me out." Victoria began chewing on her bottom lip but stopped herself. "Are we sure there's no half-sister or step sister out there?"

"Sure as I can be." Rivera slid his fingers over his laptop's touchpad. "I searched for birth records under his parents' names. Unless the birth was off record or the parents weren't listed—"

"Haven't we all seen and heard enough to convince us Harrison knew Kristen?" Mr. Heslin said. "Which makes him a liar at best. Although I think his offenses extend far beyond. So, what next? When do we call Sheriff Hayes?"

"Not yet," Victoria answered. "I want this information wrapped up in a bow, or close to it, before we hand it over to the local authorities. After what we've found out here tonight, it will be soon. Very soon."

Her father covered a yawn with his hand. "I'm going to sleep. After the scare last night, I'm exhausted. You know where the guest room is, Rivera. Make sure my daughter isn't up all night. Please." He walked over to Victoria and kissed the top of her head. "I love you, darling."

"I love you, too, Dad. I'll go to bed soon. I promise."

"And until then, you're in capable hands," he said before leaving the room.

From the corner of the first floor, the master bedroom door clicked closed.

They were alone.

Rivera set his laptop on the coffee table. "You should probably go to sleep, too." He stood and stretched his arms forward. "You need the rest."

She stared at Rivera, her pulse quickening. There was something special about him being at her father's house.

She took a few steps toward him, then stopped. Their eyes locked.

He'd made his feelings known, in a subtle way. He wouldn't make the first move.

Slowly, she crossed the few yards separating them.

"Would you mind if I did this?" she asked as she placed her hands on his shoulders, their faces only inches apart.

"I think you know the answer," he whispered.

They leaned towards each other.

His lips pressed gently against her own.

Chapter 30

Victoria woke up alone, her flannel pajama bottoms and soft T-shirt twisted around her body. Her mind replayed the scene from last night. They'd only kissed. She'd wanted more but Rivera was concerned about her concussion and the pain pills she was taking. Said he didn't want Victoria or her family to think he came all the way there to take advantage of her. Now, in the light of morning, those kisses seemed like a big deal. It meant they had finally crossed the line keeping them safely in the realm of just being colleagues.

What will it be like seeing Rivera now?

Guess I'm about to find out.

The time on her phone said 9:45.

Victoria did a double take, having trouble believing she had slept so late.

The dogs were lying around. No whining. No pleading eyes.

"Why are you all so content when your normal breakfast time came and went hours ago?"

Victoria intended to hurry downstairs and feed the dogs, but one look in the mirror changed those plans.

I look terrible and every muscle and bone in my body aches

Her black eye and the bruises on her forehead had darkened overnight. She shook out her hands, realizing she'd skipped her physical therapy exercises the last three days.

After showering, she put on a few touches of makeup. Nothing special, no different than if she was going to work. She didn't want Rivera to think everything about her was suddenly going to change.

Don't let this be weird.

Her skin still warm from the shower, she stopped at the top of the stairs and looked down.

The house was silent.

Rivera sat in the breakfast nook by the windows, his back to the stairs. Knowing him as she did, he'd probably already gone out for a run and showered. He wore jeans and a crisp, white shirt with his sleeves pushed to his elbows. His laptop was open in front of him, but his gaze focused through the back windows toward the lake. He looked strong and fresh, the opposite of how she felt.

She walked down the stairs with one arm on the railing and one across her waist. Her dogs barreled down around her.

Rivera swiveled in his seat and smiled up at her.

She smoothed strands of her damp hair over one ear and cleared her throat. "Good morning."

"Good morning. You have great coffee here." He held up a mug that said, *if my greyhound can't come with me, I'm not going.* Victoria had bought the mug for her mother.

Stopping a few yards away, she arched her brows and gave him a slight smile. His eyes were a little red and irritated.

A dash of dark movement out the window caught her attention. Oscar trotted across the patio, tossing his head and swirling his tail.

"The donkeys are in a good mood, I think." Rivera took a sip from his mug. "How are *you* feeling?"

"Actually, I'm stiffer and sorer than I was yesterday." She stopped in the middle of the room and stretched her arms overhead, suddenly self-conscious.

Should I go over and give him a kiss?

If I have to ask myself first, the answer is probably no. I want it to be natural.

She lowered her arms back to her sides and then crossed them over her chest. "My head isn't killing me anymore. It's already down to an annoying but normal headache. So...that's a good thing. Did you sleep well?"

"Yes. The guest room bed might be the most comfortable one I've ever used."

"You have my mother to thank. All the beds in this house are amazing. And dogs haven't been in the guest room in years, so hopefully your allergies got a break." Victoria scanned the countertops for evidence anyone else was around. "Did my father go out?"

Rivera took a folded tissue from his pocket. "He fed your animals and then went to the hospital to bring your brother home."

Her dogs sprawled over the couches and chairs. Sansa, Arya, and Oscar peeked out from their shelter, munching on hay.

"Oh. I guess that explains how I could sleep so late." She was glad her family wasn't around to witness these initial interactions with Rivera. They needed time to figure out how to act around each other without her father and brother wondering why things were a little different. Or worse, knowing why and possibly gloating or grinning.

"How did my father get to the hospital? We only had my car here and now that's gone. Alex had a rental but...it's a long story."

"He has my car. And I'm here to watch over you."

"Oh." Wishing she wore a belt; she gently tugged her pants up so they didn't slide any further over her hips. "Thanks for letting him use your car."

Crap, this is awkward. Although not for him, he seems totally relaxed.

"Of course. My pleasure."

She averted her gaze to the presentation on his computer. "What are you working on?"

"Murphy asked me to give a training to the rookies. It's on effective interview and questioning techniques."

"Maybe I can help you with it, if you want." She went to get a mug from the kitchen. "Oh, and, unfortunately, I have to buy a new SUV to get home. I better call my insurance company today."

"Can I help? You're supposed to be resting."

"I got a lot of sleep. I'm good." She grabbed a mug, stuck it under the coffee machine, and pressed the button for the strongest brew. "But thanks. I really appreciate you being here."

I wish I didn't feel guilty.

It occurred to her that Rivera had shown up without actually being invited, after she specifically told him not to come. What if Ned did the same? What if he looked up her address and drove to the mountains, worried after hearing about the accident, and surprised them all with a knock at the door? With all that had gone wrong at Lake Lucinda, she should be prepared for the unexpected. An unannounced visit from Ned would be humiliating for all of them. The thought of it made her stomach turn.

We're not officially dating. Never once has there been any talk of a commitment.

And yet, Victoria felt like a scoundrel. The feeling was ruining any happiness she might have otherwise experienced.

I should call Ned and make sure he doesn't come. Then, when I understand what's going on with Rivera, I can communicate things in a way where no one gets hurt or embarrassed. If that's even possible. She laughed to herself. *Maybe I'm giving myself way too much credit, and neither of them cares what I do.*

She placed a bagel in the toaster oven and then rolled her neck forward, working out the kinks across her shoulders.

"Are you ready to get back to work on the investigation?" Rivera asked. "The case that isn't ours but sure feels like it is now."

"Yes. Absolutely." The glowing rods inside the toaster oven held her attention. "It's already gone on too long and I don't want to stand by and see who dies next."

Getting to work was something she was sure of, which was nice compared to the uncertain feelings her personal life was cultivating. Once they understood what was happening at Lake Lucinda, she could go back to work. Alex could go back to Colorado. Their father could go home.

And then what?

Victoria ate mostly in silence, barely tasting her bagel and aware of Rivera looking out the window but also watching her. His relaxed expression indicated he was comfortable with everything, but wouldn't bring it up unless she did. And she was grateful for that.

A knock came from the front of the house.

Victoria felt instantly queasy. The tingle and rush of warmth which accompanied a spike in adrenaline followed, as if she was a criminal getting caught for shoplifting.

For a secluded place with barely anyone around, there sure are a lot of visitors.

Please, please don't let it be Ned.

Rivera set his mug down. "I'll get it. Try to finish your breakfast. You need it."

"No, I'll, uh..."

"Sit. Rest," he said, walking to the door.

She wasn't hungry enough to finish her bagel before, and she definitely wasn't hungry enough now. She closed her eyes, feeling horribly ill.

"It's Sheriff Hayes," Rivera called from the front door.

Relief washed over her. She got up, pulling her pants up an inch again.

Rivera opened the door. "Sean. Hey. Nice to see you." Every word sounded sincere.

Victoria edged into the doorway beside Rivera. She hadn't seen the sheriff since he found her vehicle on the side of the mountain. She hadn't actually seen him then either, since she remembered nothing of the rescue. He stood in the sunshine now, rubbing his eyes, looking as if he'd been up all night. "We're over at the Wilson place," he said. "Searching his property again." Except for his slight southern twang, he didn't sound like the sheriff she knew. Something was different about his tone. The defensive edge was gone. He sounded friendly.

Two sheriff's department vehicles were parked on the street. The gate across George's driveway was wide open.

To the side of the porch, the bowl of food for the foxes was still full.

The sheriff checked her over. His expression reminded her of how beat-up she looked.

Victoria squared her shoulders. Thinking about the car crash fueled a surge of anger.

"Sorry about having to search your place." The sheriff reached into his coat pocket and took out the bag he'd used to collect evidence. He held it up for Victoria. "I came to return this. That's quite a diamond ring in there."

"I haven't seen it yet." Victoria took it from him. "Thanks for bringing it back."

"You're welcome. George had keys to most of the homes around here, including yours. They're all labeled. We'll give yours back later. I've also got an update for you."

An update? This is quite the change in attitude.

Rivera opened the door wider. "You look like you could use a cup of coffee. Come on in and sit down."

Rivera seemed to have formed a cordial and professional working relationship with the sheriff while Victoria was in the hospital. She wasn't sure how she felt about it. The sheriff might still be the person who had framed Alex. Maybe he found their SUV on the side of the mountain before anyone else did because he was the one who ran them off the road. Bottom line—even though Harrison seemed guilty of something—she still didn't trust the sheriff. But she couldn't expect cooperation from the local authorities if she and the sheriff weren't getting along. She had to hand it to Rivera; he was being smart about the situation.

"Yes, please come in." She suppressed the urge to add, *Lead the way, you already know your way around the house, don't you?*

261

The sheriff accepted the invitation, took his hat off, and trudged inside. "How is Alex?"

"He stayed an extra night in the hospital, but he'll be home soon. My father is picking him up now."

The sheriff walked alongside Rivera to the kitchen. "We found the truck that ran you off the road. It belongs to a trucking company. It was returned with a dent in front that matches the damage to your car and your paint."

"Who drove it?" Rivera asked, ending his question with a few sniffs.

"I'm still workin' on that. One 'a the employees got paid to do it, is what I think. Dozens of 'em had access to the keys. And everyone on this peninsula has the kind of money to pay others to do their dirty work. No offense, but that's the truth."

"This time you know it wasn't us," Victoria said. "We're one household you can rule out."

"Send me the list of employees, anyone who has access to those trucks." Rivera started the coffee machine. "If any of them recently deposited extra cash into their accounts, anything like that, we'll find out. It's what we do. If you get a confession, that information could help back it up."

"Okay. I appreciate that." Hayes leaned against the counter and watched the coffee brewing. "Someone from our department is interviewing employees right now. I'll have her send you the list."

Victoria was glad to see the sheriff had come around and accepted their help. She wasn't sure what changed things.

"Milk or sugar?" Rivera asked the sheriff.

"Black works for me."

Victoria stared at Rivera, asking him a question with her eyes.

Is it time to tell the sheriff everything we've learned?

Rivera nodded.

"We found some new information," Victoria said. "About Harrison Daughton, the man who lives in Lucinda Lee's former estate."

The sheriff frowned. "The man you were with on New Year's Eve."

Out of the corner of her eye, she saw Rivera's hand tighten on the handle of the mug.

"I wasn't exactly *with* him," she explained for Rivera's benefit. "He heard me yelling for my donkey"—*why does it sound so ridiculous when I say it out loud?*—"and came out to see what was going on. Or so he said. Maybe he was already out there. The next day, he acted concerned about me. Said he didn't realize I was an agent. Now I'm not sure if he was telling the truth or not." Victoria told the sheriff what they knew. "If he's involved with Kristen and her death—which he definitely is, although I'm not sure how—he might have been playing me for information and framing Alex all along."

The sheriff set his hat on the quartz counter and accepted the mug from Rivera. "Has he been here to see you or ask about you since the crash?"

"No." Victoria leaned her elbows against the other side of the kitchen island. "I haven't seen him since before the accident."

"I'll call for back up and then go talk to him." He took a sip of the coffee. "Wow, this is good."

"You don't need back up," Victoria said. "You've got us."

"I don't think you're in any shape to be chasing down killers right now." The sheriff took another drink of his coffee. "And no offense, but I noticed you're right-handed and missing half your trigger finger. Can you handle a gun with that hand?"

263

"I can shoot well with both hands."

"I'll go with you." Rivera straightened and tapped the counter with his fist. He looked ready to march out the door, but deferred to Sheriff Hayes for a response.

"Yeah. All right." The sheriff set his mug down and rubbed his beard. "But I'll do the talking."

Rivera had a way about him and had somehow brought the sheriff around. Or maybe the sheriff was sexist and the only thing Rivera had done right was being born male. In any case, Sheriff Hayes was right about one thing—she wasn't one hundred percent at the moment, although she hadn't felt too bad with Rivera last night. A shiver ran through her just thinking about his hands moving over her body.

"Good luck," she said. "And remember, if he is guilty, he's one heck of a good liar."

Chapter 31

Victoria inhaled the cool mountain air in the backyard. If time outside at the lake didn't leave her somewhat refreshed, nothing would. With dark sunglasses and a cap to shield her eyes, the daylight didn't bother her.

She threw a stuffed porcupine toy toward the woods. Her dogs raced after it, chunks of dirt and grass flying out behind them. The animals had really messed up the yard in the past few days. It had been uniformly greenish when they arrived, as healthy as a yard could be in December. Now it looked like a minor battle had occurred there. The rain had softened the soil, making it easier for their hooves and paws to tear it up. Thank goodness her father wouldn't care. At least not much. He'd have it replanted and in great shape by the time he returned, whenever that might be. And he'd already had the fence repaired.

Voices came from the driveway, growing closer. Rivera and the sheriff. The side gate clicked open.

"That didn't take long." Victoria threw the porcupine one last time and walked to meet them.

"Harrison wasn't there." Rivera walked toward her. "No car in his garage either. And he's not answering his phone. He seems to have disappeared right after your *accident*."

Victoria frowned. "We know he's guilty of something, like not telling us what he knew about Kristen. But he might not be a criminal. I sure hope he didn't disappear the same way George did."

The sheriff had stopped outside the fence, one hand resting on top of the gate. "I'm going back to my office. I'll contact the police in Connecticut and have them visit his home there."

"Let us know if we can help." The dogs surrounded Rivera, wagging their tails and sniffing at his clothes. "If Harrison kidnapped Kristen and took her across state lines, the FBI has jurisdiction."

"Sounds good." The sheriff lifted and lowered the brim of his hat, his way of saying goodbye. "I'll be in touch this afternoon."

Victoria waved to the sheriff. Once he was out of sight, she said, "Care for a little adventure, Agent?"

Rivera cocked his head. "What do you have in mind?"

Tucking her hair behind her ear, she walked toward the back patio, scanning the ground. "I want to see what's inside Harrison's house."

Rivera went with her. "The sheriff can get a warrant."

She stopped walking, tore a dog waste bag off the roll from her pocket, and slipped her hand inside. "I'm glad you and the sheriff seemed to hit it off. I'm glad he's cooperating. Believe me, this is a big turnaround with his attitude from before we got in a car accident. But I still don't completely trust him. If he gets a warrant, he'll be the one doing the investigating. If we get it, he'll want to come with us." She crouched down and picked up a small mess from one of the dogs. "We should go alone. We'll wait until it gets dark, since I have no idea who else on the peninsula is watching us. And we'll need a little help from Sam with the security system because I'm sure Harrison has a good one."

As if he hadn't heard a word she said, Rivera stared at the blue bag she was tying into a knot. "This is part of life with dogs, huh?"

"You mean this?" She held the bag up.

He scrunched his nose and leaned away.

"You betcha. A big part of life with dogs. So, what about my plan?"

"Sounds like you've already decided we're doing this. I can go alone because—"

"Seriously?" Still standing a few feet away from him, she dropped the waste bag on the ground and took his hands in hers.

Rivera slid them out of her grasp and stepped back. "I don't think so." He laughed. "Not until you wash your hands."

She laughed and lifted her arms. "Okay, okay. Anyway, I was worried people would start questioning my ability to do my job after the plane crash. But I didn't think that would come from you. So, I can't tell if you're worried about my psychological state, or if you think I won't have your back, or if it's about what happened with us last night. I'm still an agent and I haven't forgotten how to do my job."

"Aside from the plane ordeal, you just got out of the hospital after crashing over the side of a mountain and you look like you went ten rounds...*if* we're adding up the valid reasons for concern."

"You trust me, don't you?"

He moved back to her, closing the distance between them. "I do. You know I do. In fact, so much that I'm telling you now, I brought an extra gun here with me."

She widened her eyes. "You brought an extra gun but not my laptop?"

"Hey. You didn't ask."

She laughed and tugged the front of her cap, pulling it down a bit. "I'm joking. But you did bring an extra weapon?"

"Yes. Is there a shooting range around here?"

Arya ambled toward Rivera and snorted, flicking her long ears forward and back.

"Why?" Victoria studied her colleague. "You think I need practice?"

"Yes. I won't let your drive put you in harm's way before you're ready. Doing some target practice seems like a fair compromise."

Arya came closer and stretched out her neck, braying at Rivera and exposing her long, brownish teeth.

Victoria nodded, amused by the donkey's curious behavior. "There might not be a shooting range, but there are a few hundred acres of woods where hunting is allowed. We can set up targets. Let's go. It will be good for me. And after I prove myself, we head to Harrison's place as soon as it gets dark."

Victoria was nervous about this test. All of her physical therapy had been with the goal of being able to handle a weapon. Now she'd have to find out for sure how well it had worked.

▼▲▼

As soon as the sun was down, the agents headed to Harrison's house.

Clouds obscured the moonlight and darkness enveloped the peninsula. Wearing black clothing, they blended in.

Victoria appreciated the weight of Rivera's gun against her hip. She pulled the waistline of her coat down to make sure the gun was covered.

To anyone who had inquired, she'd been adamant about retaining her ability to accurately use a weapon—and after an hour of target practice in the woods, any lingering concerns were vanquished.

"What type of vehicle does Harrison drive?" Rivera asked.

"He has a silver Range Rover. A new model."

"Range Rovers are quiet. Even with a diesel engine."

"Then let's be really quick."

Victoria led Rivera through the woods separating Harrison's home from the one owned by the Steeler's player. "When I played here as a kid, there was a gate somewhere nearby leading into the yard."

"So, you've been breaking and entering since you were a kid?"

"I guess I have. Thanks to Phoebe's dares. The gate wasn't locked, so not actually breaking. Just entering. Trespassing anyway."

There wasn't much of a path anymore, the woods were thicker, but Victoria pushed through, moving branches aside, straight toward Harrison's fence.

"We don't have to do any breaking tonight either." Rivera moved quietly behind her. "George had the code to Harrison's house."

"The sheriff gave it to you?"

"Not really. But I got it."

"Good. I won't ask how. So, we didn't need Sam to get involved?" She turned to look at Rivera but without shining her light on him, she couldn't see his face in the darkness.

"No, it's better if Sam shuts the security system down. Better to have it look like the whole system had a glitch and went off temporarily then to have a record of Harrison's code being entered at a specific time. But if Sam can't get it shut down, we have a backup plan."

"Which we shouldn't need because Sam can pretty much do anything," she said as they reached the fence. Victoria pressed the home button on her phone. "Flashlight on."

With the small light, they crept along the perimeter searching for the gate.

"Here it is." Rivera handed Victoria a pair of gloves and then pulled on a pair of his own. "It's got a padlock. The owners must have gotten wise to you little hooligans sneaking in." Rivera held the heavy lock. "Not a problem for us—because FBI trespassers come equipped with the proper tools."

Victoria stretched the gloves over her hands. She could tell he was grinning. "The more you joke, the sketchier my idea seems."

"It's not sketchy. Clause 12.1.58 of the FBI field manual states that with adequate probable cause an agent may use reasonable means to enter suspicious locations."

"You can recite the clause number? You just made that up, didn't you?"

Rivera shrugged. "I'm not a lawyer so I can't say what's a reasonable suspicion, but I'd say we have more than enough to justify it. Can you shine your light here so I can find the right tool?"

Alert for an approaching vehicle, Victoria held her light steady in front of Rivera while he made quick work of dismantling the lock.

Inside Harrison's backyard, they hurried straight to the guest house. The shades were drawn and the house was dark inside. Another heavy padlock hung from the back door.

"If there ever was a place to hide someone or something away—this place is it,'" Victoria whispered. She waited in the darkness at the side of the guesthouse, keeping watch again while Rivera dealt with the second padlock. Strangely anxious, she rested her hand on the gun Rivera had given her.

Rivera signaled he was ready. The padlock and the door's internal lock were open.

The agents went in. There was no alarm system. The inside of the residence smelled musty. They kept the lights off and their flashlight beams low.

"Don't touch anything," Victoria said. "There's a layer of thick dust everywhere."

The rooms were empty. No furniture. Nothing inside the kitchen cabinets. The fridge was unplugged. Pieces of cardboard held the doors slightly open, exactly as Mr. Heslin had done with the extra fridge in the lake house garage to keep mold from growing inside.

Victoria wasn't sure what she expected to find—Kristen's body in a freezer? Evidence the sheriff and Harrison and Judith were all part of some strange conspiracy? Harrison slumped over his desk with a suicide note next to him?

"Don't be disappointed yet," Rivera said. "We still have the main house and the garages to search."

"Now you're reading my mind?"

In silence, they locked the guest house back up and crept along the side of a large hedge to the main house and a side door with another simple lock. In less than a minute, Rivera had it open.

This was the moment of truth.

Let's hope Sam succeeded in disabling the security system.

They hurried in, closing the door gently behind them.

Victoria held still, her back against an interior wall, bracing for any sign of a functioning alarm. Silently, she counted to ten. "I think we're good."

They peered into a large pantry. A few boxes and cans sat on the wall-to-wall shelves. Not a lot of supplies, but what Victoria expected of a bachelor's second home. In the renovated kitchen, the fridge was running and various condiments lined the shelves, but it was empty of all perishables. A new garbage bag covered the inside of the trashcan below the sink.

"I hope he didn't take every bit of incriminating evidence with him," she said, moving through the first floor, shining her light into the corners and shelves, over sparsely furnished, tidy rooms.

In the master bedroom, Victoria crouched and looked under the bed. Nothing but small dust bunnies. The bathroom was beautiful, but there was nothing unusual there.

Rivera moved his light around the contemporary walk-in closet. Men's clothing hung from the rods and sat folded on the shelves, filling only a small fraction of the space. "Nothing to see here either, but we're just getting started. Plenty of places to hide secrets and skeletons in this big house."

"If we get caught..." she whispered.

"We're not going to." Rivera headed toward the stairs. "And I told you...clause 5.4.69."

She chuckled. "The clause is in a few different places in the manual, huh? Not sure if Murphy will care much about the supposed clause since he told me I couldn't work this case." She headed for another door. "Over here."

Inside the four-car garage, a freezer chest sat in one corner. Victoria rushed to it. "No lock." Heart beating fast, she lifted the lid and peered inside.

A few packages of meat with grocery store labels lined the bottom. A box of frozen pizzas.

She frowned, biting down on her bottom lip. "I was really hoping..."

"Don't worry. If there's something to find, we're finding it."

She checked her phone. "We've already been here five minutes."

"Come on." Rivera hurried back inside and to the center staircase. Together, they crept up.

The old stairs creaked under every step.

Victoria guided her flashlight around the first bedroom at the top of the landing. It wasn't as dusty as the guest house, but if Harrison employed a cleaning company, they hadn't been to his home in months. The bed was loosely made. The dresser top was clear. In the attached bathroom, a spiderweb crossed from the wall to the shower head and small bug carcasses littered the tub.

The next bedroom was similar. And the next as well. Victoria shook her head, frustrated because the meager contents of the home were about as standard and unexciting as they could get.

What am I hoping to find?

Down the hall from the other bedrooms, with the best upstairs view of the lake, Victoria entered a fully furnished room. Against one wall, a queen bed held only a mattress but no bedding. An armchair sat in one corner. A desk and a desk chair against another wall. The door to the walk-in closet was open, and the interior was bare.

Cardboard moving boxes sealed with tape sat together in the middle of the room. One said *Clothes*. One said *Shoes*. The largest box said *Books*.

Victoria sat on the floor and Rivera crouched next to her. She opened the box labeled books as Rivera kept his flashlight beam on the contents. It contained paperback novels, the type of mystery thrillers Victoria devoured when she was younger, the ones found not only at book stores but on the shelves at grocery stores, pharmacies, and airport kiosks—Koontz, Patterson, King, McPharland.

"I'll be right back." Rivera stood. "I'm going to the front to make sure no one is coming."

Shining her light on the box, she lifted several books out and placed them on the floor. A paperback she recognized stared up at her—one of Judith's first novels. Victoria opened the cover. Judith's autograph in sprawling cursive covered the page. Only her signature and nothing more.

Victoria squinted toward the dark doorway, unnerved by the soft creaks and groans caused by movement on the old wooden floors.

It's only Rivera walking to the front of the house, isn't it?

As she set Judith's novel down, a bookmark fell to the floor. A cracked piece of yellow, laminated paper with typed lines. The laminate in one corner was peeling back and the plastic parts were cloudy with age. Across the top, bold and underlined, were the words *Stay Safe*.

She attempted to pick the bookmark up, instinctively pinching it with the tip of her index finger that no longer existed. Readjusting her grip, she lifted it by the bottom corner and moved her phone light over it.

Below the *Stay Safe* header were four numbered points.

1. Don't talk to anyone.
2. Don't tell anyone your real name.

3. Don't trust anyone or you will end up dead like your mother.

4. They won't stop searching for you.

Victoria read through the list again, then sprung up at the sound of footsteps near the door.

"I'm back," Rivera whispered.

She held the bookmark out for him to read.

He let out a short, quiet whistle. "Good work, Agent Heslin."

Victoria took a picture of the bookmark before pocketing it. She stacked the novels back inside the box and carefully reapplied the tape.

"I've got a printing kit in my car," Rivera said. "Let's see if we can't get prints off that bookmark to match the ones the sheriff took from Kristen."

They hurried out the same way they had come in. Rivera relocked the back door and padlock and called Sam to turn Harrison's security system back on.

The roads were dark and empty as the agents walked back to the Heslins' house. The wind screeched through the trees. Victoria patted her coat pocket, feeling the outline of the bookmark under the fabric. She couldn't wait to test it for Kristen's prints.

"What are you thinking now?" Rivera asked.

Words from the bookmark repeated themselves in her head: *Stay safe. They won't stop searching for you.*

"Assuming it was Kristen who lived in that room, what we found explains her crooked teeth. A dentist's office might be the only place Harrison wouldn't risk taking her because he wouldn't want her dental records on file."

"That makes sense."

"And if Kristen was living with him, it's his motivation that's still unclear to me. Harrison either went above and beyond to protect Kristen's life rather than involve the police, or he's a disturbed and manipulative kidnapper who created an elaborate web of lies to keep Kristen dependent on him. If it's the latter, he's also likely a killer."

Chapter 32

With Rivera close behind her, Victoria eased the front door open.

Alex was in the kitchen eating a sandwich. "Hey." He set his sandwich down. "Dad got a platter of these for everyone, if you're hungry. It's in the fridge. There are a few with no meat."

Victoria studied her brother —his bruises, the cast on his wrist, his wrinkled shirt and disheveled hair. "How are you doing?"

"Could be worse, right? Still got both my legs and as soon as my wrist heals, I can get back to working ski patrol. I thought you had a concussion. Did it miraculously disappear or something?"

"I feel okay." Victoria rubbed her brow, where a lingering ache had settled behind her eyes. "Where's dad now?"

"In his office. And where have you been?" Alex looked from Victoria to Rivera. "Because it's super unusual for you to take a walk without your dogs."

"We took a peek inside Harrison's house." Victoria opened one of the cabinet drawers, grabbed a Ziplock bag, and slid the bookmark inside. Grinning, she set the bag down in front of Alex. "This is what we in the FBI call a clue, little brother, and it's exciting. We're hoping to get fingerprints off this. Kristen's fingerprints."

Alex read the list of bullet points. "Stay safe? Harrison was protecting her?"

"We don't know yet."

"Protecting her makes more sense with what I saw. Kristen didn't act like she'd been kidnapped or was being held hostage."

"Except...she asked you how far away the airport was," Rivera reminded Alex. "Sounds like she might have been trying to figure out a plan. And she probably wasn't sure who she could trust."

"I can't wrap my head around this. The whole situation is so way beyond bizarre." Alex ran a hand over his head and looked at his sister.

"Same here. My thoughts have been going around and around in circles trying to explain it," Victoria said. "We need some professional insight. I want to call the psychiatrist the FBI assigned to me. Dr. Monroe. She's good. I like her. I want her take on what we found."

"Good idea." Rivera opened the fridge. "I'm getting a sandwich. Would you like one?"

"No thanks, I'm good. I should have told you to make yourself right at home. Better late than never." Victoria opened her arms in a sweeping gesture. "Make yourself right at home."

"No worries. Your father already told me to." Rivera opened and closed a cabinet, opened another, and took out a small plate.

The dogs surrounded him, eyeing his sandwich. Rivera chuckled. "Guess they know who has the food."

"Yep. That's how it works. You're their new best friend until you finish eating." She grabbed a bottled water from the fridge. "Let's make the call in the dining room."

Rivera set his plate down. He pulled several tissues from his pocket in time to cover a succession of sneezes.

Victoria heard him blowing his nose as she went into the dining room. She flipped the switch, illuminating the chandelier and casting a soft light around the gorgeous space. Pulling out one of the tall dining chairs, she sat down at the marble pedestal table.

Rivera spoke from the doorway. "Did you take my sandwich? I put it on the counter a few seconds ago."

Victoria shook her head. "Oops. That was basically an open invitation to steal it. Get another one. You can't turn your back on food for a second."

He laughed. "These dogs are going to take some getting used to."

Rivera returned with another sandwich and sat down. "There's no way for us to tell who did it?"

"Are you asking about who killed Kristen? Because maybe we're getting ahead of ourselves. Until we get prints from the bookmark, we can't say with complete certainty that Kristen and Harrison knew each other."

"I mean, which of the dogs stole the food. There's no way to determine the guilty one?"

"Oh. I'm almost positive it was Izzy, the Galga, but since I didn't see it, I can't reprimand any of them." She turned to the dogs, staring right at Izzy. The pitch of her voice rose. "You did it, didn't you?" Her voice changed back to its normal tone as she swiveled back around and said, "I'm calling Dr. Monroe now…after hours or not."

"We've never had defined hours. She works for the FBI, too." Rivera picked up his sandwich and then looked down at the dogs. "Oh, no you don't, bud. This one is all mine."

After three rings, Dr. Monroe answered.

"Hi, this is Agent Victoria Heslin."

"Hello, Victoria. Is everything okay?"

"Yes. I apologize for calling you so late. I could use your help and this shouldn't take long."

Rivera's nose was running. He sniffed as he took two orange pills from his pocket, put them in his mouth, and took a swig of water.

"It's all right," the psychiatrist said. "I'm here for you when you need me. However, it might be best if we met in person."

"This isn't about me. It's about a case."

Rivera jerked his head to the side and sneezed.

"A case. Aren't you on leave right now?"

"Sort of. Dante Rivera and I are working on a local case in West Virginia." A stretch of the truth, but not a lie. "I wanted to get your insight. I'm going to put you on speaker so Rivera can hear, too."

"I'm listening."

Victoria pressed the button for speakerphone.

Rivera put his sandwich down and covered it with his hand. "Good evening, Dr. Monroe."

"Good evening. Sounds like you have a cold. Hold on. I'm going to close my door." A rustle of movement came through the phone and then a door clicked shut. "You were a profiler, Victoria. You should have a good grasp on the psychological aspects of your suspect."

"I think so, but I don't want to bias your opinion. I may have overanalyzed the situation and overlooked the simplest explanations."

"All right. I'm listening."

Victoria set her phone on the table. "Nine years ago, a single mother and her ten-year-old daughter disappeared while in New York City. There have been no signs or sightings of the mother or daughter until a few days ago. The daughter resurfaced. Here in West Virginia."

"The daughter would be eighteen now. Have you interviewed her?"

"Unfortunately, when she reappeared, she was already dead. She drowned."

"I see."

Rivera raised his sandwich to his mouth. Victoria glimpsed hives on the underside of his wrist.

"Still no trace of the mother," Victoria said, "but we believe the daughter has been living with a man who is now in his late thirties. Traveling back and forth between his secluded properties in Connecticut and West Virginia. There are no records of her being in school, none with her name or his last name or any students residing at either of his addresses. She doesn't have a license. We're in the dark about her relationship with the man. We don't know if he kidnapped her or if there was some sort of...arrangement. From what we can tell, she's had opportunities to ask for help or run away but didn't take them. She doesn't seem to have been a prisoner, exactly, but there's something odd going on. We'd like to have a better understanding before we confront the man. In case we're way off or missing something."

"I'll try to help. Of course, it's all speculation, since I haven't met these people."

Victoria told her everything and finished with the list of bullet points from the bookmark.

"Let's hypothesize that Harrison kidnapped the girl to replace his sister," Dr. Monroe said. "Taking her would be an attempt to assuage an irrevocable sense of guilt and loss. Now if that's true, he's someone with deep-seated psychological troubles and possibly a very dangerous man."

Victoria shivered, thinking about Harrison's teary eyes when he spoke of his sick sister.

"She was a child when she disappeared," Dr. Monroe continued. "A grown man can easily convince a girl she can't leave, and she's only safe with him. I'm familiar with many cases where it's happened. Now, as the girl matured, she would remind him less and less of his sister, who would remain as a perpetual child in his mind. And she would become more difficult to control, harder to keep hidden. Maybe she's noticing people and stepping out beyond the boundaries he set for her, so he can't trust her anymore."

Victoria straightened in her chair. "Kristen's visit with Alex might have been the last straw for Harrison, the thing that made him realize he couldn't keep his secret any longer."

Rivera leaned closer to the phone. "Is it possible someone *was* after her? And Harrison was trying to protect her all these years? That he loved her?"

That was the only explanation Victoria could think of that made Harrison seem okay. She wanted to believe it.

"It's possible," Dr. Monroe said. "The two of you are more equipped to answer that question than I am. And on the subject of love—most murders are crimes of passion. It's more likely he killed her *if* he loved her."

Victoria shifted in her seat as she tried to poke holes in Dr. Monroe's logic.

"This has been interesting, and I hope I've been a little helpful at least," Dr. Monroe said. "Make an appointment to see me in person. We need to talk about you. Although, it appears as of now, you're able to focus on your job well."

"I think so," Victoria said. "I'll make an appointment. Thank you so much for your time." She ended the call and looked up at Rivera.

He pulled a tissue from his pocket and wiped his nose, again. "Sounds like you want to believe Harrison was protecting her, so let's explore that possibility. Who from?"

Victoria lifted her shoulders. "Her biological father? The mob?"

"And once she died, why didn't he say he knew her?" Rivera inhaled sharply, a shallow wheezy sound.

Victoria lost her focus. *Is he having trouble breathing? Is he that sick?* "Uh—It's possible he didn't acknowledge her because he didn't want them to come after him next. That makes sense to me. Because the thing is…Harrison seemed shocked when we found George."

"Right, but wasn't he near the burial site when George was found?"

"True."

"It's all pretty strange but we've heard and seen stranger, haven't we?"

"Yes, we have." Victoria stood up. "I want to talk to Alex, see what he has to say now that we have more information. Then let's go outside for some fresh air. You need it."

Alex wasn't downstairs any longer, but her father was.

"Have you seen Alex?" she asked.

"In his room on the phone. He's talking to Minka."

"Oh." She hoped that was a good thing. "We're getting closer to the truth. I think. We've got some theories."

Victoria and Rivera alternated telling Mr. Heslin about their conversation with Dr. Monroe.

"Excellent." Her father looked pleased. "You two work well together."

"Yes, we do." Rivera's voice was hoarse. He sounded a little like Sheriff Hayes had when Victoria first met him, when his cold must have been at its peak.

"Let's go outside and sit on the patio," Victoria said.

Rubbing his eyes, Rivera followed her to the mudroom for coats.

Their case was coming together, but he was falling apart.

Chapter 33

A cold wind rattled the trees and blew a few dried leaves across the patio stones. Victoria held her hand against the crown of her head to keep her hair from blowing into her eyes.

"Ready to go back in?" Rivera asked. "I'm feeling better."

"You go ahead. I'll be there in a bit. I need to make a phone call."

"Okay." He scooped up their empty beer bottles and smiled at her before heading back inside.

Victoria pulled her thick cardigan tight around her. Trailed by a few dogs, she walked to the water where she would have more privacy. Small waves lapped against the shore, soft and methodical. An owl hooted from somewhere up in the trees.

On the dock, she brushed debris off a swivel chair and sat down.

Her dogs stared at her, not wanting to lie down on the hard boards.

A gnawing sensation had been building up inside Victoria since last night, since she and Rivera kissed, and it wouldn't let go its grasp. With only one way to ameliorate the confusion she was experiencing, she called Ned.

They chatted, Ned saying he'd just finished a surgery at the free clinic. Her mind was elsewhere, wanting to say what she needed to say, but dreading doing so. She realized Ned wasn't talking. He'd asked her something.

"Sorry, Ned—I didn't catch the last thing you said."

"I said, since you're staying longer than planned, I should come out. I can leave tomorrow morning. I don't have another doctor appointment until next week."

She swallowed hard. "Thanks, Ned. But you don't have to come all the way to the lake. Rivera is here working on the investigation, sort of."

There was silence on the other line. When it almost reached the point of being unbearable to her, Ned spoke again. "Of course. I understand." He cleared his throat. "You're on a case and…I get it. You focus on that." His cheerful tone sounded forced. "Because as soon as you solve the case, you can come home."

She winced. "Yes. And I think we're getting close to the bottom of this. In the meantime, enjoy your time off until I get back."

"I will. The clinic asked me if I could come back tomorrow. They've over scheduled their neuters—all those dogs who came from Santa."

"Oh, good. Just don't let anyone else steal you away. Don't forget, I'm still paying you."

She cringed. *Why did I say that? It came across so wrong, like I'm your boss and that's it.*

"Don't worry, I'm not going anywhere, Victoria."

He gets it, right? Or does he? Do I even get it?

"I'm sorry Ned, I'm kind of confused about everything right now."

"What?"

"The case. I'm confused because the case is on my mind."

When the call ended, Victoria sat alone, feeling worse than before she called. With a heavy sigh, she stood. "Come on, dogs. Time to go in."

Through the back windows, Rivera stood in the brightly lit family room, talking and laughing with her family.

Her father smiled as he delivered a slow, soft punch to Alex's arm, the one without the broken wrist.

This—the relaxed laughter—is what I imagined this trip would be like when we first arrived at the house. Except Minka was supposed to be here.

The dogs followed her inside as if she was the Pied Piper. She closed the door behind them. "What did I miss?"

Her father raised his beer. "Your brother has some good news to share."

Alex grinned, an expression she'd sorely missed over the past two days. "Minka has regretted the error of her ways and returned to me. Or, she accepted my groveling. Either way, we're back together."

"Sometimes groveling is what it takes," Mr. Heslin said.

"It was actually the money I spent on the ring that she was so upset about. Except she didn't know it was for the ring. I made something up, didn't think it would be a big deal, but I guess it was. I should have just told her the truth."

"I'm sorry I gave you a hard time about it, too, Alex," Mr. Heslin said. "Do you still want to marry her?"

"I never *didn't* want to marry her. I've wanted her to be my wife since our first date. She knows I have the ring now. Valentine's day is coming up. That will be a nice time for a proposal." Alex patted Victoria's shoulder. "Sorry your younger brother might tie the knot before you."

"It's great news and I'm thrilled for you. Or I will be when it happens."

Rivera was smiling despite his eyes watering again. His allergies had to be annoying him, but he hadn't complained. "As long as we're celebrating," he said, "I have some good news to share, too."

Victoria's smile disappeared. She had no idea what Rivera planned to share, and she was suddenly uncomfortable.

"Two things, actually. I talked to Murphy. An FBI team is waiting on a warrant to search Harrison's estate in Connecticut. They should have it in the morning. If Harrison is hiding anything there, they'll find it. And I also spoke with Sheriff Hayes. The prints on the bookmark are definitely a match to Kristen."

Victoria inhaled deeply and felt a wave of relief. Then she mentally replayed every conversation she'd had with Harrison, starting with meeting him at the grocery store. The man was a phenomenal liar. Unless he actually believed the things he'd said, which was even scarier because it meant he was profoundly disturbed. Either way—he was a psychological mess. There were still many unanswered questions, but confirming Kristen lived with Harrison was a big start.

"A lot of good news for one night," her father said. "Who wants to play cards?"

Alex and Rivera agreed right away, then Victoria.

They'd played five hands of poker when Alex stood up, a wide grin stretching across his face. "Read 'em and weep! Three of a kind!" He tossed his cards onto the table, displaying three queens.

The others groaned and dropped their cards.

"And that's it for me tonight." Alex stretched. "I'm going to call Minka again. There's something I forgot to tell her."

Leaving the cards on the table, Mr. Heslin stood up. "I think I'll head into my room to watch some television."

Everyone conveniently disappearing at once seemed a bit suspicious.

She and Rivera were alone again.

He stood up and went to her.

Victoria tensed, though she wasn't sure why.

Rivera gently brushed her cheek with his finger, then ran his hand slowly over her ear and down through her hair.

She melted under his soft touch.

His gaze ached with longing, yet he held back, as if he wasn't sure it was okay to cross that imaginary boundary again.

And she wasn't sure if she was ready for everything to change.

A frenzy of commotion came from the dog door.

Izzy burst inside and leaped onto the couch. She spun around in circles, stopped and made playful growling noises, then spun again.

The other dogs barked and pushed against each other to get to her. Their tails wagged like mad as they huffed and snorted.

"What's going on?" Rivera asked.

"I'm not sure. She's excited about something."

Izzy jumped from the couch. She took one bouncing stride on the ground, sending a throw rug careening across the floor, and bounded onto a leather chair, panting.

Rivera grimaced. "Victoria, do you smell that? Because even with my nose stuffed—"

"Oh, my God!" She covered her nose and mouth with her hand.

289

Izzy kept running around the room and spinning on the furniture.

Rivera looked puzzled. "What's that terrible smell? What is going on?"

"I think she got sprayed by a skunk. No, it's different. Maybe a fox. They have a strong, musky smell like—"

"Like what we're smelling?"

"I think so."

"So, what do we do?" Despite all the horrible things they had experienced, she'd never seen Rivera look so shell-shocked.

"Izzy, come here. Come." Victoria tried to catch the ecstatic dog but Izzy was so pleased with herself and the disgusting smell she now carried that she wouldn't listen. She raced around, snorting and huffing, hopping from one piece of furniture to the next. She'd riled up the other dogs. They celebrated the new fragrance with renewed energy.

"Izzy, no! Izzy, come!" The closer Victoria got, the stronger the smell. Izzy seemed to think they were all playing a game.

"I think trying to catch her is making it worse," Rivera said.

Victoria stopped chasing and threw her arms up in surrender. She and Rivera stared at each other. Her frown changed to a grin. She covered her mouth to stifle a giggle.

Rivera burst out laughing.

Her giggles quickly changed to belly-aching heaves of laughter, forcing her to bend over. She slapped her legs. Tears streamed from her eyes.

She stopped laughing suddenly. Her eyes widened. "Oh, no. I hope the donkeys didn't get sprayed, too."

As Victoria rushed to the back door, Rivera said, "So I guess this is another thing you can expect in a life with dogs?"

"Yep." And then she was laughing with Rivera again.

The all-encompassing laughter momentarily erased all her worries.

Chapter 34

The trail narrowed, forcing Victoria, Alex and Rivera to walk in single file. Victoria's dogs marched ahead of her, crammed shoulder-to-shoulder, none of them willing to concede the lead.

Alex pointed to several massive rocks rising from the side of the path ahead. "We usually get our cell service back once we pass that point. I don't know about you two, but I'm dying to learn what your FBI friends found at Harrison's estate."

"I'll call Murphy if we don't hear from them soon," Victoria said

"Good. I want to go home to Colorado as soon as I can. Not to mention that the whole lake house stinks." Alex stepped over a deep rut in the trail. He walked with a bit more caution in his step, making Victoria think he still ached from the accident, something she could relate to. Sore or not, at least they were both alive and out soaking in the fresh mountain air.

Victoria lowered herself down a steep drop on the path. "According to the internet, the scent will eventually fade."

"How long is eventually?" Alex asked.

"Um...months?" Victoria answered.

Alex snorted. "Between your cookie burning and the skunk or whatever, thank God we can leave."

"We shampooed that dog three times," Rivera said. "And used the only can of tomato sauce. Then we washed all the dog sheets and any of the furniture covers we could remove."

"Sounds like the two of you had a fun night. Unless that's your idea of fun, Rivera."

"It was a memorable night," Rivera said. "I don't think I'll ever forget it. That's for sure."

And it had been fun.

Hours of laughing and cleaning had left her and Rivera too tired to do anything other than go right to sleep. The pungent smell did not lend itself to a romantic evening. In the morning, Rivera helped her find a new SUV online. The dealer was bringing the vehicle to the lake house tomorrow, trailer hitch already attached. She'd tried to spend the rest of the day outside so Rivera wouldn't get any sicker.

A little farther past the rocks on the winding path, everyone's phones beeped with new voicemails and texts. They walked to a spot where the trail widened, then stopped to check their messages.

Rivera stared at his phone. "I've got two missed calls from Murphy."

They gathered together as Rivera called Murphy and put him on speakerphone.

"I called to tell you about the search in Connecticut," Murphy said. "Your guy, Daughton, lives on a massive, old-money type of estate. It has an actual family graveyard. Daughton's parents and sister are buried there with headstones worthy of royalty. The agents found an unmarked grave nearby containing human remains from about a decade ago."

"Whose remains?" Victoria asked. *Mallory Bozeman?*

"They might know once they run the DNA," Murphy said.

293

"What did Daughton have to say about it?" Rivera shifted his weight.

"He wasn't there," Murphy said. "There's an APB out for him. He has the resources to go anywhere, but he's piqued the FBI's interest now for sure, so we'll find him. He must have known it was only a matter of time and that we're looking for him."

Victoria leaned toward the phone in Rivera's hand. "Murphy, is there any proof someone was searching for Kristen Bozeman because they wanted her dead? Any reason to believe Harrison was her guardian angel or something like that?"

"They don't know. We'll all have to wait and see what Daughton has to say when they catch him. Listen, I have to go," Murphy said. "I have my own cases to work. You can call Jennifer Marachi in the Connecticut office for the details. She's the lead on this. I'm sure she'll want some information from you, too. They'll also be in touch with your local sheriff to get everything he has on the case. However, this isn't his investigation anymore. It's too big now. Hey, I've got to take this call. I'll get back to you."

The front of the phone changed to the home screen.

"So, I'm officially off the hook here, right? No longer a person of interest?" Alex looked back and forth between the agents. "I can go home to Colorado?"

Oliver lifted his head and straightened his ears at something in the woods.

"I should think so," Rivera said. "I'd say you are just that—in the clear. Let's call the sheriff when we get back to your house. He can officially dismiss you."

Alex scrunched up his face. "But your boss said it's not his case anymore."

Victoria opened her mouth to speak, but Rivera beat her to it. "It's good for closure."

Exactly what she was going to say.

Back on the neighborhood streets, Rivera studied the homes as they passed. "I'm not sure what Harrison's estate in Connecticut is like, but this place is the perfect spot for hiding someone. So much seclusion. Barely anyone around."

"No one except George watching," Alex said. "And look where that got the poor guy. His property will be on the market soon. Someone will tear down his trailer and build a mega mansion across from Dad's place. I might even miss that chain-link fence. There will never be another like it here again."

"Do you remember the man in Cleveland who kidnapped a woman and kept her locked in his basement for over a decade until she escaped?" Victoria asked. An image of the house that had been all over the news flashed into her mind. A small two-story row house on a crowded street.

"I do," Alex said.

"So do I," Rivera said.

"Ten years with people coming and going around her. No one suspected. No one ever heard her scream. So yes, this might be the perfect place, but any place will do." Victoria shivered, but not from the cold.

"That's really sad." Alex shook his head. "People are so messed up."

Rivera turned to Victoria. "Who were your calls from, Tori? Did Murphy try to call you, too?"

"I didn't look yet." Her dogs switched sides, forcing her to spin around and uncross their leashes. "I'll check when we get back and my hands aren't so tied up."

▼▲▼

"Victoria!" Alex called from downstairs. "We're getting takeout from The Mountain Grill. What do you want?"

Victoria stopped packing and walked out to the balcony. "Give me a minute to check their menu. I'll text you my order."

"Okay, but hurry."

"Did you get Rivera's?"

"I have everyone's but yours," Alex shouted.

She returned to her room and sunk into the corner chair with her phone, typed in her passcode, and found the menu for The Mountain Grill. She scrolled through the salads and selected one, then typed Alex a message with her order.

She had a voicemail from an unknown number. A call that had come in while she was hiking.

Probably a marketing call. Unless it's about the delivery of my SUV.

She hoped there wasn't a delay. As soon as the new car arrived and she packed up, they would leave. Alex had already booked his flight home and Rivera had offered to drive him to the airport.

She went to voicemail and selected the most recent message.

"Hey. It's me, Harrison. I had to return to Connecticut this week. My sister had a relapse and my niece needed me. I'm sorry I didn't get to say goodbye. I hope we'll cross paths again. And I think we will."

The recording clicked off.

Victoria stared at her screen as goosebumps rose on her arms.

He could not have sounded nicer or more normal.

296

She saved Harrison's number in her phone, just in case he contacted her again. Then she forwarded the voicemail to Jennifer Marachi, the lead special agent in Connecticut.

Catching Harrison wasn't her concern. The case wasn't hers. It never was.

But that didn't mean the questions would leave her alone.

Did Harrison kill Mallory and Kristen Bozeman? Did he kill George? Did he frame Alex? Did he have Alex and I run off the road? If he didn't do those things, who had? And why? Was he only protecting Kristen?

She had to know.

Chapter 35

"Thanks so much for agreeing to drop me at the airport, Rivera." Alex scraped the last of his scrambled eggs into one of the dog bowls. He still hadn't shaved since returning from the hospital. A mixture of blonde and brown stubble covered his chin.

"Yeah, no problem." Rivera stuck his plate in the dishwasher and closed the door. "It's the least I can do. I appreciate the hospitality. And the boat ride this morning."

Alex turned on the faucet and washed his hands. "My flight leaves at two. Ready to go in about forty-five minutes?"

"Yep." Rivera leaned against the counter.

Victoria came up between them and put her hand on her brother's arm. "I need to borrow your new best friend for a minute. Excuse us."

"Sure thing," Alex said.

"Can you walk out to the dock with me?" she asked Rivera as she slid her hands into her pockets.

From the way Rivera looked at her, she could tell he was already suspicious. She offered a weak smile as they went outside.

The dogs burst through the dog door and followed the agents across the yard toward the dock.

Although clouds gathered above the mountains, for the first day since she'd arrived at the lake, the sun was shining. A red speedboat skimmed across the water in the distance. And near the shore, at the edge of Enticement Cove, a couple was fishing off a pontoon boat.

"This is an incredible property." Rivera set his hand on the dock railing. "Would be sort of sad if your father sold it."

Victoria leaned her knee on one of the swivel chairs and put her hands together. "So...the other night. It was really nice."

"It was."

She shifted on her feet. "I've been doing a lot of thinking since then."

"And?"

"And...You're such a great guy." Her shoulders slumped as she chose her words. "You're smart and fun, you're kind. You're easy to talk to. My family loves your company. And you've been the best sport ever about my dogs. The absolute best."

Big Ed nudged Rivera's hip. The agent stroked the dog's ears. "They're growing on me."

"You are a really excellent guy."

"I have a feeling there's a 'but' coming."

She raised her eyes to meet his. "Working with you is a privilege. Our work is important, and if you look at everything we've accomplished together, it's amazing."

"Yeah. Yeah, it is." Rivera flexed his jaw, staring down at the grain in the wide wooden planks. A muscle twitched across his cheek.

I hope that's not resentment brewing inside him. Please don't be mad at me.

She placed her hand over her heart. "I want you in my life."

He turned to her. "I feel the same way. Unfortunately, I get the impression you mean it differently than I do." He shrugged and shook his head. "You know me. I won't try to push you into anything." He stared out at the quiet lake. "What doesn't work between us? Is there something about me that doesn't...do it for you?"

"I didn't say it was you. It's not. It's definitely, definitely not that." She dropped her head into her hands.

"Is it because of work?"

"I don't know right now. I'm confused."

Rivera extended his arm as if he was going to hug her or give her a pat on the back, but changed his mind. He leaned both elbows against the railing. "I don't want our professional relationship to be awkward for you. Yet my feelings for you won't change. I guess I'd be stupid to tell you I'll wait for you, but...if that's what you need, I'll do it. I'll keep being me and hope you come around and talk to me some day like you talk to your dogs. You're worth waiting for. Everybody who knows you knows that."

"Thank you." Rivera didn't act hurt or resentful. He seemed to understand what she was saying, maybe even more than she did.

"Come on, we'd better get going." Rivera put his hand on her upper back. "Your brother has a flight to catch and someone might think I'm out here proposing." He laughed. "Can't have that."

Chapter 36

The dogs barked as Victoria was doing a final cleanup of the backyard. During the past hour, the sky had changed from cloudless to overcast.

Sheriff Hayes walked toward the fence and stopped at the gate. He touched the brim of his hat and dipped his head. "Hey."

"Hi, Sheriff, what can I do for you?"

"I see you got yourself a new car. It looks good."

"Thanks. Less than seventy miles on it."

"And you've got your trailer hitched up. You taking off?"

"Very soon. My brother and Agent Rivera already left."

"Oh." The sheriff looked toward the house, rubbing his beard. "I'm disappointed that I missed them." He turned back to Victoria. "Listen, I wanted to tell you and the rest of your family, especially Alex—I'm sorry I put you through all of this. I hope you can understand."

"I understand you were doing your job."

"Yeah. I'm not sure if we would have solved this on our own. It's the strangest case I've ever seen. Anyway, I've been communicating with some of your other FBI colleagues as they take over the case. They all have great things to say about your work. Which made me question some of my own biases. Not because you're a woman or anything, I don't think, but because you have a house here on the peninsula, I guess."

"It's all right. No hard feelings."

"I expect the FBI will find Daughton soon."

"I expect they will, too, Sheriff. I appreciate you coming out here."

The sheriff touched his hat again, then turned on his heels. "See you around, Agent Heslin. When you come back, be sure to drop by my office and say hello."

▼▲▼

Victoria brushed Arya's neck with one hand and held her phone with the other. She hit the home button and said, "Call Ned."

"Hello," Ned answered.

"Hi. I'm calling with an update. My father and I are leaving in a few minutes. I'm going back to the office full time starting Monday. Does that work for you?"

"Works for me. What time do you think you'll get home? I'll stop by tonight."

"No—I mean, you don't have to do that. I have to drop my dad off first. I'll see you Monday."

Izzy raced across the yard, barking at a squirrel running along the fence.

"That's Izzy, isn't it? I recognize the raspy bark."

"It is. She got herself sprayed by a wild animal two nights ago, something musky and terrible that stunk up the entire house. Talk about an unpleasant surprise. You'll get a little whiff of it when she gets back, but I'm telling you it's not anywhere near as bad as it was. That's only one of the *many* reasons we're all eager to get out of here."

"I can't wait to see you. And the animals."

"They're all going to go nuts when they see you."

Mr. Heslin stepped out on the patio. "Victoria!" He spotted her and waved.

"Hey, Ned. I've got to get the donkeys in the trailer. I'll see you Monday morning."

"Monday morning. Drive safely. Be careful. *Extra* careful. Text me when you get home so I know you made it."

"I will. Take care."

She ran her gloved fingers through Arya's thick fur and leaned closer to hug her.

The donkey jerked from her arms with a snort and backed away.

"Guess you're not as crazy about me yet as I am about you. It's okay. That can change. I just need to be more patient, don't I?" Victoria took hold of Arya's halter and led her toward the trailer.

After loading the animals, she and her father went back inside to do a final check of the rooms, take out all the trash, and lock up the house. The donkeys whinnied almost the entire time.

"Sounds like they don't like being in the trailer," her father said as he set the alarm system.

"Guess not."

"Well, we're ready to go."

Outside, delicate snowflakes fell from the sky and swirled in the wind, creating a sense of calm she hadn't felt during the trip. The snow was pretty, but Victoria was happy to leave before any accumulated.

The donkeys were snorting and kicking the sides of the trailer as she checked the latches one last time and locked the back before climbing into the driver's seat. After starting the car, she drove slowly down the long driveway.

"That was not at all the trip any of us imagined." Her father stared ahead at George's property. Yellow crime scene tape wrapped around the metal gate. "But I'm glad you were here. Do you think you'll ever want to come back?"

"Hmm." She laughed and reached over to pat his shoulder. "Ask me next year and I'll give you my answer."

A fox ran out of the bushes ahead of the car, its little ears pointed and its tail up behind him, watching them leave.

Chapter 37

It was dark when Victoria dropped her father off at his house, then headed to her own.

Twenty minutes later, she stopped in front of her iron gate and keyed in the security code, hoping there was something edible in her fridge. The gate slid open. She drove in and waited for it to click back into place before she continued up the long driveway.

Parking outside, she got out of the car and detached the trailer. The donkeys had been active and restless for most of the trip home and she didn't want to wait any longer than necessary to get them to their paddock. She spied Oscar's nose through the front window, his nostrils flaring. "We're home, fellas. Hang on. I'll be back to get you out of there in just a few minutes."

She got back into her Suburban, drove into the garage, and let the dogs out. They rushed inside and straight to their dog bowls as she keyed in another code, shutting off the interior alarm system. After setting her phone and keys on the counter, she made a quick trip to the bathroom, then went back outside for the donkeys.

"Sorry for the wait, guys," she said as she unlocked the trailer door. "I didn't forget you."

As she swung the door open, Harrison jumped up from a crouch, his gun aimed straight at Victoria's heart.

She gasped. "What the—?" *No wonder the donkeys were making such a fuss when I was locking up the lake house.*

Harrison moved closer, holding up the hand that wasn't brandishing a weapon. "I just need to talk to you. That's all this is."

She glanced around, afraid to take her eyes off him for more than a split second. Her thoughts raced. She was glad she'd told Ned not to meet her at the house tonight. The last thing she wanted was for him to walk into this. If she could just get inside, a safe near the door held her FBI-assigned weapon. Her personal weapon was in her bedroom.

"You don't need a gun. Just let me get these guys out of the trailer and put them in the paddock." She tried to sound calm as her adrenaline spiked. "Then we can talk."

Harrison grunted and kept the gun trained on her. He wore a large winter coat. Something bulged from one pocket.

She moved forward, hands up. "I'm just going to take them out of the trailer now."

He stepped out onto the driveway and stood to the side, keeping the gun aimed at her. His finger rested on the trigger. She hoped he knew how to use a firearm and wouldn't discharge it by accident.

She walked into the trailer, using her peripheral vision to scan for anything to use as a weapon. There was nothing inside except the donkeys and hay. Controlling her breath, she unclipped Arya and Sansa and led them out. Eyeing the open garage, she judged the distance and how long it would take her to sprint there. If he was a decent shot—too long.

Harrison followed her to the paddock. "Don't try anything. I might not hit you with the first bullet, but it would be hard for me to miss your donkeys. I know you don't want that."

306

"I won't try anything." Her heart pounded as she opened the paddock and let Sansa and Arya loose inside. "I'm going back to the trailer for Oscar."

"The one who ran away, right?" He smiled, like all of this was normal, like he hadn't just hidden in her trailer all the way from West Virginia to hold her at gunpoint.

As she walked to the trailer, Harrison stayed close.

Oscar whinnied, tossed his head, and showed his teeth, uncomfortable with Harrison's presence.

"Don't worry, sweetie," Victoria said as she unclipped the donkey's halter and led him out. "He won't hurt us." She prayed that was true.

They walked back to the paddock in silence. Inside, Oscar ran off as soon as she unsnapped the lead.

Keeping her movements slow and her hands in front of her, Victoria faced Harrison. "You have to turn yourself in. The FBI won't stop looking for you. The longer this goes on, the worse it gets."

"Yeah. Thanks to you, everyone is after me. And now you're going to fix things."

Is that what he thinks I can do? "Tell me what happened so I can help." As he stared at her, she wondered if he was delusional. "Why didn't you tell me you knew Kristen? That she lived with you?"

"I couldn't. It wasn't safe."

"Safe from who?"

He shook his head.

"How did she die?" Victoria asked. "I can't help you if I don't know what you're facing."

"You wouldn't understand."

307

"Try me. You can practice on me." She kept her voice soothing and calm, like they were in this together. "Because we're going to need to make people understand what happened, unless you want to be in jail for the rest of your life."

"That won't happen!" He scowled. "Let's get inside."

"Right. We should go inside." She didn't force a smile, but did her best to look natural.

When she opened the back door, the dogs swarmed them. Without lowering his eyes from Victoria, Harrison pushed them out of the way.

"Let's sit down," she said, entering the living room. Her bedroom and her closest gun were just beyond it. "Tell me what happened."

"Over there. Sit." He gestured to a chair in the sparsely furnished living room.

Victoria perched on the edge of an armchair. Harrison stood a few yards from her. Far enough away that he could fire off a round before she reached him.

"If I tell you what happened, will you call off the FBI?" he asked.

"I can try. How about putting the gun down?"

He shook his head.

Victoria tried to recall the takeaway points from a seminar on hostage negotiation. She hadn't forgotten the most important strategy—shut up and listen. "Why don't you start from the beginning."

"What I need you to understand is that none of this was my fault. I did what had to be done." His voice took on a panicked tone.

"Tell me." She rested her hands on her thighs so he wouldn't see them shaking. This wasn't the first time someone had pointed a gun at her inside her home, but she was still afraid. She was pretty sure she knew what he was capable of doing.

Harrison opened his mouth, then closed it and pressed his lips together before speaking. "I used to have a family. A real one. In an instant, they were taken from me in a car accident—my parents and my sister. I was only sixteen years old. And the worst part of it is that I was driving." He touched the deep scar on his face. "When they died, I was lost. You can't imagine what it was like."

Understand and empathize—two more things from the hostage seminar. "I'm so sorry. I know what it's like to suddenly and violently lose someone—my mother. It's something we never fully get over."

Harrison raked his free hand across his head. "I spiraled into a dark tunnel of guilt and self-loathing. I drank a lot to get through each day. I couldn't stop, even though I would have done anything to find a way out."

"I know." *Be patient—another point the seminar emphasized.*

Big Ed sniffed Harrison's leg. Harrison pushed the dog away with a swipe of his leg. "An opportunity came when I saw Kristen and her mother at my family's business. I rarely visited the New York offices. Seeing them that day was destiny. Except for her beauty mark, Kristen was the spitting image of my sister, Katherine."

Victoria studied Harrison, waiting for him to let his guard down, if only for a second. His eyes seemed to glaze over as he told his story. But his grip on the gun hadn't faltered.

"Kristen's mother was doing temp work. She'd brought her daughter along, making her sit by herself in the office. What sort of mother leaves a child alone with strangers in a big city?"

Victoria huffed to encourage him.

"I followed them to a cheap apartment in an awful area. It wasn't much better than that dump George called home. Everything there suggested a way of life that was unacceptable for a little girl. I saw a chance to give her a much, much better future."

Here it comes...

Harrison grimaced and looked away.

Victoria prepared to leap up and smash the gun from his hand, but in the blink of an eye, his focus returned to her.

"The only problem was Kristen's mother. She wanted me. In those days, before Kristen, I was so wasted most of the time, I can barely remember what I did...but I know Mallory wanted more from me than I wanted to give her. In a way, when she died, I was acting in self-defense." Harrison's face scrunched and he let out a low moan, like the memories pained him, which meant he wasn't a complete psychopath. "I didn't want Mallory Bozeman to die, and I didn't enjoy taking her life, but I had to. I strangled her."

Victoria had to look away. Harrison was a killer. There was no longer any lingering doubt that he had merely been protecting Kristen.

"After that, there was no turning back. Kristen needed me. I never took another drink. I had a new purpose—protecting her. I made up a story about the *bad man* who killed her mother and wanted to kill her, too. And it was the truth because the drunk who killed her mother, that wasn't really me. That's not who I am. Taking care of Kristen brought me back to my former self. I took her to my estate in Connecticut and gave her everything my sister would have had."

"I'm sure you did your best. All these years, and no one else knew?"

"No one. It's amazing that our arrangement worked out as long as it did, but as you and your family can attest, money has a way of making the impossible exist. Except, everything comes to an end, doesn't it?"

"Yes, it does."

His grip tightened on the gun. He came closer, leaning toward her. "Over the past few years, as *my niece* matured into an adult, I could see things couldn't go on as they were. Kristen began doubting me. She wanted the two things I couldn't safely allow—freedom and the truth. The night she died, I left her alone. I told her I had to make a quick trip to settle some family business. She was supposed to stay inside the lake house. Instead, she defied me." Harrison's eyes flashed with anger. He spoke without pausing. "She said she didn't tell your brother anything that could hurt us, and I believed her. But what about the next time she disobeyed? And the time after that? What we had—it simply wouldn't work much longer. The little girl was long gone and the secrets we kept were in jeopardy. I loved Kristen like she was my sister, but her time was over. And honestly, if I'd never taken her in, she probably would have died of neglect years earlier, or ended up on the streets."

Victoria hid her revulsion. She had to get to her gun. And if she did, she wouldn't hesitate before firing.

Harrison waved his weapon. "Now do you understand?" His question came out loud and forceful.

"Yes. I understand." *That you're completely insane.* "Harrison, please put the gun down. I'm going to help you out of this situation, but I can't do it at gunpoint."

Shaking his head, he glared at her. "Get up."

311

Something had changed. She stood slowly, desperate to calm him down. "What's wrong?"

"I'm not sure if I trust you." He cocked the weapon. "Why should I? This is your fault. You and your brother."

"You can trust me." Sweat trickled down her temple. For once, she regretted having little decor around her house. A heavy vase or metal sculpture would suffice to smash the gun from his hand, if she moved fast enough, and if only there was one. "I understand everything you told me. I want both of us to get through this. Otherwise, we can't work anything out."

"Go in there. In the bathroom." He gestured toward the open door. "Move."

She headed toward the powder room.

He grabbed one of the kitchen chairs and dragged it behind him. "Stay in there while I think about this…about what needs to happen next."

Victoria backed into the room.

Harrison slammed the door.

She locked it from the inside and quickly pressed her back against the side wall. Her heart pounded as she let out a deep breath and contemplated her next move. He was calling the shots, but she was still alive, and no one was hurt. "Let's both take a few minutes to think about what to do next," she said, grasping for the right thing to say.

"Yes. Let's do that."

Outside the bathroom, something scraped against the floor and then rattled the door. The doorknob jerked.

Victoria heard the rustling of material and thought Harrison might be removing his coat and settling down. Something pushed against the bottom of the door. Her gaze darted to the floor. A torrent of liquid droplets rushed up toward her, accompanied by the hiss of an aerosol spray.

She jumped away and yanked her shirt over her mouth and nose. There was nowhere to go in the small windowless room.

"Goodbye, Victoria."

"Wait!" Holding her breath, she hurried back to the door, fumbled with the inner lock, and tried to get out. The door didn't budge. She threw all her weight against it, but he'd jammed it.

Her dogs barked on the other side of the door.

Think. Think!

There was a small vent in the ceiling. The only other opening. She moved to climb on top of the toilet to breathe fresh air, but before she could get even one leg up, she was falling.

Victoria coughed, rubbed the back of her head, and moaned.

Her eyes flew open.

I'm alive!

She stood, slowly, and looked in the mirror.

It must have been chloroform or something similar. Not a fatal gas.

She didn't know how much time had passed. The house was quiet. She crept toward the door. "Harrison?"

He didn't answer. A chorus of barking erupted.

"Harrison? Are you still here? Open the door."

Still no response except the dogs going crazy.

Rattling the doorknob accomplished nothing. She alternated between throwing her full weight against the door and jerking the knob, hoping the chair would slip away.

"I'll be out as soon as I can," she said to the dogs. "If one of you could move the chair, that would really be a great help."

On the bright side, she had plenty of water to drink and Ned should arrive in less than twenty-four hours to let her out. Aside from needing to go after Harrison, she actually felt worse about not being able to feed the dogs than being stuck in the bathroom longer.

But was Harrison really gone?

She grabbed the toilet brush from inside the cabinet. Over the next thirty minutes, she smashed it against the porcelain sink and used the edge of a brass candle holder to pry the brush's plastic handle apart until it was small enough to fit under the door. Sweating and cursing, she jammed the hard plastic repeatedly against the back chair legs. The chair finally slid out and smashed to the floor.

When she flung the door open, the dogs jumped all over her.

"Believe me, I'm as thrilled to be out as you are to have me." She grabbed her phone off the kitchen counter and checked the time. "I was in there for hours!"

Before she could call the FBI, she spotted Harrison's name on her phone screen. He'd left her a new message.

Trembling with anger, she pressed the play button.

As with his last message, Harrison sounded completely normal. "It's me. Harrison. I borrowed your car and left it at the airport in short term parking. Floor D. I decided I won't be needing your help after all."

In the background, a woman's smooth voice announced, "Esta es la ultima llamada para abordar el vuelo—"

"It was nice seeing you again." Harrison's voice rose. He spoke quickly, making it impossible to hear the rest of the woman's announcement. "Take care."

The message ended.

He was on the run.

Victoria replayed the message.

Esta es la ultima llamada para abordar el vuelo—

This is the last call to board flight—

Victoria hadn't been able to hear the flight number.

Had he boarded the first flight to Mexico? Spain?

She swiped through her phone screens to find the number for Jennifer Marachi to tell her Harrison had already left the country.

Chapter 38

The FBI offices were usually bustling. The first Monday of the new year was no exception.

Victoria stopped at Sam's desk and pointed to the string of battery-operated Christmas lights attached to the wall of his cube. "Hey, there. You going to leave these until next December?"

"Victoria! Welcome back." Sam took his hands out of his sweatshirt pocket, got up from his chair, and gave her a hug. "It's great to see you."

"You, too." She filled him in on the events that had transpired at her house.

Sam shook his head. "This happened last night?"

"Yes."

"Unbelievable. I'm glad he left you alive."

"I just heard they tracked him to Buenos Aires and have agents on the ground looking for him."

"They'll find him."

"I hope so. And when they do, I'll have to testify about everything he told me. Anyway, I'm on my way to see Murphy. I hope he has something good for me. Not a desk job."

Sam sat back down. "Oh, I'm sure he'll have something interesting for you. But sitting at a desk isn't the worst thing that can happen, is it?" He grinned and spread his arms wide, encompassing the perimeters of his small work area. "I'm the king of *all this*. Interesting things come my way every day."

"That's true." Victoria let go of the side of his cube and backed away. "I'll see you later."

In the corner office, the door for the Special Agent in Charge was closed. Through the window blinds, a woman's upper body was partly visible on the other side of the desk from Murphy.

Victoria went to a nearby empty cubicle to log in and check her work emails while she waited. Sitting down, she pulled out her laptop and powered it up.

"Victoria, hi!" Payton Jennings from Forensic Accounting stood next to the cubicle, slim and elegant in a pencil skirt and matching jacket over a silk blouse. She was with Rivera.

He looked healthy and handsome. Gone were the red and irritated eyes, the raw, runny nose.

Victoria's knee bounced under her desk until she made it stop.

It's good I'm seeing him right away. Now I'll know if things will be awkward or not.

"Hey, Payton. It's great to see you, too." Victoria nodded at Rivera. Tucking her hair behind her ear, she returned Payton's friendly smile. "It's really nice to be back. And I wanted to thank you for all you did to help get me home from Greenland."

"Of course." Payton adjusted the rim of her glasses. "I mean, it's my job, but when it's one of your own, there's that extra incentive. Everyone was so worried about you. And Rivera was the one driving the effort, for sure." Payton beamed up at Rivera. "I don't think he slept for a week."

"I know. I hope—I hope I've thanked him enough."

"Like Payton said, one of our own, right?" Rivera crossed his arms. His voice was clear again. "We're all glad to see you back, Victoria." He smiled. "We're on our way to a meeting, so—" He moved his hand up and a bit to the side, a sort of wave, then he and Payton walked off together, talking.

Victoria blew out a long, controlled breath, appreciating Rivera's graciousness yet again. He seemed relaxed. He'd acted as if nothing unusual had happened between them.

I think we're good.

She watched the agents walk into a conference room and close the door. Standing up, she checked if Murphy's door was still closed. It was.

Back to my email.

Her laptop was ready for her. She logged in and scanned her emails.

Jane Norell, Human Resources Update.

Darren Jones, Training Recertification.

Sydney Pyler, New Case File Deadlines.

The next one sent a shock through her. The sender was Harrison Daughton.

Victoria's hands shook as she opened the email and leaned forward to read.

Dear Victoria,

I trust you're okay or you wouldn't be reading this.

In the end, my efforts weren't enough to protect my secrets. It was all getting too complicated. Which got me thinking, too late, why do I care anymore? So here is everything else you probably want to know. Consider it my peace offering for trying to frame Alex and ruin your family. It feels good to have things off my chest.

About George—he minded his own business, but with you and the sheriff poking around, trying to figure out where Kristen had come from, it was only a matter of time before he told someone he'd seen Kristen and me together. I killed him with his shovel a few days earlier and had just finished burying him and dumping the shovel in the lake when you came running through the woods. I'm willing to bet no one except George and I had walked through his woods in decades, but you were there with your dog that same night. It's beyond ironic. Perhaps that was also destiny.

Victoria closed her eyes, feeling deep sadness for George, and then returned to reading.

I'm joining my family now. It's long overdue, as I should have been the one who died in that accident instead of them. I have another foolproof plan (yes—I'm laughing, too) but this one will work.

Take care, Victoria.

Sincerely,

Harrison Daughton IV

Victoria's eyes flew up to the email's time stamp.

Seven thirty a.m.

It had come through an hour ago.

She grabbed her phone and called Jennifer Marachi. "This is Victoria Heslin calling about Harrison Daughton again." She stood up, her heart racing. "He's about to commit suicide. You have to hurry—"

"We've already found him," Jennifer said.

Victoria gripped the edge of her laptop screen, about to close it. "You found him? Before he…?"

319

"No. After our agents in Buenos Aires got a call about a man on the roof of The Four Seasons Hotel. It was Harrison. He didn't survive."

"He jumped?"

"I'm afraid so."

Victoria sank back into her seat.

"Agent Heslin? You said he sent you another confession?"

"Yes." She stared at the note on her screen, the words blurring. "Are you sure it was him they found?"

"His Connecticut license was in his wallet. We'll check DNA, but we believe it's him. Send me the email."

Victoria hit the forward button, typed in Marachi's email address, and hit send. "It's sent."

"Thank you, Victoria. I'm sure we'll be in touch about this again, but Harrison's death means this case will wrap up much sooner than I expected."

Victoria set her phone down and leaned back in the creaky office chair.

She had all her answers.

She never had to face Harrison again.

It was time to move on.

Chapter 39

"I'm back," Victoria called, although there was no need to announce her return. All the dogs were scrambling noisily to the door and greeting her as if she'd been gone a month rather than a day.

Ned wasn't there when she left for work in the morning, but his SUV was in her garage now. He rounded the corner behind her pack of excited animals, wiping his hands on his pants, the sleeves of his long-sleeved T-shirt pushed up. After their plane crashed, he'd lost more weight than she had, but he'd gained most of it back. His arms were more cut than usual, his jaw and cheeks more defined. His skin looked rough and reddish, but so much better than when they'd first returned from Greenland.

"Welcome home, Victoria." He glanced toward the bathroom. "What happened to that door? It's like the paint got scratched off."

"Long story." She stood with her hands by her sides, taking in every inch of him and loving what she saw. "Your face is healing so well."

"It is. How was work?" Ned wore a pleasant and relaxed-looking smile. "Did they give you a new case?"

A few of the dogs left Victoria and trotted over to Ned, nuzzling him and sharing their excitement.

"Not yet. I mostly had paperwork to do. I think they'll put me on a case tomorrow. Unless Murphy is waiting for something new to come up." She couldn't stop smiling and was starting to feel rather silly about it. Seeing Ned in her house, surrounded by her dogs, felt right. "How was everything here?"

"Good. Myrtle limped a bit when she came in from a run. Not to worry yet, but if it persists into tomorrow, I'm taking her to the clinic for an x-ray. And Big Ed has something he can't wait to show you." He tousled the dog's spotted ears. "Don't you, big boy?"

They were still standing there, the hallway between the garage door and the kitchen separating them. That was all right. She didn't want to ruin the moment.

"Ned." She took a deep breath, summoning the strength she needed to take a risk, to put herself out there so that things between them might be clear. "I missed you. This is strange of me to say, because I'm like your boss..."

"You are unequivocally my boss, Victoria."

"And I don't want to mess things up there, except, if you're okay with it. I mean—"

"I'm a good vet. I can get hired at a dozen clinics in Virginia tomorrow, or start my own practice, if that's what I wanted to do." His voice was soft, not bragging. "So, don't worry, if that's where I think you're going with this." He laughed. "And I won't be filing any sexual harassment claims against you. We survived something incredible together, like it or not, we're bonded for life."

With a half-smile, Victoria took slow steps to him, taking in every feature along the way. When they were inches apart, she gazed into his brown eyes and cradled his cheek in her hand. For a few moments the only sound was their breathing, then Victoria said, "That's all I needed to hear."

If you enjoyed this book, Victoria's next adventure in this series is *The Groom Went Missing*.

ACKNOWLEDGEMENTS

Writing a book is one thing, but getting it polished and publication ready is another. For me, it's the most time-consuming part of the writing process. I have many people to thank for their help. My critique partners, Dan Alatorre, Jim Boatner, Reita Pendry, Susan Wilson, and Alex Whitney. My editor, Allison Maruska. My beta readers, Blaise and Linda Bisaillon, Mary Vassallo, Karen Scioscia, and Caryn Sutorus. My entire ARC team—some of you have been with me for this entire series and I'm so grateful for your support! My audio book narrator for this series, Stephanie Dillard, who always finds mistakes in my manuscript, even after so many sets of eyes have combed through it. I'm super appreciative for the help they all generously provided to make my work better.

BOOKS BY JENIFER RUFF

The Agent Victoria Heslin Series
The Numbers Killer
Pretty Little Girls
When They Find Us
Ripple of Doubt
The Groom Went Missing

The FBI & CDC Thriller Series
Only Wrong Once
Only One Cure
Only One Wave: The Tsunami Effect

The Brooke Walton Series
Everett
Rothaker
The Intern

Suspense
Lauren's Secret

ABOUT THE AUTHOR

Jenifer Ruff is a USA Today and international bestselling author of thriller novels who writes in three series: The Brooke Walton Series, The Agent Victoria Heslin Thriller Series, and the FBI & CDC Thriller Series.

Jenifer grew up in Massachusetts, has a biology degree from Mount Holyoke College and a Master's in Public Health and Epidemiology from Yale University. She worked as a management consultant for Price Waterhouse Coopers and for IBM Business Consulting before discovering her love for writing. An avid hiker and fitness enthusiast, she lives in Charlotte, North Carolina with her family and a pack of greyhounds. For more, visit her website at Jenruff.com.